THE REMEMBRANCE OF KINGS

Volume I: The Song of Lemuria

by C.B. Conklin

Cover design by C.B. Conklin
Interior layout by C.B. Conklin

ISBN (Paperback): 978-1-0690842-0-0
First Edition
Printed in the United States of America

For those who remember,
and for those who are just beginning to.
For the dreamers who wake with echoes of other worlds,
for the wanderers who feel ancient songs in their blood,
and for every soul on the long road home.

May these words be both spark and mirror—
a remembering, a recognition, a return.

Table of Contents

The Remembrance of Kings

Volume I: The Song of Lemuria

By C.B. Conklin

Series Invocation

Before the mountains rose and the rivers carved their song,
before the stars scattered themselves upon the endless night,
we made a vow.

A vow to descend.
A vow to scatter.
A vow to forget—so that remembering would carry the weight of truth.

Across worlds and bodies, across lifetimes and centuries,
through the fires of war and the stillness of prayer,
we wander.

Yet always the Spiral calls us back.
Always the Song awaits.
Always the vow returns,

golden and unbroken,
woven through the voices of those who remember.

This is that remembrance.
This is the vow made flesh once more.

Introduction

There are moments in the long arc of the human story when the earth itself seems to awaken, when stones hold their breath, when rivers carry not only water but memory, and when the sky bends low to whisper truths too vast for ordinary hearing. This tale begins in one such age: the twilight of Lemuria, when memory was not yet fractured, and the soul's vow still shone like fire threaded through the marrow of all who lived.

Lemuria was not a place in the way we now think of place. It was a realm of resonance, a great weaving of earth, water, fire, air, and star. Here, the human soul did not yet imagine itself separate from creation. Every stone was kin, every wave a teacher, every tree a living archive of song. To walk the land was to walk through remembrance. To breathe was to touch the vow. In that age, existence itself was devotion, and life was the language of eternity.

At the heart of this remembrance stands Kael'Thorin. He is no king, no prophet, no chosen hero in the mold of later tales. He is, instead, a vessel — a young soul asked to carry a promise older than mountains, older than fire, older than the stars. His journey is not one of conquest, but of surrender: to be shaped, broken, and remade by the memory that stirs within him, a vow spoken long before his birth. The thread of this vow is what carries him, and through him, what carries us all.

Yet Kael'Thorin does not walk alone. Around him gather the Five Guides — not guardians in the sense of command, but mirrors of what lies latent in every soul, each bearing a facet of the remembrance. Their presence does not shield him from pain, nor spare him the burden of choice, but illuminates the path he must walk. To know their essence is to glimpse the deeper tones of this story.

Thalan'ar is the seer of lines, the one whose vision pierces veils of shadow and time. His presence is clarity: the cool brilliance of starlight breaking through cloud. He does not simply see what is — he perceives what weaves beneath, the hidden geometry that guides both star and soul. His gift to Kael'Thorin is not certainty but orientation, teaching that even in the vastness of ruin, there are constellations to follow. His tone is steady, austere, a compass pointing ever toward truth.

Seraphiel is the radiant heart of flame. In her lives both tenderness and ferocity, for fire is not one thing — it destroys, it purifies, it warms, it illuminates. She comes with wings of light, folding around Kael'Thorin not as a shield but as a balance, reminding him that compassion is not weakness, and courage is not rage. Her presence is the heat of devotion, burning away what is false and igniting what must endure. Through her he learns that balance is born not of avoidance, but of standing fully within the fire.

Amari'el Shae'Lumae is the singer of waters, keeper of sacred song. Her voice is a river — soft as rain upon stone, fierce as torrents rushing toward the sea. She awakens memory not by command, but by melody, drawing forth what has been forgotten with gentleness and ache. In her presence, Kael'Thorin feels the weight of grief, yet also the promise of renewal. Her tone is not merely sound but resonance, the way silence itself bends when song is near. Through her he learns that to remember is to heal, and that every sorrow carries the seed of song within it.

Odric is the keeper of stone, vast in his silence. His gift is endurance — the patience of mountains, the stillness that outlasts storm and flame alike. In his presence there is no urgency, no haste. He teaches by weight, by the immovable truth that what endures need not prove itself. Kael'Thorin feels in him the deep gravity of vow, the knowledge that to remain steadfast is its own form of power. Odric speaks seldom, but when his silence settles, it steadies the soul. His tone is the slow breath of earth itself, reminding that even in ruin, there are foundations which cannot be erased.

And then there is Ka'el — the wind between worlds. He cannot be grasped, cannot be caged. He is motion, liminality, the breath that carries across thresholds. Where the others hold, Ka'el releases; where they root, he reminds that all must move. His presence is felt more than seen, a stirring at the edge of perception, a whisper across the skin. He is the uncertainty that is also invitation, the reminder that between every ending and beginning there is a passage, and that passage is holy. His tone is the exhale of the infinite, teaching that mystery itself is guide enough.

Together, the Five are not simply companions to Kael'Thorin. They are the echo of what every soul carries: the memory of a vow. Through them the story unfolds, not as myth locked in the past, but as resonance alive in the present. For each flame, each stone, each song, each wind, each vision is a mirror — inviting us to see ourselves not as strangers to this tale, but as participants in its weaving.

This vow — the golden thread of Lemuria — is not bound to that land alone, nor to a single age. It ripples outward across the vast sea of time, scattering through centuries and continents, reappearing in fragments of myth, dream, and song. Its resonance surfaces in temples, in firesides, in lullabies, in the sudden ache of recognition when we meet a stranger's eyes. It is the promise that binds all journeys of remembrance.

This book does not ask you to believe in Lemuria as a matter of history. It asks only that you listen. For within the rhythm of these words, within the unfolding of Kael'Thorin's path and the voices of the Five, you may feel something stir. A thread tugging at your own soul. A memory that belongs not only to them, but to you. And if you follow that thread, it may lead you not only into the story that begins here, but into the remembrance of your own vow — the vow that has always been waiting beneath the surface of your life, calling you home.

Part I: The Beforefall

Chapter 1: The Waters That Remember

The Grove did not simply exist—it breathed

It exhaled with the mist, rising in curling tendrils from the moss-laden ground, wrapping gently around the trunks of the Eldertrees whose crowns vanished into heavens not seen but remembered. Each leaf, a rune. Each gust of wind, a whisper of names long since woven into the roots of Lemuria.

Kael'Thorin moved slowly now, letting the hush of the Grove seep into his bones. There was a reverence required here, not imposed, but known. Like entering the chamber of one's own soul and remembering it had always been sacred.

The other five had long since passed through the thresholds of the spiral stones. But even their silent passage had left imprints in the song of the forest—faint notes that only the heart could detect.

Kael'Thorin paused before the sixth stone.

It was carved from deep obsidian, flecked with flecks of gold and emerald, as though the stars themselves had embedded into its face. At its center, a sigil glowed faintly—a glyph that mirrored the one he often saw in his dreams: a spiral enclosed by a teardrop, encircled by three concentric lines. The Mark of the Rememberer.

He reached out and touched it.

The stone warmed instantly.

A vibration—subtle, like the purring of an unseen beast—moved through his fingertips, up his arm, and into the center of his chest.

His eyes fluttered shut.

He saw the face of his mother—not of this life, but another—singing to him in the old tongue, the language of water and breath. She had taught him then, in a life long buried beneath the sands of forgetting, that the Grove was not a place on a map, but a moment in the soul's unfolding.

And now, here it was.

He stepped forward.

Immediately, the light changed. What had been filtered sunlight through canopy turned iridescent—pale greens and blues, mingling with the violet shimmer that only appeared when the veil between dimensions was thinnest. The forest no longer just looked alive—it was alive. Watching him. Welcoming him.

"Enter whole," a voice murmured—no louder than a thought. "Or do not enter at all."

Kael'Thorin nodded, the vow already forming within his marrow.

"I enter as I am," he whispered. "In truth. In fracture. In fire and water."

And the Grove allowed him passage.

His footfall made no sound.

The moss beneath his soles was so soft it felt like stepping on memory itself—gentle, fragrant, ancient. Trees leaned inward, not out of menace, but intimacy, like old friends drawing close. Blooms opened in his wake—cerulean and silver—each releasing a faint chime like temple bells.

Far ahead, through a parting of the trunks, he saw it:

The Spiral Pool.

It lay in a hollow of stone and root, encircled by the five who had gone before him. They did not speak. They did not need to.

He was the final note in a chord long composed.

And now the harmony could begin.

The Spiral Pool was unlike any water Kael'Thorin had ever seen.

It did not reflect the sky above—but the stars that lived within things. Not constellations of burning gas, but the memory-stars of each soul, each moment, each truth lived and lost and found again. The Pool shimmered not in light, but in story.

He slowed as he approached, eyes never leaving its surface. Around the edge, five stones stood—each a seat, each aligned to one of the five.

Odric stood at the northern point. He was tall and wide-shouldered, clad in robes the color of granite and ash. His presence was grounding, like the gravity of mountains. He held his arms crossed over his chest, one hand resting lightly on a stone pendant carved with the runes of the Old Tongue. A protector of the vow, and of Kael'Thorin.

To the northeast stood Seraphiel, whose hair shimmered like copper fire and whose robes danced with threads of gold and violet. Her eyes held stars of remembrance, and when she looked at Kael'Thorin, he felt his bones vibrate with ancient chords. She had once been his sister in a lifetime lost to wind.

Thalan'ar, at the eastern mark, was the stillest of them all. Dressed in layered tunics of midnight blue, his hand never strayed far from the hilt of a ceremonial blade that had not tasted battle in a thousand years. He was not a warrior in function, but in fidelity—to truth, to balance, to the spiral of becoming.

Amari'el Shae'Lumae stood to the south, her form fluid, like the sea made flesh. She bore a circlet of woven kelp and crystal, and her voice—when she spoke—carried the tones of a temple bell struck beneath deep water. Her role was memory's keeper, the sacred feminine who reminded Kael'Thorin of what it meant to feel the story, not just know it.

And Ka'el.

He was not visible as the others were.

But his presence moved in the trees, stirred the surface of the

Pool, whispered behind Kael'Thorin's right ear when doubt tried to take root.

Ka'el was the wind between worlds.

The Watcher between veils.

The First Spiral.

Kael'Thorin inhaled deeply and stepped forward into the center.

No words were spoken.

Each of the five extended their palms toward him, and light—woven of color and tone—streamed forth, encircling him in five intersecting spirals. The strands did not bind him. They reminded him. They aligned him.

A tone rose from beneath the pool, low and sonorous.

Kael'Thorin knelt.

And placed his hands upon the Waters That Remember.

The moment Kael'Thorin's fingertips touched the water, it ceased to be water.

The surface remained still, but it was no longer liquid. It became *memory*, boundless and pulsing, layered like the rings of a great tree—each ripple a life, a vow, a forgetting.

The Grove dimmed.

Not into shadow, but into depth. Light itself softened, bending around the Spiral Pool as though to make space for something older than illumination.

Kael'Thorin's breath caught.

He was falling—but not down. Inward.

Within the stillness, vision bloomed.

He stood once more in a crystalline city, towers of opal and gold gleaming in the rays of a triad sun. Music wove between the spires—living tones that healed, that taught, that remembered. He wore white robes threaded with silver. Children ran around his feet, their laughter blending into the song of the air. They called him by a name he had not yet remembered.

Then—

A battlefield. Red soil. The cries of the wounded echoing off black stone. Kael'Thorin crouched beside a dying man whose face mirrored his own. A twin. A brother. A reflection. The man grasped his hand and whispered a name—"Aelin"—before the light left his eyes. The Spiral burned across Kael'Thorin's palm.

Another ripple—

A great ship crossing a sky of shifting auroras. He stood at its helm, flanked by beings whose eyes held galaxies. He was not captain, but translator—of star-song, of the unspoken. They descended to a world of coral forests, bearing the first glyphs of

Lemurian remembrance.

The images came faster.

A woman with hair like spun copper, holding him as fire engulfed a temple.

A child carving spirals into river clay, alone, but guided by invisible hands.

An old man—himself—kneeling beneath the same Hollow Tree he would soon walk to, eyes closed, heart open, whispering the vow to remember once more.

Then—

The Five.

Not as they stood now, but in forms from other ages.

Odric as a giant cloaked in bark and iron, wielding a hammer that sang mountains into form.

Seraphiel as a priestess in robes of flame, dancing atop a burning lake without fear.

Thalan'ar as a silent sentinel, eyes blind but seeing truth through stone.

Amari'el as a healer with coral-threaded hair, weeping over a dying dolphin's song.

Ka'el as the wind itself, the dream itself, the nothing that touches all.

They had always been with him.

Across ages. Across worlds.

He opened his mouth to speak—but the Pool did not allow words.

Only tone.

A note escaped his lips—unbidden, unfamiliar, and yet utterly his. It rang out across the Grove. The birds stilled. The trees leaned closer.

The water glowed.

And from its depths, a spiral of light emerged.

It coiled around his form—not to bind, but to *remember with him.* Each loop brought back a vow.

"I will remember."
"I will return."
"I will serve the Spiral."
"I will not forget, even when I forget."
"I will love through lifetimes."
"I will carry the seed."

The Pool accepted.

The Grove exhaled.

Kael'Thorin collapsed forward onto his hands, breath ragged, sweat glistening on his brow. But his eyes were lit from within. He looked up—first at the Pool, then at the Five.

"I'm ready," he whispered.

Seraphiel stepped forward and placed a hand to his heart.

"You've only just begun."

The Hollow Tree was not far, though Kael'Thorin's legs felt unsteady as he moved.

The Five had departed, not in footsteps or rustling leaves, but in presence. A shift in the Grove's breath. As if the scene had closed its sacred circle and was now allowing the initiate to step into solitude, to meet what must be met alone.

He followed the path revealed by Odric's gesture. It was not a trail so much as a thinning of trees, a gentle winding through silver ferns and moon-root vines, their soft bioluminescence lighting the way like starlight filtered through memory.

Kael'Thorin moved slowly. His feet carried him, but it was his breath that guided the way—deeper, slower, quieter. The Grove seemed to respond to each inhalation, parting slightly with every exhale. A symphony of silence wrapped around him, broken only by the distant murmur of water.

He crested a ridge and saw it.

The Hollow Tree.

It towered impossibly high, its trunk wide enough to hold a village within. Its bark was etched with glyphs older than language, glowing faintly with a moss-colored light. Vines wrapped its base like offerings, and small creatures—spirits of the forest—nested among its upper boughs, watching silently with eyes that glimmered like dawn.

Kael'Thorin approached the opening at its base.

It yawned like the mouth of a cave, yet it felt warm—not forbidding. Like a womb returning him to Source. He hesitated only a breath before stepping inside.

The air within was still, but charged. He could feel the resonance of lives lived here, vows spoken in whispers and in sobs, feet that had knelt where he now stood. The inside of the tree was not hollow by absence, but by intention. A space *made* for remembrance.

A bed of moss awaited him in the center. Beside it, a shallow bowl carved from ancient driftwood, filled with crystalline water that shimmered like the Spiral Pool. Above, one glyph burned softly in the bark—one he now recognized as the Spiral of Becoming.

He sat.

Then knelt.

Then folded into stillness.

Not sleep. Not trance.

But communion.

Within minutes—or hours—his breath synced with the hum of the Hollow Tree. It was not a sound he heard with ears, but a knowing he felt in bone.

Visions came again, but not as images. As sensations.

The heaviness of a body left behind on a battlefield. The weightless joy of being held by a lover in a world now forgotten. The terror of a death not yet processed. The grace of forgiveness extended through time.

It all moved through him.

Not to harm, not to overwhelm.

But to remind.

He was not broken.

He was becoming.

And that becoming was holy.

He awoke to light.

Not the sunlight of the physical world, but an inner glow—warm, golden, and humming at the edge of hearing. It took Kael'Thorin several long moments to remember where he was, not because he had forgotten, but because he had gone so deep within that the outer world had faded into mist.

The Hollow Tree had not released him. It had birthed him anew.

He stood slowly. His body felt lighter—not in weight, but in burden. His shoulders no longer carried the ache of unseen expectation. His chest was open, his breath fuller, as though he had remembered how to breathe for the first time in many lifetimes.

A soft rustle behind him. He turned.

It was Amari'el.

She stood in the entrance of the Hollow Tree, illuminated by the forest's soft bioluminescent light. She did not speak. She simply extended her hand.

Kael'Thorin took it.

Together, they walked in silence through the Grove. Birds called out with slow, melodic notes as they passed, as if singing the ending of a rite and the beginning of another. The path shimmered faintly, guiding them back toward the Spiral Pool.

But they did not return to its edge.

Instead, Amari'el led him down a narrow passage he had not seen before—winding through tree roots and low-hanging ferns. The air grew cooler. More still.

Then it opened.

Before them stood a stone altar, half-covered in moss, glowing faintly with spiral markings that echoed the Pool and the Tree. This was not a place of ritual. It was a place of vow.

Amari'el spoke.

"Every soul must vow itself anew, in every lifetime, in every layer. You remembered in the water. You remembered in the tree. Now you must remember in your will."

Kael'Thorin stepped forward.

His heart beat loudly in his chest.

"I vow," he said slowly, "to carry the seed of remembrance. To walk the Spiral not for myself alone, but for all who are still forgetting."

He placed his hand upon the altar.

The stone pulsed beneath his palm.

"I vow to speak the name of the Lost when others have silenced them. I vow to choose courage when fear seduces. I vow to remain open to love even when sorrow darkens the sky."

Amari'el stepped beside him and placed her hand over his.

"And we vow to walk with you," she whispered, her voice a song. "In every shadow. In every dawn."

The altar's light brightened, then dimmed, then disappeared.

The vow had been accepted.

Kael'Thorin turned to her. "Is it done?"

She smiled, and her smile was ancient. "Now you return to the world."

And together, they stepped back into the Grove.

As they walked, the trees of the Grove parted more easily, sensing the shift.

Kael'Thorin no longer moved like one newly returned, but as one rethreaded into the weave of what was. The Grove, alive and ancient, recognized the difference. Its leaves hummed subtly with approval.

They emerged onto a small rise that overlooked the wider expanse of Lemuria's eastern forests. From here, a shimmering river carved its way toward the horizon, catching the light of the twin moons that had begun to rise. The air held that rare silence—one not born of stillness, but of reverence.

Waiting for them on the rise were the others.

Odric, Thalan'ar, and Seraphiel stood side by side. Their faces were unreadable, but their eyes held depth—a kind of sacred solemnity, as if they, too, had once stood where Kael'Thorin now stood. Perhaps they had. Time, in Lemuria, was never so linear.

"Brother," Thalan'ar said, his voice like stone meeting water.

"Welcome," said Seraphiel, her voice like a string plucked in the heart.

Odric nodded once. "The vow is made. Now the Spiral turns."

Kael'Thorin stepped toward them.

There was no ceremony here—only presence. And presence, in this land was more sacred than ritual.

Together, the five gathered in a circle, Kael'Thorin in the center. Amari'el remained at the edge, watching with eyes that glimmered—not with tears, but with knowing.

A breeze stirred.

Kael.

His presence returned, as it always did in liminal moments. The wind turned warm and whisper-soft, brushing against their skin, curling around their words before they were spoken. Kael was listening.

Thalan'ar stepped forward and extended something wrapped in cloth. Kael'Thorin took it.

He unraveled the cloth slowly to reveal a blade—slender, elegant, forged from orichalcum and etched with spirals so fine they seemed woven rather than carved. The handle was wrapped in sea-silk and glowed with inner blue light.

"This is not for war," Thalan'ar said. "This is for memory."

Kael'Thorin nodded, reverently taking the blade in hand.

Odric moved next and placed a thick leather bracer on Kael'Thorin's left forearm. It bore the same spiral etched in silver.

"To ground you when the sky pulls too hard," he said.

Seraphiel offered a pendant shaped like a teardrop, filled with crystallized water from the Spiral Pool.

"For truth spoken when silence tempts."

Then Amari'el stepped into the circle. She held nothing.

She placed both hands over Kael'Thorin's heart.

"For love," she said.

They stood in silence for a time—no longer Five and One, but a Circle. A beginning.

Then Kael'Thorin lifted his gaze to the horizon.

There, in the fading light, shimmered something strange.

A ripple.

A disturbance in the peace.

"Do you see it?" he asked quietly.

They did.

The time of peace was ending.

The ripple was not visible to the untrained eye.

It shimmered only briefly, like heat bending air, like memory slipping between thoughts. But Kael'Thorin saw it—felt it. So did the Five.

The horizon held its breath.

They descended the rise together, no longer in solemn formation but as companions, eyes trained toward the disturbance. They did not rush. Rushing was not the way of Lemuria. But the urgency had begun to hum beneath the stillness.

As they moved through the ancient woods, the trees leaned in, leaves whispering warnings not in words, but in song—an octave lower than joy, a key turned half-shadow. The animals had vanished. Not in fear, but in respect.

The Grove, too, could feel it.

At the forest's edge lay a clearing known as the Mirror Field. It was once used for initiations of resonance—where adepts would sit in absolute stillness and learn to see themselves not through reflection, but through frequency. It had not been used in centuries.

Until now.

In the center of the field, the ripple widened.

The air thickened.

Kael'Thorin slowed as he stepped into the circle of ancient stone markers. Each was inscribed with the same spiral—worn by time, but still glowing faintly.

He felt it before he saw it.

A tear. Not in the sky, not in the world, but in the veil.

A thin, flickering line began to form—vertical, luminescent, pulsing. From its center came a sound not heard with the ears, but felt behind the sternum. It was not malevolent.

But it was foreign.

Not of Lemuria.

Thalan'ar reached for the hilt of his blade, though he did not draw it. Seraphiel's eyes narrowed, lips moving in silent invocation. Odric stood like a monolith, anchoring the space. Amari'el sang low under her breath—a tone of weaving and soft boundaries.

Kael'Thorin stepped forward.

"Let me."

They did not stop him.

He knelt before the ripple and placed his palm upon the grass.

"I see you," he whispered.

The ripple responded.

It pulsed, then opened—slightly. Not wide enough to pass through, but enough for something to *pass out.*

A beam of light emerged—then condensed.

A shape.

A child.

Naked. Eyes wide. Breathing heavily.

It was a boy, no more than five or six years in appearance. But his eyes—

Kael'Thorin staggered back.

Those eyes were stars collapsed into form.

The child fell forward, and Kael'Thorin caught him.

The boy looked up at him.

"Help me," he whispered.

Then his eyes rolled back, and he went limp.

Silence.

The Five surrounded Kael'Thorin as he cradled the child.

Seraphiel broke the silence. "He is not from here."

Odric nodded. "But he is not enemy."

Thalan'ar frowned. "He is before."

Kael'Thorin looked at them all.

"No," he said slowly, voice firm. "He is after."

The Grove stirred.

Kael's wind rose in the trees.

The spiral had turned again.

The child slept for three days.

Not in the way of human children, but in the way of celestial crossings—his body motionless, breath barely perceptible, suspended in a state between worlds. The Grove adapted instantly, wrapping him in warmth and resonance, as if the land itself understood the significance of his arrival.

Kael'Thorin did not leave his side.

He sat beside the boy, legs folded, hands resting lightly on his knees, matching his breath to the child's. He watched over him as a guardian would, but also as a student—every twitch of the boy's fingers, every subtle hum in his chest, was a lesson.

"Who are you?" Kael'Thorin whispered on the second night, voice low and reverent. "Or… who will you become?"

The Five kept their distance, not from disinterest, but respect. They knew the space was sacred. It was Seraphiel who visited the most, bringing tinctures brewed from memory blossoms and water drawn under moonlight. Amari'el, too, sang over him—tones of anchoring and rebirth.

On the morning of the fourth day, the boy awoke.

He sat upright without warning, gasping—as though surfacing from a great depth.

Kael'Thorin startled, hands reaching out. "Easy…"

The boy looked at him. Really looked. His gaze was no longer filled with starlight—but with the flicker of remembering.

"Where am I?" the boy asked. His voice was soft, unsure.

"You're safe," Kael'Thorin said. "You're in Lemuria."

The boy blinked slowly, tasting the name. "Lemuria…"

He touched his chest. "I was... I was flying. But not with wings. With thought. With... light."

Kael'Thorin's eyes narrowed. "Do you remember your name?"

The boy hesitated, then shook his head.

"No. But I remember her face."

"Whose face?"

The boy looked toward the trees.

"She sang to me before I came. Her voice was fire and water. I think... I think she sent me here."

Kael'Thorin's breath caught. He turned to see Seraphiel standing at the edge of the Grove, unmoving.

The boy's eyes followed his gaze.

"That's her," he whispered.

Kael'Thorin's heart thundered.

Seraphiel stepped forward, slowly, as if walking across threads of fate. She knelt before the boy and touched his cheek.

"I did not call you," she said softly. "But I was there when your path crossed ours."

The boy leaned into her hand.

"Then why do I feel like I've known you for lifetimes?"

Seraphiel's eyes misted. "Because perhaps you have."

Kael'Thorin looked between them, his mind awash in unspoken knowing.

The Spiral had not brought them a visitor.

It had brought them a return.

The child's name returned before the sun fully set that same day.

He had wandered alone to the edge of the Mirror Field, standing before the worn spiral stones. Kael'Thorin watched from a respectful distance, allowing the boy's remembrance to unfold without interference.

The wind stirred gently—Ka'el, ever present, whispering through the grass like an elder humming a lullaby.

The boy tilted his head, eyes wide, and placed both hands on the spiral-marked stone.

"I remember," he said aloud.

Kael'Thorin stepped forward. "What do you remember?"

The boy turned to him, expression calm and ancient.

"My name," he said. "It is Auren."

The word echoed through the Grove.

Amari'el, seated beneath a flowering lunaria tree, stilled mid-song. Seraphiel, in meditation beside the Spiral Pool, opened her eyes and whispered, "So it begins again." Odric paused in the shaping of a sacred tool. Thalan'ar looked skyward, mouth set in thought.

Kael'Thorin repeated the name. "Auren."

It vibrated in the space between them—like something returned to its rightful place.

Auren stepped away from the stone. "I am not from this time, am I?"

"No," Kael'Thorin said gently. "But you are of this world."

Auren nodded. "Then I must learn how to be here."

Kael'Thorin smiled. "And I will teach you."

From that moment, Auren was no longer the lost one—they were now two: a bearer and a seed, a remembering and a becoming.

They returned to the Grove, side by side.

That evening, the Five gathered once more beneath the Great Canopy, firelight reflecting in their eyes. Kael'Thorin sat with

Auren beside him, the boy quiet, observant, heart still humming from the day's revelations.

Odric leaned forward, elbows on knees. "What came through the veil was not an accident."

Thalan'ar nodded. "Something has shifted. The veil thins too early."

"It is not too early," Seraphiel said calmly. "It is on time. The Spiral has quickened."

Amari'el looked to Auren. "Then he is both messenger and message."

Kael'Thorin said nothing. His hand rested lightly on Auren's shoulder.

The fire crackled.

The Grove listened.

And above them, the stars shimmered with a brightness not seen in many seasons. A brightness that whispered of paths soon to fracture, truths soon to be buried, and hearts that would one day forget.

But not yet.

Not tonight.

Tonight, they remembered.

And the remembering was enough.

Days passed, then weeks.

The Grove began to shift.

Not in appearance, but in tone. Its resonance deepened, like a drumbeat preparing the ground for something vast. The elders noticed it. The animals moved differently. The wind, Ka'el's breath, carried new notes—more minor chords, more silence between gusts.

Auren adjusted quickly.

He learned with a speed that surprised even Seraphiel. Words came easily to him. Energies, even more so. He could call light to his palm before he knew how to shape clay. He asked questions no child his age should know to ask.

But Kael'Thorin saw what others did not.

Auren did not sleep easily. He woke often with his brow soaked in sweat, eyes wide with stars again, whispering names that Kael'Thorin didn't recognize. Names that made the air around him shiver.

"Are you dreaming?" Kael'Thorin asked one morning, gently brushing the boy's hair back.

Auren looked at him. "No. I'm remembering."

"Remembering what?"

The boy hesitated.

"A place of glass towers and burning skies. Where no one listens to the trees."

Kael'Thorin went still. "Atlantis?"

Auren nodded. "I think… I think I was there. Or I will be."

The Five convened again.

This time, it was not around the fire, but deep within the Echo Cavern—where words were spoken only if they could withstand the resonance of truth. The chamber glowed with lines of crystal, humming softly as each voice entered.

"He remembers Atlantis," Kael'Thorin said plainly.

Thalan'ar's jaw clenched. "Then the threads are fraying faster than we feared."

Seraphiel closed her eyes. "Auren may be more than a return. He may be a bridge."

"To what?" Odric asked.

"To what comes after the fall," she said.

Silence bloomed in the cavern.

Kael'Thorin's voice broke it. "Then we must prepare him. Not as a child. As a key."

A beat passed.

Then Thalan'ar stepped forward, his voice like stone meeting truth. "Then he begins the Rite."

Amari'el's breath caught. "So soon?"

"There is no soon or late anymore," Thalan'ar said. "There is only now."

Seraphiel nodded. "The Spiral demands it."

Kael'Thorin looked up at the crystal ceiling. Its facets glimmered with echoes of what had been, and what would be.

"Then let it begin," he said.

The Spiral had turned again.

The Rite of Spiral Initiation began not with ceremony, but with silence.

At dawn, Kael'Thorin and Auren walked alone to the edge of the Spiral Pool. The air was still, heavy with expectation. Mist clung to the water's surface, whispering secrets of those who had come before.

Auren wore no adornments, save a woven strand of lunaria around his wrist—Amari'el's quiet blessing. Kael'Thorin carried no blade, no staff. This was not a rite of power. It was a rite of listening.

At the edge of the pool, Kael'Thorin knelt and traced the spiral pattern into the earth beside them.

Auren watched closely.

"What is the spiral?" he asked softly.

Kael'Thorin looked up, his voice steady. "It is not a shape. It is a promise."

"To who?"

"To yourself. To your Source. To the song you are still remembering how to sing."

Auren nodded, understanding more than his years should allow.

Kael'Thorin gestured toward the water. "Step in when you're ready."

The boy did not hesitate.

He walked into the Spiral Pool, water rising to his knees, then to his waist. The mist curled around him like arms. As he reached the center of the spiral, a soft glow spread from beneath the water—ancient glyphs lighting one by one around him.

Kael'Thorin watched, heart full.

Auren tilted his face to the sky. His eyes closed.

And the Grove responded.

The leaves trembled. The waters hummed. The very air shimmered as though all of Lemuria held its breath.

Then Auren spoke—not loudly, but with clarity that cut through dimensions.

"I vow to remember, even when all light fades."

A ripple spread across the pool.

"I vow to remain true, even when the world forgets."

Another ripple.

"I vow to carry the spark forward, even when my name is no longer known."

The spiral glowed brighter.

And then, silence.

Kael'Thorin stepped into the water and placed his hand on the boy's head.

"It is done," he said.

When they emerged, the Grove bowed—not with movement, but with resonance.

The Spiral had accepted him.

The boy who came through the veil was no longer merely a child.

He was Auren, Spiral-borne, soul-remembered.

And in the distance, unseen to them all, the first fault lines began to form beneath the towers of Lemuria.

They returned from the Spiral Pool just as the sun crested the eastern cliffs, painting the Grove in gold.

Auren walked a step ahead now, his stride more grounded, his posture taller—not with pride, but with integration. The Spiral had etched itself into his bones.

Kael'Thorin followed in silence, watching, sensing the subtle shift in the weave. The boy was no longer becoming. He had begun.

At the edge of the Grove, the Five waited.

Thalan'ar stood with his arms crossed, nodding once as Auren approached. "You bear the vow well."

Odric gave him a single clap on the shoulder—firm, grounding.

Amari'el kissed his forehead, whispering a tone only the trees could understand.

Seraphiel knelt and took his hands in hers. "What you carry now will echo beyond this world."

Auren met each gesture with quiet grace and then turned to Kael'Thorin.

"What happens now?"

Kael'Thorin looked toward the horizon, where the sky shimmered unnaturally. A haze. A bending.

"We begin watching the weave," he said. "Because what is woven can be torn."

Later that day, they gathered at the Circle of Calling—a sacred site once used to consult the deeper intelligences of Lemuria. Carved from sky-stone and nestled into a hilltop shaped like a crescent moon, it was the place where truths were drawn forth by frequency, not force.

Each member of the Circle stood in a point aligned with one of the five harmonic elements: stone, fire, water, air, and memory.

Auren stood in the center.

The platform beneath him began to vibrate, subtle at first, then increasing. His body remained still, but his inner vision flooded with light.

A vision opened.

He saw a city of towers—glittering, glass-like, suspended above sea and stone. He saw scholars dressed in gold, and children born in tubes of light. He saw machines humming with breathless rhythm. But he also saw something else.

A shattering.

Not from war. From forgetting.

The vision cracked. Auren stumbled, eyes wide.

Kael'Thorin caught him before he fell. "What did you see?"

Auren trembled. "A place where soul is traded for brilliance. Where the sky itself weeps but no one listens."

Seraphiel exhaled sharply. "Atlantis."

The Circle dimmed.

The vision had confirmed what many feared.

The spiral wasn't just turning.

It was unraveling.

The days that followed the vision at the Circle were marked by quiet urgency.

The Five moved with new precision. Conversations grew shorter, more purposeful. The Grove itself, sensitive to the currents of soul and time, changed its rhythm. The flowers closed earlier. The winds shifted eastward.

Kael'Thorin spent his nights in deep meditation, sometimes

waking with tears on his face and words from lifetimes past on his tongue.

Auren grew restless.

Though still a boy in form, something within him had accelerated. His gaze lingered longer on the sky, as though searching for constellations yet to form. He wandered into the edges of the Spiral Forest alone and returned speaking of symbols in bark, of voices that told riddles in the wind.

One morning, Amari'el found him carving into stone with nothing but his fingertip.

"What are you doing?" she asked softly.

Auren didn't look up. "Remembering."

She knelt beside him, brushing away the stone dust to reveal a spiral not unlike the sacred ones, but with differences—more complex intersections, more branches breaking away from the center.

"Where did you see this?"

"In a place I haven't been yet," he replied. "But I will go. I think I must."

Amari'el looked at him, truly saw him. "You are beginning to fracture."

"I know," he whispered. "But it doesn't feel wrong."

She nodded and touched his shoulder. "We'll hold you as you do."

That night, the Five met privately with Kael'Thorin.

"He is beginning to drift between echoes," Seraphiel said. "His soul is slipping forward and back."

"He is tasting futures not yet sown," Odric added. "And pasts not fully buried."

Thalan'ar frowned. "If he keeps drifting, he could forget this life entirely."

"No," Kael'Thorin said, resolute. "He will not forget. He is the memory."

Amari'el whispered, "Then we must become the roots."

The meeting ended with a silent agreement: they would stay close, steady, and guide Auren through what was coming.

For something was coming.

It could not yet be named, but it was felt—like the static before a great storm, like the tremor before a mountain cracks.

And so they watched.

They waited.

And they prayed, not to gods, but to the Spiral itself—that the boy would hold.

That the vow would endure.

That memory would be stronger than forgetting.

That evening, the sky broke.

Not in storm, not in fire—but in tone.

A resonance moved across the land, low and trembling, like the sound of a temple bell rung beneath the ocean. It passed through every root, every tree, every breathing thing. The Spiral Pool shimmered darkly. The air grew heavy with knowing.

Kael'Thorin woke instantly.

He wasn't alone.

Auren stood in the threshold of his dwelling, eyes wide, voice low.

"It's calling."

Kael'Thorin rose and moved to him. "What is?"

But Auren was already walking, barefoot, shirtless, drawn by a thread older than language.

The Five were already waiting at the heart of the Grove when they arrived.

No words were exchanged.

Each of them knew.

It was time.

Auren walked to the Spiral Stones once more and stood at the center. The glyphs around him flickered but did not glow. This was not the Rite. This was something else.

A convergence.

The wind stopped.

Ka'el was listening.

Auren raised his arms slowly, as though the heavens were suspended from his fingertips. His voice rang out—not loud, not forceful, but true.

"I open the gate."

Nothing happened.

Then the air tore.

Not violently—but like silk parting to reveal an ancient scar.

The Grove gasped.

From the sky descended a shimmer—not a being, not a vessel,

but a presence.

It did not speak.

But it was heard.

The Five dropped to one knee. Kael'Thorin stood firm, though his breath caught in his throat. Auren remained unmoved, face lifted, eyes glowing silver.

"I remember," he said.

And the presence pulsed in acknowledgment.

Images poured through the sky—visions of futures that had not yet come to pass. Towers falling. Oceans swallowing temples. Flames dancing in sacred halls. A great forgetting.

And then—stillness.

A child in a city of glass.

A flame passed from hand to hand.

A name spoken across lifetimes.

Auren.

He was not just a child.

He was not just a key.

He was the seed.

And the Spiral had chosen to awaken him before the Fall.

The light receded.

The air mended.

But nothing would be the same.

The Five rose slowly, their faces pale, their eyes full.

Kael'Thorin placed a hand on Auren's back.

"What did you see?"

Auren turned to him.

"Everything."

The days that followed were both luminous and heavy.

Auren no longer wandered. He walked with intent—as if remembering his purpose with every step. Animals began to follow him in quiet procession. The trees bowed slightly in his presence, and even the elder stones whispered differently when he passed.

Yet beneath the awe was a current of sorrow.

Kael'Thorin felt it most. It was subtle—like the fading scent of rain before the drought arrives. He knew the Grove's song well, and it had changed. The tones that once spiraled upward now held a descending cadence. Not despair—but preparation.

One evening, as twilight bathed the land in violet, Kael'Thorin and Auren stood at the edge of the Grove where the land fell away into the Valley of Seedlight.

The boy—no longer merely a boy—spoke without turning his head.

"You feel it too."

Kael'Thorin nodded. "Yes. Something draws near."

Auren's voice was soft, crystalline. "It's not war. Not yet. But forgetting."

Kael'Thorin turned to him. "And will we be the ones to remember?"

Auren finally looked up at him. "You will be the last to forget."

Kael'Thorin's chest tightened. "And you?"

"I won't have the choice."

The wind stirred, carrying the breath of Ka'el across the valley.

"I see pieces," Auren continued, "like shattered glass. Lemuria. Then Atlantis. Then… other lands. The North. The steppes. The rivers. And always, a vow… carried in silence."

Kael'Thorin closed his eyes.

"What must we do?"

Auren reached for his hand and placed something within it.

A seed.

Glowing faintly. Pulsing with memory.

"Plant this the moment the towers begin to fall," he said.

Kael'Thorin opened his mouth to protest, but Auren was already turning away.

"I won't remember you next time," Auren said, his voice nearly lost in the wind.

"But I will find you."

Kael'Thorin stood in silence as the boy walked back toward the Grove, the last light of the sun catching in his hair like flame.

The vow had begun its descent into shadow.

And the soul of Lemuria was preparing to fracture.

The Spiral Pool stirred that night.

No wind touched its surface. No stone fell. Yet ripples moved across the water like breath, like thought. The Grove's creatures kept to their hollows. The canopy stood still. Even Ka'el's whisper was absent, as though the wind itself had paused to listen.

Auren knelt at the water's edge.

His reflection shimmered strangely, as though it did not quite match his form. Eyes of silver, yes—but beneath them, a thousand eyes flickered in and out of focus. Older versions. Younger echoes. Other lives waiting in the wings of time.

He pressed his fingers into the water.

The surface welcomed him, parting gently. Not with splash, but with surrender.

And then—his mind fell inward.

Through memory.

Through lifetimes.

He stood in a city of towers. Then a forest soaked in dew. Then a wide plain where men on horseback shouted words he did not understand. Then snow. Then fire. Then stone. Then silence.

Then—Kael'Thorin's face.

He clutched the memory and pulled it close. Not for clarity—but for anchor.

Because the Spiral was trying to scatter him.

A voice rose from within the water—not sound, but frequency.

"Will you carry the vow?"

Auren answered without hesitation. "Yes."

"Even when it burns?"

"Yes."

"Even when it betrays?"

"Yes."

"Even when it is forgotten?"

A pause.

Then—"Especially then."

The ripples stopped.

The Spiral accepted.

Auren fell back from the pool, gasping. Kael'Thorin was already at his side.

"What did you see?"

Auren's voice was hollow. "All the ways I will die."

Kael'Thorin knelt. "And what did you feel?"

The boy looked at him, eyes wet with starlight.

"Gratitude."

The vow was sealed.

And the soul of the future had kissed the waters of the past.

Kael'Thorin did not sleep that night.

He sat in stillness at the edge of the Spiral Pool, watching the reflection of the stars shimmer and shift. His mind returned again and again to the boy's final words—gratitude—and the weight they carried. Gratitude not for joy, but for knowing.

The knowing of what was to come.

The next morning, he gathered the Five beneath the Great Canopy.

There was no formality, no rite. Only presence.

Auren stood among them, not as an initiate, not even as a ward—but as one who had become mirror and flame. The Spiral was in him now. His voice, though quiet, carried a gravity that none could ignore.

"I saw the seed," he told them. "And the many soils it will pass through."

Seraphiel bowed her head.

"You must scatter us," Auren continued. "Not in exile, but in purpose. Each of you carries an echo. A tether. A piece of what will survive."

Amari'el touched her chest where a spiral pendant rested. "What of you?"

"I must forget," Auren said.

Thalan'ar stepped forward. "You know what that means?"

"Yes," he said. "It means I will need you to remember me."

Kael'Thorin stepped forward last.

He held out the seed the boy had given him days before. "And this?"

Auren reached for it, then stopped. "No. You keep it. You'll know when."

Silence passed through the group like a shadow.

Odric finally broke it. "Then the time is near."

"Yes," Auren said. "The song is already changing."

He looked to each of them.

"You will forget this meeting. But you will remember the sound of this moment."

Then he closed his eyes—and began to sing.

It was not a song of language, but of tone and resonance. A frequency layered with memory and light. The Five knelt. Kael'Thorin wept.

And when the song ended, the Grove held its breath.

For it knew what none dared say aloud:

This was the final day of peace.

That night, the stars sang louder than usual.

Kael'Thorin sat in the high boughs of the listening tree, the one oldest in the Grove, where bark folded like mountain ranges and time passed differently. He could hear the echo of Auren's song woven into the night air.

But it was not the boy's voice that haunted him.

It was the truth beneath it.

Auren had given them a gift wrapped in inevitability—memory sealed in tone. And like all sacred things, it was already slipping into myth.

The Grove remained still, reverent, unaware of just how near the ending truly was.

Thalan'ar sharpened his blade beneath the moonlight, not for battle, but for clarity. His discipline had become ritual. Each pass of the stone against steel was a prayer to remain grounded in the storm to come.

Amari'el retreated to the Singing Groves, where the flora pulsed with light. She wept into petals and turned her sorrow into melody, feeding the roots with her grief. Even as she mourned, she wove blessings into every leaf, preparing the land for remembrance.

Odric sat among the elemental forges, etching sigils into stone and fire, whispering protections into tools he would never wield.

Seraphiel fasted and faced the Spiral Pool alone, eyes open to visions even she did not yet understand.

And Auren?

He slept.

Peacefully.

As if he had given all that he could for now, and the world would carry him the rest of the way.

Kael'Thorin watched over them all.

The Grove.

The Five.

The Seed.

He held the vow in his hands now, tangible and pulsing.

And he whispered to it.

"I will not forget."

Not this time.

Not ever.

Far from the Grove, deeper into the wilderness of Lemuria, Auren walked alone.

The trees here were older, more quiet, as though they remembered the stars before they had names. Moss covered the stones like whispered secrets. The sun filtered through thick canopy in fractured beams, revealing floating particles of light like ancestral dust.

Auren felt no fear.

Only a strange sense of reunion.

As though he had walked this path in another life—or many.

He followed the subtle pull of the Spiral, not through direction, but through resonance. His steps responded to the tone beneath the soil. A turning here. A pause there. Each choice intuitive. Remembered.

He came at last to a clearing shaped like an eye.

In its center stood a single obelisk, unlike any in the Grove. Darker. Angular. Older than Lemuria itself.

Auren approached slowly.

The obelisk shimmered as he neared it, its surface responding to his presence. Glyphs lit one by one—not Lemurian, not Atlantean, but something deeper. Precedent. Primordial.

He placed his hand against it.

A wave of energy surged through him.

He fell to his knees.

Flashes of lifetimes.

A mother with hair like raven feathers. A horse beneath him on an endless plain. A battle cry. A forest of heather and fog. A river iced in moonlight. A cave of glowing salt. A star falling into his open hand.

Then—stillness.

And a voice.

"You are the song. We are the remembering."

Tears fell.

Auren looked up.

And from the base of the obelisk, a small green shoot broke through the stone and began to grow.

The seed had stirred.

He smiled.

And though the Grove was far behind him, Kael'Thorin looked up at that exact moment, sensing the shift in the web of memory.

The Spiral was holding.

And the vow, though scattered, had begun to bloom.

As dusk descended once more, the air shimmered with a quiet magic.

Auren made camp near the obelisk, though not out of necessity—he felt no hunger, no chill, no fatigue. He built no fire. Still, he stayed. The clearing had claimed him, and the Spiral had not yet released its hold.

He lay on the moss, eyes open to the stars breaking through the canopy.

One star in particular pulsed—brighter, then dim, then bright again.

A rhythm.

A pattern.

He reached out with his mind, not in thought, but in tone.

And the star responded.

His body remained still, but his spirit lifted, pulled through a corridor of light that bent around time. He flew past the temples of Lemuria, through the crystalline channels of Atlantis, across snow-covered plains, past the whispering cedars of the northern lands…

…until he stood at a river's edge.

A child's hand reached for his.

The child was him.

And not him.

Wearing the same soul, yes—but shaped by another time, another culture, another vow.

The child smiled.

Auren knelt. "Who are you?"

The child did not speak, but placed a feather in Auren's palm.

It shimmered with the light of all the lifetimes they had shared.

"You are me," Auren whispered. "And I am you."

The river bent, winding upward into the sky.

The child ran into the current and vanished.

Auren blinked—and he was back beneath the trees.

He sat upright, clutching the feather still glowing in his hand.

Kael'Thorin, now far away, stirred in his sleep.

In the Spiral Grove, Amari'el looked to the stars and began to hum without knowing why.

In the elemental forges, Odric's flame bent sideways.

The vow echoed.

Across time. Across forms.

The Spiral had begun to stitch its pattern beyond Lemuria.

And the soul's journey—unfolding, remembering—was now truly underway.

Back in the Spiral Grove, change was stirring.

The elders—those who did not speak much, who communed more with wind than with words—began to shift their gatherings to the outer trees. They walked slowly, listening with their feet. They placed hands on trunks and whispered their farewells in spirals of sound that only the land could interpret.

Kael'Thorin stood beside the ancient Cedar of Memory, feeling the pulse of something irreversible.

"The gate is thinning," Seraphiel said, appearing beside him.

Kael'Thorin nodded. "He's opened it wider than we imagined."

Amari'el joined them, holding a bowl of singing water, the surface trembling with frequencies not native to this realm.

"He's calling the echoes," she said. "Not just ours. All the fragments of his soul across time."

Thalan'ar, standing nearby with Odric, frowned. "Can he survive that?"

Seraphiel looked up at the sky, now streaked with strange clouds—threads of blue fire, gold mist, silver weavings.

"If the Spiral holds, yes. If not..."

Her voice trailed off.

Kael'Thorin spoke with certainty. "It will hold. It must."

That night, the five gathered once more. But not in the Grove. They followed the tones carried on starlight to the very place Auren had entered days earlier—through forest, across stone, to the clearing of the obelisk.

It was glowing now.

The shoot at its base had grown into a sapling.

And in its leaves, symbols shimmered—Atlantean, Mongolian, Celtic, Cree—languages from timelines far removed, yet humming in harmonic unison.

Auren was not there.

But his presence was.

Kael'Thorin stepped forward and touched the bark.

A vision flooded him: Auren standing on a cliff beneath a burning sky, holding a scroll of light and a sword made of air.

Then: Auren in chains.

Then: Auren teaching.

Then: Auren dying.

Then: Auren returning.

The Spiral was speaking.

And the story was just beginning.

Auren walked for three days and three nights, though no sun marked the sky in the way of men's calendars. The forest deepened, folding in on itself like the pages of an ancient tome. Sounds grew older. Even the wind began to speak in voices long thought lost.

He reached the edge of a vast glade.

At its center stood a circle of thirteen stones, each inscribed with sigils that pulsed with a low hum. The space between them shimmered, not with light, but with potential—a veil of becoming.

Auren entered the circle and sat cross-legged in its center.

He placed the feather from the vision at his left side, the glowing seed at his right. Then he closed his eyes.

The Spiral opened.

He did not travel this time. Instead, it came to him.

One by one, fragments of himself stepped from the veil: a Lemurian child, an Atlantean sage, a horseman cloaked in wolf fur, a druid with eyes like winter, a boy chasing ravens along a frozen riverbank.

Each sat beside him.

He did not ask them questions.

He only listened.

And from them, he heard not stories—but tones. Resonant fields. Frequencies of memory held in form. He felt the weight of fire, the grace of water, the ache of loss, the thrill of discovery, the sweet cut of love.

Together, they hummed.

One tone.

One Spiral.

One vow.

And then—each stood, placed a hand on Auren's heart, and returned into the veil.

He opened his eyes.

He was alone again.

But no longer separate.

He stood slowly and lifted the seed.

It pulsed with the light of all that had been remembered.

And as he stepped beyond the circle, the stones began to sing—soft and low, like lullabies beneath the earth.

The song of Lemuria had been awakened.

Chapter 2: The Path of the Spiral

The first light of morning in Lemuria did not come from the sun.

It came from the land itself.

Veins of bioluminescent rootfire pulsed beneath the mossy floor of the Spiral Grove, casting a soft amber glow through the predawn mist. The trees, tall as mountains yet silent as breath, shimmered faintly with dew that glowed like memory.

Kael'Thorin stood barefoot on the threshold, just beyond the boundary stones.

He did not move.

The Spiral Grove was not a place one entered casually. It called. And when it called, it was both invitation and initiation. A summons and a surrender.

His breath moved slow, deliberate. His cloak of obsidian-threaded wool hung heavy with night's moisture, and the air buzzed with the scent of cypress, myrrh, and something older—an undercurrent of ozone and flowered decay, the perfume of things dying beautifully.

Behind him, the night receded in silence.

Ahead, the Spiral whispered.

It was not a sound, but a pressure. A rhythm. A pull. It touched his sternum and the space between his shoulder blades. It called to the marrow of him, not just to walk forward—but to remember.

He looked down.

The path was not visible.

There were no stones or tracks. Only soft earth and petals drifting like thoughts unspoken.

Then a hand touched his arm.

Amari'el Shae'Lumae.

She wore a robe of riverwoven silk, the color of early twilight. Her hair was braided in the Lemurian fashion—interwoven with single strands of lightroot. In the growing brightness, she shimmered like something not entirely of this world.

"You're trembling," she said.

Kael'Thorin did not deny it. "I remember… and yet I don't."

She nodded. "That is the path."

Then she released his arm and stepped forward into the Grove.

The air parted for her.

The Spiral accepted her.

Kael'Thorin inhaled sharply, letting the scent of the sacred flood his lungs, and then followed.

Behind them, the stones sealed.

The Spiral Grove had no walls, yet it held its own kind of architecture—one built of resonance, not stone.

Each step Kael'Thorin took was met with a response from the land. Not sound exactly, but a shift in sensation. As if the Grove recognized him. As if the soil remembered.

He had walked here once before, in a time veiled from thought, in the life-before-lives. The memory of that moment tugged at the edge of his perception like smoke—present, but always moving.

The path bent toward a clearing surrounded by ancient songwood trees, their trunks curved like chalices lifting into the morning mist. The air here carried a gentle pressure, a kind of sacred density. Kael'Thorin slowed his steps.

Amari'el was already waiting at the center of the spiral ring.

She stood barefoot upon the central glyphstone, arms lowered, eyes closed. Her breath was even, like a river carving silence into the air. She was not praying. She was listening.

Kael'Thorin moved toward her, stepping into the Spiral's center—an act that would have been forbidden to any uncalled soul. But he had been summoned. That made all the difference.

When he stood beside her, Amari'el opened her eyes.

"There are many who walk the Spiral," she said, "but few who let it walk them."

Kael'Thorin searched her expression, seeking more than the meaning of her words—seeking the deeper invitation within them.

"And I am to be walked?" he asked.

"No," she said. "You are to be woven."

A silence stretched between them—thick, luminous.

Finally, he nodded.

"I accept."

From the edge of the clearing, four other figures began to emerge.

The Five were gathering.

They came not as strangers, but as stars drawn back into constellation.

First was Thalan'ar, broad of shoulder and deep of gaze, his body painted with the red ochre lines of his mountain kin. A silent weight preceded him, as if the Grove bowed slightly in his presence. He bore no weapon, but his very stillness cut the air.

Then Seraphiel, cloaked in blue-gray mist, her silver hair drifting like smoke above her shoulders. Her feet barely touched the moss, yet her presence pressed inward like a tide—gentle, insistent, inevitable. The Grove hummed in harmony with her arrival.

Odric emerged next, walking with the slow confidence of stone. His robe was worn and layered, part ritual vestment, part traveler's dustcloak. A shard of crystal swung from his belt. He nodded once to Kael'Thorin—brother to brother, soul to soul.

And finally, Ka'el—though he did not walk as the others did.

He appeared as wind before form, his figure crystallizing in the shimmer between leaf and light. Cloaked in the everturning ether, Ka'el was not entirely there, and yet more present than any of them. His gaze, when it settled on Kael'Thorin, held galaxies.

Amari'el stepped forward, arms wide.

"We are gathered."

Her voice was both announcement and invocation.

The Five took their positions around the glyphstone, forming a perfect star around Kael'Thorin.

"This Spiral is not for knowledge alone," Amari'el said. "It is for seeding remembrance into the blood and bones of the world."

"And in doing so," Seraphiel added, "he will forget."

Kael'Thorin stood in the center, still and strong.

"I do not fear forgetting," he said. "Only that I might not return."

Thalan'ar's voice rumbled like deep earth. "You will return."

"And when you do," Odric said, "we will remember you first."

The Spiral flared beneath them.

The weaving had begun.

The Spiral took shape not through motion, but through memory.

Beneath their feet, the glyphstone pulsed in rhythmic light—runes igniting and fading in sacred sequence. Each spark told a story, not in language, but in essence. The Spiral was a library, an archive of souls.

Kael'Thorin knelt at the center as Amari'el began the First Turning.

She moved clockwise, fingers brushing the air, weaving patterns that shimmered like liquid threads. With each pass, a ring of light encircled Kael'Thorin, sealing him into the ritual—not as prisoner, but as seed.

Seraphiel stepped next, lifting both hands toward the canopy above. Her breath became song, and the song became shape—a resonance that softened the space between what was and what would be. The Spiral responded, rippling with tones of wind and ocean and longing.

Odric moved in from the west, kneeling opposite Thalan'ar, palms pressed to the ground. Stones answered him, rising in tiny pillars from the moss. They circled Kael'Thorin like sentinels of remembrance.

Thalan'ar did not move.

Instead, he watched.

Not with his eyes, but with his entire body. He was the witness. The anchor. His role was not to add, but to hold—to become unmoving so all else could move around him.

Then Ka'el passed through them all.

He did not walk.

He shimmered, whispered, flickered. He entered Kael'Thorin not like a spirit taking hold, but like wind filling sails. And for one brief instant, Kael'Thorin's body lifted from the glyphstone—hovering an inch above the spiral center.

His eyes flashed open.

They glowed.

And then—he wept.

Not from fear.

But from awe.

He had touched the edge of all that was to come.

And then, just as gently, he returned.

Feet to stone.

Breath to chest.

Tears to skin.

The Spiral Markers led them across the plateau like a constellation scattered upon the earth. Each one pulsed faintly when Kael'Thorin passed, as though recognizing him—not his face, not his form, but the essence he carried.

The wind grew softer here, warmer, carrying the scent of blossoms that did not grow anywhere else in Lemuria. It was the scent of the grove's edge, of a place older than memory and guarded by the vow of countless souls.

They descended into a shallow valley, where the air itself seemed denser, filled with a quiet power. At the far end, beneath the arching limbs of ancient trees, the Spiral Path coiled inward like the shell of a great sea creature. At its center, a light shimmered—not the cold light of stars, but a living radiance, gold threaded with green.

Amari'el paused at the edge of the first curve. "Beyond this point," she said softly, "the grove will see you as you are. It will know what you carry, both burden and gift. You cannot step inside without being seen."

Kael'Thorin's gaze met hers, steady. "Then let it see me."

They stepped forward together. The spiral closed around them, each turn drawing them deeper into the heart of the land's memory. Above, the branches swayed, whispering in a tongue older than the stones.

And somewhere, carried on the wind between worlds, Ka'el's presence moved—silent, unseen, but watching.

Interlude I: The Divide of the Two Towers

The sea knew before the councils did.

On the nights when the moons crossed, the tide pulled strangely along the Inner Sea, as if some great creature were turning in its sleep. Fisher-monks of Lemuria said it was the continent dreaming; Atlantean pilots swore it was the deep machines breathing. Both were right, and neither would yield.

Along the Lemurian coast, signal braziers were kept unlit by order of the High Tower—an act of restraint. Across the water, the Atlantean Lighthouse of Sevrion burned white-blue, its beam combing the waves in a lattice of command. Where light met darkness, a third band appeared: silver, neither surrender nor dominion, a seam in the world that widened each season.

Messengers crossed that seam in quiet craft with muffled keels. They carried not scrolls, but songs impressed into crystal—records of harvests, tremors felt in the stone, births of storm-whales, sightings of sky-barges. Trade still flowed; curiosity was not yet a crime. But what the crystals truly carried was apprehension: Lemuria's reports grew filled with omens read from wind and root; Atlantis' returns thickened with inventories and yield projections. One listened for the soul of the world. The other measured its power.

In the High Tower, Eldress Tymae stood at the western window and watched Sevrion's beam comb the black. She did not curse it. She counted its beats—one, two, three—and set a small bell to ringing on the fourth, so that the room filled with alternating waves of light and sound. "Harmony requires difference," she told the novices. "But difference without listening becomes fracture."

Across the sea, Archon Valceran of Atlantis walked the gallery of the Lighthouse and marked the bell tolls faintly drifting from the dark. He did not curse them. He logged their interval in a brassbound ledger, alongside wind speeds and barometric drift. "Patterns precede control," he told his engineers. "And control is the precondition of peace."

Between tower and tower, the seam widened.

It was not hatred that pulled them apart, not at first. It was fidelity—to different readings of the same world. Lemuria believed the great forces would obey if honored. Atlantis believed they would obey if mastered. Both loved the sea. Both feared losing it. And fear, like tide, is obedient to the moon.

On a rainless night, a courier skiff from Sevrion cut the silver seam, bearing a crystal sealed with the Archon's mark. The Lemurian pilot accepted it in silence, set it in the Pool of Translation, and watched the light unfurl into glyphs:

Notice of Expansion.
Installation of second tower approved.
To safeguard shared waters.

Tymae's bell did not ring that night. In its place, she set a bowl of river stones at the window and turned each one over with her thumb, whispering a name—of coves, of estuaries, of villages that would feel the new glare.

Across the water, Valceran's ledger closed on a page inked with triumph and unease. He ordered the engineers to sleep in shifts. He ordered the beam kept bright.

The sea kept its counsel.

It lifted, then settled, like breath before a word.

The announcement of a second tower rippled outward like a stone dropped into still water. Most in Lemuria did not yet feel its weight. Fisherfolk along the outer isles only knew that new currents swirled beneath their keels, strange and contrary. In Atlantis, merchants toasted the news in glass halls, speaking of safe passages and expanded reach.

But there were others—those who walked between worlds—who felt the seam widening in their bones.

On the high plateau of Lemuria's Inner Reach, Thalan'ar knelt beside a cairn of wind-smoothed stones. His hands rested on the topmost one, eyes closed. The stone's memory was long, and it murmured to him of currents gone restless, of salt torn from the sea's own skin. He opened his eyes to the slow sweep of Sevrion's light across the far horizon.

"It begins," he said.

Far to the south, in the Singing Groves, Amari'el Shae'Lumae stood among branches heavy with starfruit. She sang to the leaves, and they trembled with silver light, passing whispers down through root and stream. The water's song had changed—less fluid, more strained. She felt it as one feels a dissonant chord in a beloved melody.

"Something presses against the heart of the world," she murmured. "We must be ready."

Odric, stationed along the Shore of Echoes, watched the tide pull back farther than he had seen in many seasons. He did not speak to the sea; he listened. A deep, slow pulse beneath the waves told him the sea was holding its breath. He gripped the haft of his spear and turned inland.

High above them all, in the Axis Grove, Seraphiel stood at the base of the central pillar—a living trunk older than any record. Her gaze lifted to the canopy, where unseen winds moved. They were not the winds of Lemuria alone. Ka'el, the wind between worlds, had carried him fragments: glints of metal unfamiliar to these shores, the taste of coal smoke, the hum of engineered light.

Seraphiel's voice was low. "The pattern sharpens."

None of the five had yet convened. They moved in their own spheres, but each knew the others would be feeling the same summons. The second tower was not just a structure—it was a turning in the spiral of events, a casting of a new shape upon the waters. And shapes, once cast, drew the world to fit them.

On the decks of Atlantean galleons, envoys rehearsed speeches about cooperation and safety. In Lemurian council chambers, scribes etched warnings about overreach and imbalance. Between these words, the quiet envoys walked—those who crossed without flags or treaties, guided by currents known only to the soul.

One such envoy, cloaked in sealskin and salt, slipped through a hidden cove to meet a companion in the moonless dark. A Lemurian by birth, an Atlantean by oath, he bore no emblem. Only a carved token—a spiral broken at its midpoint—rested in his palm.

"They will not stop at two," he said.

His companion, a woman with eyes like tidepools, closed her fingers over the token. "Then we must decide where we stand before the third."

Above them, the stars turned slowly, indifferent yet watching.

The night air over Lemuria carried a strange tension, as though the ocean itself sensed the slow turning of fate.
By the time the five had gathered in the Grove of the First Light, the moon hung low, its silver wash catching the delicate threads of mist weaving between the ancient trees. No formal summons had been sent—yet each of them knew, without message or herald, that they were meant to be here.

Kael'Thorin arrived first, his stride measured, his eyes reflecting the same restless gleam that had followed him since the council's decree to raise the second tower. He carried no weapon, only the weight of memory—visions that had haunted his sleep and shadowed his waking hours.

Thalan'ar emerged from the eastern path, silent as the tide, his presence wrapped in the quiet authority of one who had walked the corridors of power for far too long. He clasped forearms with Kael'Thorin in greeting, though his expression betrayed nothing of the turmoil beneath.

From the shadows of the grove, Amari'el Shae'Lumae stepped forward, the moonlight catching the silver strands of her hair. She bowed her head slightly—not in subservience, but in acknowledgment of the gravity that drew them together. Her gaze swept the gathering place, as though measuring the balance of forces in play.

Odric came next, his boots heavy with the scent of the docks, carrying the salt and wind of Lemuria's outer edges. He spoke little, but the sea seemed to follow him, its unspoken warnings murmuring just beyond hearing.

Last came Seraphiel, her arrival heralded by the faint rustle of wind through the upper branches. She wore no cloak, no emblem of his station, yet the Grove itself seemed to part for her. Her eyes met each of theirs in turn, lingering on Kael'Thorin with a flicker of unguarded knowing.

They formed a loose circle, each standing at one of the five ancient stones that ringed the grove's heart. For a moment, no words passed between them. Only the soft pulse of the earth beneath their feet spoke, the slow heartbeat of Lemuria itself.

"It has begun," Thalan'ar said at last, his voice low but carrying.

Kael'Thorin's jaw tightened. "The tower?"

"The tower is only the surface," Seraphiel replied. "The deeper current runs beneath—politics cloaked as vision, and ambition draped in prophecy."

Odric crossed his arms. "And the people cheer it. They do not see the shadow it casts."

Amari'el's voice was quiet, yet it seemed to thread through each of them. "The shadow is not cast by stone and mortar alone. It is born of separation. Atlantis will not stop with a second tower. They are testing how far they can reach before Lemuria will draw the line."

Kael'Thorin looked from one to the next. "Then we must decide where that line lies."

Silence followed—not of indecision, but of the weight of choice. Each of them felt the same truth: once drawn, the line would not be easily moved.

Seraphiel finally stepped forward, placing a hand on the central stone. "Before we speak of lines, we must speak of vows. Not to the council, nor to the towers, but to Lemuria itself."

The others nodded, and in the dim moonlight, the first whispers of their unspoken pact began to take form—one that would shape not only the fate of Lemuria, but the echo of their souls through lifetimes to come.

The Grove of the First Light seemed to lean in, branches arching overhead as though the ancient trees wished to hear every word of what would be spoken next. The air was thick with the scent of earth and the faint sweetness of moonlit blossoms. Somewhere in the distance, a lone seabird cried, its call carried on a wind that felt older than the towers themselves.

Thalan'ar's gaze swept the circle. "If Atlantis is testing our resolve, we cannot simply answer with resistance. We must shape the very currents they seek to control."

Kael'Thorin inclined his head. "You speak of influence."

"I speak of presence," Thalan'ar replied. "Not in their halls, but in the hearts of our people. The second tower will stand whether we oppose it or not. But if we tend the roots, the branches will not bend so easily."

Amari'el stepped closer to the central stone, her fingers brushing its lichen-covered surface. "The roots you speak of are already fraying. The old songs are fading from memory, replaced with the rhetoric of progress. If the people forget who they are, no tower will need to fall for Lemuria to be lost."

Odric shifted, his sea-worn hands curling into fists. "Then we remind them. Quietly, at first. In the markets, in the docks, in the gatherings where the council's gaze does not reach. Let them hear the old words again, even if they think them only stories."

Seraphiel's voice was steady, yet carried the weight of a tide turning. "And we must bind ourselves to this work—not as a task, but as a vow that will hold beyond this life."

Kael'Thorin's eyes narrowed in thought. "Such a vow would call the soul across ages."

"That is the point," Seraphiel said, stepping into the moonlight. "The shadow that moves now is not bound to one age alone. If we anchor our vow deep enough, it will reach through the drift between lives."

The idea hung between them, heavy with both promise and cost.

Amari'el met Kael'Thorin's gaze, her voice soft but unyielding. "Would you carry this through the turning of worlds?"

He did not hesitate. "Yes."

One by one, the others spoke the same word, until the grove itself seemed to echo with it.

Then Seraphiel placed both hands on the central stone, her eyes closing. "So let it be written in the marrow of the earth, in the breath of the wind, in the song of the waters. What we vow here will not fade."

A low hum rose from the stones, as though the grove had accepted their pact. The air grew warmer, the moonlight brighter, and each of them felt the same quiet certainty: they had just bound themselves to a path from which there would be no return.

Far beyond the grove, unseen in the depths of the ocean, a current shifted course.

The days that followed were quiet on the surface, but beneath, something had begun to stir.

In the harbor towns, Odric's voice was heard in the murmurs of sailors and merchants as he reminded them of the old navigational chants—verses once sung to honor the sea and the sky together. A few sang them in jest, but more than one voice found the rhythm catching in their memory, humming as they worked the rigging.

Amari'el walked the market lanes, weaving through the stalls where Atlantean trade goods now glittered in the sun. She spoke not against the goods themselves, but of the stories they displaced—tales of the First Grove, of the crystal springs that fed both land and heart. To the children, she taught small songs whose meanings would unfold only with time.

Kael'Thorin kept to the outer villages, speaking little, listening much. In each home, he carried the presence of one who had not bent to the rising wind of change. His eyes held the steadiness of the deep roots Thalan'ar had spoken of, and in their reflection, others began to remember their own.

Seraphiel moved like a shadow along the coast, tending to the Axis Grove where the ley lines of the island converged. He whispered to the waters, to the stones, to the unseen threads that bound Lemuria's spirit. It was not his words that traveled, but the resonance they carried, filtering into dreams and sudden moments of clarity.

As for Thalan'ar, he remained within the central city, close to the Tower of the First Light. From there, he observed the council's movements, the slow tightening of Atlantean influence in their decrees. His was the most dangerous path, for he stood where the shadow was longest.

One evening, as the sun fell and the towers glowed like twin flames against the horizon, a flock of seabirds rose in perfect unison from the water. No one marked the moment as unusual, save for the five—each seeing it from their separate places, each feeling the same quiet pulse of recognition.

The vow had begun to move.

Yet in the deep halls of Atlantis, a councilor named Drenivar, known for his keen sense of opportunity, turned his gaze toward Lemuria with new intent. Though he could not name it, he sensed resistance—like a current that pushed against his plans. And Drenivar was not a man to let such currents run free.

The first stone of the second tower was not laid in daylight.

Before dawn, under a sky the color of quenched steel, Atlantean barges slid into a crescent cove opposite Sevrion. Lanterns hooded, chains wrapped in leather, orders spoken in gestures—Drenivar's caution was absolute. He preferred facts to port rumors, foundations to proclamations. When the sun rose, he wanted the work already irreversible.

On the Lemurian side of the seam, the shoreline felt it. The tide hesitated—one long, listening breath—and then receded farther than any fisherman could remember. Odric watched from a low bluff, the sea-mist beading on his lashes. He did not try to stop what was beginning. He marked it: the angle of the barges, the rhythm of the cranes, the way the new pylons were driven not straight down, but at a cunning slant to grip the bedrock like claws.

He sent no carrier bird, lit no signal fire. He closed his eyes and spoke his accounting into the water. The Shore of Echoes would carry it inward faster than any courier.

Amari'el received it first—waking suddenly with her palm pressed to the floor of the Singing Groves. She felt the metal's bite in the seabed as one feels a knife drawn across the skin of a drum. She stood, gathered the young tenders, and changed the morning's lesson. No songs of harvest. Songs of remembering: the old chord that binds river to sea, root to rain. The children's voices trembled, then steadied, a thread drawn taut against an unseen pull.

Thalan'ar moved through the city like a man measuring a pulse. Decrees had already been posted—framed as safety ordinances for coastal trade. He read the language twice, then a third time, tracing absences: no limits on beam strength, no sunset provisions, no clause for shared oversight. He set the scroll down and understood Drenivar's game. If the second tower rose before the councils met, Lemuria would be arguing procedure while Atlantis claimed inevitability.

At the Axis Grove, Seraphiel walked the spiral paths until the wind shifted. Ka'el had brought her a sliver of another sky—the smoke-sour taste of furnaces, the hum of crystal engines forced past their harmonics. She touched the central pillar and felt a faint discord ring down the root like frost. "Not here," she whispered to the wind. "Not yet." The leaves stilled, as though they, too, were holding breath.

Kael'Thorin came last to the knowing. He stood on a ridge above the Inner Sea, the world below him only shadow and shape. He did not need light to see. The Spiral in his chest brightened, answering the pressure from across the water. He felt the choice that would be asked of him and of all who walked with him—not whether to love Lemuria, but how.

The five met without meeting. Each, in their place, laid a hand upon what anchored them: stone, root, tide, wind, spiral. Their vow, spoken nights before, drew tight like a net cast wide and hauled to the shore.

Across the seam, Drenivar watched the first pylon lock into place. He did not smile. He simply opened his ledger and made three neat marks: *Angle true. Grip firm. Resistance: none observed.* He did not write what he felt—a brief pressure at the base of the skull, as if the sea itself had looked back.

When the sun finally climbed the horizon, a pale band broke over the water. Men on the barges cheered. On the Lemurian bluffs, gulls lifted in a single spiral. In the Groves, children paused mid-verse, turning their heads as if someone had entered the room.

The seam had widened again.

Not by war cry. By a stone in the dark.

And the world, obedient to shape, began to lean.

For a time, the sea held its counsel.

But in the Axis Grove, the leaves had already begun to whisper—not in words, but in the slow, deliberate turn of their faces toward the inner wind.
In the Singing Groves, the last note of the morning song lingered longer than breath should allow, curling through the air like a thread unwilling to break.

On the Lemurian cliffs, Kael'Thorin drew his cloak around him. The light on the water looked unchanged to any ordinary eye, but he felt the difference.
It was as if two hands had begun to turn a vessel in opposite directions, the strain yet gentle—but growing.

He knew what the others would know. The seam was no longer a line. It was a direction.

And directions, once taken, are not easily turned.

Interlude II: The Blade and the Song

The training hall opened to the sea like a breath held wide. Pillars of pale stone arced over the floor, each veined with threads of mica that glittered whenever the tide sighed against the cliff. Ropes of bellweed hung between the arches, their seed-pods tuned to the wind. When the breeze shifted, the hall answered with a soft chiming—Ka'el's whisper passing through the listening place.

On the sand-polished floor, a circle of blade-bearers moved in slow, deliberate forms. Their knives were ceremonial, leaf-shaped and unsharpened, forged to catch and carry sound rather than cut flesh. With each measured step, a blade tilted, caught a ribbon of morning light, and sang a faint, bright tone. The tones intoned a pattern; the pattern was a vow. Around the circle, singers held a drone in the chest and throat, shaping harmonics that felt more like tide than music.

Odric walked among the blade-bearers barefoot, the long scar on his ankle pale as chalk. He did not clap or count. He breathed, and the circle adjusted without looking. "Let each edge learn its own mercy," he said, voice low enough to lie flat against the sand. "The hand that rushes wounds at the wrist. The hand that listens makes even a blade into shelter."

Across from him, Amari'el Shae'Lumae lifted a palm and the drone opened into intervals—a luminous stair. Some voices widened into the upper air, some settled like pebbles in a riverbed. "Hold the tone, not the fear," she murmured to the singers. "Let the song cradle the edge until both remember they are servants of the same promise."

Kael'Thorin stood near the seaward arch with Seraphiel and Thalan'ar, a step behind the line where salt spray turned the floor dark. From here he could see the entire practice like a map: the eddies of breath, the slipstreams of gaze between Odric and Amari'el, the slight tremble in a novice's left shoulder as she tried not to grip. Seraphiel's presence at his side felt like cool sunlight—feminine, steady, exact. Thalan'ar's attention moved more slowly, as if he were reading the stones, page by page.

A bellweed pod clicked softly, out of turn. The wind had shifted nearer the cliff face. The chime thinned, then returned—almost the same, not quite. Amari'el's eyes flicked toward the arches and then back to the singers. She deepened the root of the tone. The hall answered with a warmer resonance, like light through honey.

Odric stopped in front of the trembling novice. "Let it tremble," he told her quietly. "Let the body tell its truth in this breath, then give it another truth in the next." He raised her wrist with two fingers—no force, only direction. "Feel the blade receive the room. Don't make the room receive the blade."

The novice exhaled, and a sliver of brightness slid along the metal, clean as a gull's cry.

Kael'Thorin felt the echo ring inside his chest. The resonance found the Encoding that lived along his bones since the vow at the grove—an answering note, small and sure. He closed his eyes to listen, and behind the music he heard the sea describe the long curve of a coming weather. Not storm, not yet; a pressure at the edge of the horizon, like a thought arriving from far away.

"Again," Amari'el said, and the singers lifted the intervals one notch higher. The blades moved with the voices, tilting their edges into the harmony as if tasting. Odric's hand rose, and the circle pivoted counterclockwise: twelve blades, twelve breaths, twelve soft tones that braided with the drone until the hall held a single, gently turning chord.

Something in the turning misaligned.

It was small as a hairline in glass. Kael'Thorin felt it first as a coolness on the left side of his neck, then as a shimmer that didn't quite land where it should. Seraphiel's brow furrowed. Bellweed chimed, but one pod sounded like a cracked bell. The novice's blade caught not honey-light but a thin blue flicker that left the air tasting of iron.

Odric's eyes narrowed. "Hold."

The circle froze mid-breath. Amari'el kept the drone alive with a fingertip against her own sternum, then lowered it by a breath-width. The cracked-bell overtone softened, but did not vanish.

Thalan'ar knelt and set his palm to the floor. "Not the stone," he said. "The air."

Seraphiel turned her face to the sea. Her voice, when it came, had the softness of a hand smoothing a child's hair. "Ka'el?"

The wind moved through the arches like a thought reconsidered. The bellweed gentled. The thin blue flicker winked out, and with it the iron taste. Odric lowered his hand. Amari'el's intervals returned to their luminous stair and the chord gathered itself again, whole.

"It will come again," Thalan'ar said without standing. "From outside the hall."

"From outside the island," Seraphiel added, sorrow in the knowing but not despair.

Odric placed two fingers against the novice's blade and then against his own throat, as if calibrating metal to voice. "Then we will practice until what comes finds us listening," he said. "A blade that listens does not answer a lie with a wound."

Amari'el met Kael'Thorin's gaze across the circle. For a moment the hall fell away and there was only the thread between them, river-clear. In her eyes he saw the two vows nested: to protect and to sing, to refuse what does not belong and to welcome what does. He nodded once—yes, I hear it too.

The practice resumed, quieter. In the arches, the wind delayed and then went on, skimming the cliff face toward the lighthouse whose noon beam would soon be tested again on the far water. Kael'Thorin laid his hand flat over his heart and kept time with the turning chord. The air remembered. The blades remembered. The song waited with its hands open.

Somewhere beyond the horizon, the pressure gathered patience.

When the turning chord faded, Odric asked for the hall to clear by halves. Singers sat along the seaward wall; blade-bearers knelt by the landward pillars. The space between them held a wide swath of clean floor where light pooled like water. Amari'el stepped into that brightness and touched her throat, then the hollow behind her ear, then the center of her breastbone—three points, three breaths.

"We practice the seam," she said. "Where edge meets song and neither breaks."

Odric nodded. "Pairs," he added. "Each blade-bearer with a singer. Name what you carry; offer it to the other; receive what they give."

They moved quietly, used to this kind of instruction. Kael'Thorin found himself across from the trembling novice from earlier. She had stopped shaking, but her fingers still rested too far from the blade's leaf. Opposite her, a singer no older than Kael'Thorin pressed his palm to his ribs and found the drone there like a remembered footpath.

"Name what you will not cut," Amari'el said, walking the line.

The novice swallowed. "My mother's patience," she whispered.

"Name what you will always allow to pass," Odric said.

The singer answered without thinking. "A child's fear."

"Begin," Amari'el murmured.

The singer set a breath-wide tone. The novice raised her blade until its flat caught a sliver of light. The tone and the light searched for each other. Kael'Thorin watched the moment of finding—the tiny easing at the corners of the novice's mouth—

and felt something in his own sternum mirror it.

Around them, pairs began their practice. Names rose like small lanterns and floated to the roof: What I will not cut. What I will allow. A fisher's muscle-memory. A widow's quiet. A sailor's laughter. The first green of terraces in spring.

"Listen for when the edge arrives before the song," Odric called, bare voice against the sea's hush. "That is when harm happens."

"And listen for when the song tries to drown the edge," Amari'el added. "That is when truth is lost."

Kael'Thorin and his partner began. He kept his breath simple, not climbing, not insisting. The novice lifted the blade a little closer to the tone. It hummed, faint as a bee at a distance. The bellweed answered with a mild chime that felt, finally, like agreement.

Then, once more, the hairline arrived.

Not as a blue flicker this time, but as a high, thin whine that seemed to ride above the tone, as if a wire had been strung from horizon to horizon. The novice's wrist jittered. The singer's breath hitched and flattened. Kael'Thorin felt the line slice the room—not cutting flesh, cutting choice.

Seraphiel was at his side before he had the thought to call for her. She did not speak. She turned her face to the arch and let the wind travel over the fine bones near her temple. Her eyes softened, then narrowed to a blade's width. The whine persisted for three heartbeats more and evaporated like mist struck by noon's spear.

"What did it refuse?" Kael'Thorin asked, voice low.

Seraphiel's answer was a chord, not a sentence. He heard it as words only after the chord had settled. "It refused to be measured into corridors," she said. "It refused a name that turns a round sea into a straight line."

"Corridor," Kael'Thorin repeated, feeling the word trying to lay itself across the hall like a ruler.

"They will call it safety," Seraphiel said. "They will draw lanes of light and ask the wind to obey. The wind will not."

Across the floor, Thalan'ar had not moved from kneeling. His palm remained on the stone, but his listening had widened until Kael'Thorin could feel it tug at the tide itself. "Words gather before they are spoken," he said softly, to the stone or to anyone. "We felt the gathering."

Odric walked back to them, sand clinging to the callus at his heel. "Practice again," he told the pairs. "Answer the wire with breath, but do not chase it. Keep the vow. Edge in the hand, song in the chest." He looked at Seraphiel. "If the wind refuses, we follow the wind."

Amari'el's mouth curved. "And teach those who insist on straight lines what a circle can do." She lifted her hand, and the singers opened the drone like a harbor mouth. Tones braided, never forcing, never yielding, and the blade-bearers moved until metal sang without brightness, like a river softened by silt.

Kael'Thorin's pair found their balance again—two breaths cupped together, the blade settling into a listening angle that felt more like prayer than defense. The high whine did not return, but he could feel where it had tried to plant itself, a scar waiting for a wound.

When the practice ended, the hall exhaled. Odric dismissed the pairs to water and rest. Amari'el remained in the open floor, fingertips resting lightly at the base of her throat, eyes half-closed as if finishing a conversation only she could hear.

Seraphiel touched Kael'Thorin's wrist. "Walk with me."

They stepped into the arch and along a narrow balcony carved from the cliff. The sea lay far below, slate-green and restless, the sky gathering light in folded panes. A thin spray salted their faces. Bellweed clicked behind them like beads in an unseen hand.

"The wind refused a command shaped like care," Seraphiel said once they were alone. "That is the danger, Kael'Thorin. Not blunt force. Persuasion. A word that says 'I will keep you safe' and then hangs a chain across the water."

"Can a chain be made of sound?"

"It can if enough voices call it law." She rested her palms on the stone rail. "They will sing a corridor into the air and teach sailors to believe it is kinder than fog."

Kael'Thorin thought of the harbor, of fishermen who measured by taste and memory, of skiffs steered by fathers teaching sons night currents with their hands. "What happens when the first boat disobeys the corridor?"

"The corridor will not allow disobedience," Seraphiel said. "It will call disobedience error. And the sea will be asked to correct it." She closed her eyes and listened. "But the sea belongs to no law that begins with fear."

They stood without speaking while the tide combed the rocks below. A gull drew a clean arc and vanished into brightness. Far out, the lighthouse caught a seam of light and gave it back to no one in particular.

"Do I carry blade or song?" Kael'Thorin asked at last.

"Both," Seraphiel said, and there was the faintest smile in it. "You are the place where they agree not to harm."

He nodded, feeling the truth of it settle where the Encoding lived. The admission made him briefly heavier and then, somehow, lighter—as if a weight had learned it was also a wing.

Back in the hall, Odric and Amari'el faced one another across the empty floor. No one else remained in the circle. He held a practice blade, its leaf dark with use; she held nothing but air.

"You will argue for silence," Amari'el said, not unkindly.

"And you will argue for sound," Odric replied.

"And we will end in listening," she finished, and her smile matched Seraphiel's.

Odric lifted the blade so its flat faced her like a shield. "The edge is a promise to stop," he said, voice scarcely above the water's murmur. "To stop what does not belong."

Amari'el answered with a tone so quiet Kael'Thorin felt it more in his molars than in his ears. "And song is a promise to let pass what does."

He stepped toward her; she did not move. The blade met the tone; the tone met the blade. Neither yielded, yet both softened. The air around them thickened, not with force but with agreement. Odric's eyes closed. Amari'el's shoulders eased. The blade lowered by a finger's width. The tone rounded a fraction, as if it had learned a new vowel.

Thalan'ar's voice reached them from the arch. "This is what they cannot draw," he said. "A corridor cannot carry consent."

Seraphiel straightened from the rail and joined them. "Then our teaching is simple," she said. "Teach consent to air."

"How?" Kael'Thorin asked, and the word left his mouth like a fish slipping from a net—more hope than strategy.

"Practice," Odric said.

"Practice," Amari'el echoed.

"Practice," Seraphiel agreed, and in her repetition was a benediction.

The bellweed chimed, a small, approving rain. Outside, the horizon wore a seam that might have been weather or will. Kael'Thorin looked at it and felt the old vow stir. Blade and song both lifted in him like two hands opening at once. He imagined sailors in fog refusing a straight line because their grandmothers had taught them how to listen to crooked water. He imagined a corridor turning to rope and then to thread and then to nothing at all.

For an instant—a bright, impossible breath—he glimpsed something like the end of a fall. Not prevention; remembering through it. His throat tightened. "Let us be ready," he whispered, and did not know if he spoke to the Guides, the sea, or the part of himself that would meet the corridor with a circle.

Seraphiel's hand found his shoulder. "We will," she said. "We are."

The grove lay hushed, as though the stones themselves had drawn breath and held it, waiting to see what these two would choose. The blade still shimmered faintly with the afterglow of Kael'Thorin's grasp; the song still lingered like a fragrance around Amari'el's lips.

Kael'Thorin lowered the blade slowly until its tip brushed the moss. In his hands it no longer felt like a weapon, but like an extension of his vow—an edge not to sever life, but to mark the boundary where harm must stop. The promise struck deep into him: that the blade was not destruction, but restraint; not violence, but the discipline that shields the heart from forgetting.

Amari'el stepped forward, her voice softer now, carrying only for him. "The song is not always sung in joy. Sometimes it returns as lament, sometimes as warning, sometimes as the fragile hum of breath in darkness. But always, it returns. The circle cannot be broken." She raised her hand and touched the flat of the blade, and at her touch the vibration of its edge softened into a low harmonic note, a sound like a distant shore remembering its tide.

He looked at her, and though no words passed between them for a time, something in him aligned with her vow. The spiral was not a path one walked alone—it was a weaving of edge and song, of silence and remembrance. Where his strength might become too rigid, her melody would bend it back into grace; where her voice might tremble, his arm would steady the rhythm. They were not yet bound, but they had touched the shape of what would one day be sealed.

Together they turned to the stones that circled the grove. Each stone seemed to bear a faint glimmer now, as if listening. Kael'Thorin lifted the blade in both hands, and Amari'el sang a final note. Steel and breath, edge and voice, joined in a resonance that spiraled outward, upward, and into the unseen currents of Lemuria. The grove answered with silence—not empty, but full, as though the land itself had agreed.

When at last the blade dimmed and her song faded, they bowed to one another. There was no triumph, no conquest, only recognition. The circle had been affirmed. The vow was begun, though its weight would take lifetimes to unfold.

Kael'Thorin whispered to himself, "The edge is a promise to stop." Amari'el replied, as though completing his thought, "And the song is the promise to return."

Thus the interlude closed—not with a clash, but with a chord. And the spiral turned again, unseen yet unstoppable, drawing them toward the greater vow that awaited.

— ✦ —

Blade of restraint, sing in silence.
Song of return, rise in remembrance.
Circle unbroken, vow begun.
Let the spiral carry us onward.

Part II: The Casting of Memory

Chapter 3: The Encoding

Dawn found the Grove of the First Light already awake.

Mist threaded the roots like pale silk, carrying the faint salt of the inner sea and the resin-sweet breath of the songwood trees.
No bells rang. No heralds called. Yet the paths filled—quiet feet, steady eyes, the people of Lemuria drifting into a circle without command.
News of the second tower had reached even the innermost valleys; what it meant none could agree upon. But all knew the Spiral would speak today.

Kael'Thorin stood at the center of the glyphstone, both palms open to the morning air. He felt the weight of a thousand nights settle on his shoulders,
not as burden, but as a mantle claimed. The vow he and the others had bound in the Grove was no longer a whisper. It breathed inside him, a second heartbeat.

Across from him, Amari'el Shae'Lumae stepped into the light, her robe the color of wet leaves after rain. Her gaze met his, and something eased—
the small, human assurance that even a sacred work could be held by two hands instead of one. She took her place on the outer ring, the position of Witness and Water.

Thalan'ar entered next, marked in ochre and ash—the sigils of earth and caretaking drawn across his forearms. He bowed to the four cardinal trees and set a clay bowl

between them, filled with soil from the terraces where Lemuria first learned to feed itself without harm. Odric came from the west, bearing a weathered spear and
a cloth-wrapped stone from the Shore of Echoes. Seraphiel arrived last, as the wind turned, her mantle pale as the inside of a shell. The leaves bent toward him;
without gesture, without sound, Ka'el—the wind between worlds—moved at the edge of perception, confirming the circle was whole.

The elders formed a second ring. Children—eyes wide, hands tight—stood with their guardians in the third. Beyond them, in the shadow line, lingered those who distrusted
the Spiral or feared it: traders with Atlantean glass at their belts, council scribes, two off-islanders with faces sun-bleached and skeptical. Lemuria was not one voice.
That was why the Encoding mattered.

Seraphiel lifted her hand—not high, not grand. The Grove hushed.

"The Encoding is not a shield against loss," she said, voice level. "It is remembrance planted where loss cannot steal."

A murmur moved through the rings, then settled.

Amari'el's voice followed, threaded with song. "This rite does not bind our future to a single path. It binds our hearts to what is true, that our steps—
even when we wander—return."

Odric set the cloth-wrapped stone at Kael'Thorin's feet and

unbound it. The rock was black, veined with green. Its surface held a faint sheen like river dusk.

"From the Shore of Echoes," he said. "Where the sea remembers what we say when we think no one hears."

Thalan'ar poured soil into his palm and let it sift back into the bowl. "From the terraces that fed us when the sky withheld rain. We are not kept by towers."

Kael'Thorin listened—not to their words alone, but to the harmonics beneath them, the alignment forming like facets finding one another in crystal.
He could feel the watchers in the shadow ring, the tug of difference, the ache of what might soon be asked of the land. The Spiral in his chest warmed,
not with heat, but with quiet radiance.

Seraphiel stepped backward, making space. "Begin."

Kael'Thorin knelt and placed his right hand upon the glyphstone. Lines of light rose—spiral, helix, wave—each a pattern of Lemuria's memory.
He breathed them in, not with lungs but with the whole of him, and as he did the patterns unwound through his bones, mapping themselves upon the places no knife could reach.

Images unfurled behind his eyes: the First Grove at dawn, elders threading songs through seed; the Laughing Terraces when the rains returned; the night the Skyfish leapt the reef and the children ran the strand with lanterns, guiding them back.
Not nostalgia—foundation. He felt the weight of each story settle

into him like stone in a seawall: placed, aligned, bearing.

From the outer ring, a boy's clear voice rose on its own, unbidden: a single line of an old harvest chant. Another voice joined, then a third. The melody gathered the people the way tide gathers foam,
not with force but with belonging. Atlantean bracelets flashed in the shadows and did not leave.

Amari'el moved to Kael'Thorin's left and extended her hand. He took it. The link was simple, human, necessary. A tremor passed between palm and palm—a recognition beyond words.
Around them, the glyphstone brightened.

"Let the Encoding be set in this vessel," Thalan'ar said quietly, placing the bowl of soil beside the stone. "Not to be kept from others, but to be carried for them."

Odric's spear touched the ground, the sound a soft strike that traveled outward in a low ring. Seraphiel's eyes closed; the wind stilled; Ka'el pressed at the edge of breath—a boundary, a blessing.

Kael'Thorin lifted his left hand and touched the center of his chest.

"I receive," he said.

The Grove answered.

Light did not blaze; it gathered. Threads from soil and water, wind and stone, memory and song curved inward, crossing

through him, then into the bowl, then back again—
a shuttle weaving a pattern no single thread could hold. He felt not exaltation but union: himself as part rather than pinnacle; the vow inside him no louder than anyone else's, only more awake.

When the light subsided, the bowl looked unchanged. Yet the soil at its surface had darkened to a richer hue, and a fragrance rose from it—cedar, rain, green things mending.

Kael'Thorin stood. The elders' ring opened to let the children forward. One by one, with awkward solemnity, they pressed their fingertips to the soil, then to their hearts.
Laughter trembled at the edges of reverence and did not break it.

From the shadow ring, the two off-islanders stepped closer. One removed his glass bracelet and slipped it into his pocket. The other kept hers and bowed her head.

Seraphiel lowered her hand. "The Encoding is begun."

No cheer followed. No proclamation. Only the sound of leaves turning toward an inner wind, and the far thrum of the sea reshaping its shore.

Somewhere beyond the horizon, stone met water in Atlantean cadence. Here, the earth remembered its own name.

The great hall of the Lemurian High Council was unlike any other place in the known world, a vast circular chamber carved into the living stone of the cliffs, its walls inlaid with crystalline veins that caught the light of the setting sun and refracted it into a shifting aurora of color. Each beam was alive with a hum, subtle yet steady, a reminder that Lemuria's structures were not merely built, but grown and sung into being.

Kael'Thorin stood in the center, the ceremonial dais beneath his feet resonating faintly with his pulse. Around him, the elders gathered—men and women whose lifetimes stretched beyond the memory of cities, their faces etched with both wisdom and the quiet burdens of leadership. At the far side of the circle, Thalan'ar watched with the patience of stone. Seraphiel's gaze was fixed not on the hall, but somewhere beyond it, as though she were listening for a sound only she could hear. Odric leaned lightly on the haft of his spear, the gesture more symbolic than defensive.

Ka'el, the wind between worlds, was not visible to the human eye, but Kael'Thorin could feel his presence—a cool, unseen current coiling gently around him. It steadied him, even as the moment threatened to shake the foundations of what he believed himself to be.

High Chancellor Vaedriel raised a hand, and the murmurs stilled. "Kael'Thorin," she said, her voice carrying the resonance of the hall itself. "You stand before the Council to receive the Encoding—a binding of memory and essence that will root your soul across lifetimes. What is given here will endure through the fall of cities and the silencing of seas. Do you come of your own will?"

"I do," he said, his voice quieter than he intended, though it did not waver.

"Then understand this," Vaedriel continued, stepping forward. "The Encoding is no mere gift. It is a weight. It will mark you as one who carries a seed that must one day be sown, no matter the cost. It will call to you in dreams and in waking, across the span of ages. And when it calls, you must answer."

A hush settled over the hall. The light from the crystal veins shifted, deepening into a gold touched with violet—the Lemurian colors of oath.

Thalan'ar took a step forward, his voice low and deliberate. "Once this is done, there is no return to unknowing. Your path will be your burden, your gift, and your trial. We will walk with you, but the choosing remains yours."

Kael'Thorin looked from one guide to the next. Seraphiel's eyes were a mirror of still water, giving nothing and yet holding everything. Odric gave the barest nod, as if to say, You were made for this. Amari'el's lips curved in the faintest of smiles, though her eyes were bright with something unspoken.

"I choose it," Kael'Thorin said, the words falling into the silence like a stone into deep water.

Vaedriel extended her hands, and the air within the dais shimmered. The hum of the crystalline walls deepened, harmonizing with a tone that seemed to rise from the marrow of the earth. The Encoding had begun.

The moment the Encoding began, the air in the great hall thickened, not with weight, but with presence. Kael'Thorin felt it first as a vibration in the soles of his feet, then in his hands, his chest, until every heartbeat seemed to carry a second pulse—one not entirely his own.

The crystalline walls brightened in response, their gold-violet light stretching into threads that wove through the chamber. These threads arced toward him like rivers seeking the sea, converging at the dais where he stood.

Amari'el Shae'Lumae stepped forward, her eyes luminous beneath the shifting light. She did not speak, but her presence was a balm against the growing intensity. For an instant, Kael'Thorin caught the faintest memory—though he was certain it was not his—of a shoreline beneath a twin moon sky, and Amari'el's hand reaching for his. It was gone before he could name it, but its echo settled into him like a truth remembered.

The Chancellor's voice rose above the humming stone. "Witness now the crossing of essence. Let the soul be written into the deep."

Ka'el, the wind between worlds, stirred invisibly through the chamber. Kael'Thorin felt the current lift through him, carrying the threads of light into his body. They entered not with force, but with the surety of something that had always belonged.

His breath deepened, and the hall fell away.

He stood in another place—no longer stone and council, but a vast expanse of water stretching to every horizon. The surface rippled with colors he could not name. From the depths, shapes moved toward him—great beings of light and shadow, each carrying an aspect of the world: the steady pull of the earth, the fire of creation, the unbroken flow of time. They circled him, not as predators, but as keepers.

One by one, they pressed their presence into him. Not words, but impressions: Remember. Guard. Return.

He felt himself pulled back into the hall with a suddenness that left his knees weak. Amari'el was there, steadying him, her touch brief but grounding.

"It is done," Vaedriel said softly, though her voice carried to every corner of the chamber. "The Encoding is bound. May its memory guide you across the ages."

Kael'Thorin exhaled slowly, knowing without understanding how much had just changed.

In the shadows at the far edge of the chamber, Thalan'ar's eyes glimmered. Odric's stance had shifted—less guarded now, more resolute. Seraphiel's gaze was distant, as if already charting the course ahead.

And somewhere, in the unseen spaces between worlds, Ka'el's presence lingered—silent, watchful, and waiting.

The hall emptied slowly, as though the people were reluctant to step out of the resonance that still trembled in the stones. Children lingered near the dais, touching the polished edge as if it might sing to their hands. Elders exchanged quiet nods, their faces grave but luminous. Traders with Atlantean bracelets stood longer than they intended, listening for something even they could not name.

remained at the center until the last of the crowd had drifted down the spiral ramps. The air was warmer now, settled, as if the room had taken a deep breath and released it. He lifted the bowl of darkened soil and held it to his chest. The scent of cedar and rain rose again—faint, persistent.

Amari'el Shae'Lumae approached without a word. For a time they stood shoulder to shoulder in the colored hush. The light from the crystal veins had softened to a gentle pulse, like the underside of dawn.

"Is it heavy?" she asked at last, glancing at the bowl.

"Yes," he said. "But not as weight." He searched for the right word and found it. "As gravity."

Her lips curved. "Then it will keep you when the wind asks you to scatter."

He turned toward her fully, the bowl still against his heart. "Will you walk a while?"

They left the hall through a narrow passage that opened onto a terrace cut into the cliff. Below, the Inner Sea breathed in long silver lines. On the far horizon, Sevrion's beam combed the darkening water, steady as a metronome. A second light, faint as a rumor, ghosted the sky opposite it—the first tests of the new tower's lens, sweeping in trial arcs.

Amari'el's gaze followed the distant light. "They will call it protection."

He set the bowl on the stone rail. "Protection from what?"

"From chaos," she said. "From storms. From the old uncertainty." She looked at him carefully. "But not from themselves."

The wind curled around them, and with it the unmistakable pressure of presence. Ka'el—the wind between worlds—moved along the
edge of the terrace like a river of cool air. Feathers of the cliff swallows rippled. The bowl's surface stirred and settled.

Kael'Thorin closed his eyes and listened. The Encoding had sharpened his inner hearing; the world felt nearer, more articulate.
Behind the steady promise of the vow, new threads emerged—thin, taut lines of consequence tugging at the horizon. He felt one draw tight toward the Groves, another toward the Shore, and a third, finer than hair, pulling toward the city's heart where decrees were inked before they were spoken.

"Thalan'ar will need watchers in the council," he said. "Quiet ones."

Amari'el nodded. "He has them. But watchers do not change the river. They only map its bend."

"Then we move before the river is bridged."

She studied him in profile. In the half-light he looked older, not in face but in bearing. The Encoding had placed something in him that refused to be smaller than what was asked. It would keep him upright when the ground slipped.

“Kael’Thorin,” she said softly. “The vow can make a person forget they are a person.”

He met her eyes. “I won’t.”

“Promise?”

“Promise.” The word felt simple and absolute between them.

Below, a fishing-boat’s mast rang once as the swell turned. The sound seemed to answer the promise, marking it in the night.

They walked the terrace’s arc until it narrowed into a stair that wound down toward the water. At a landing carved like a crescent, Amari’el stopped and touched the stone. A shallow basin had been cut there long ago to catch rain. She dipped her fingers and traced a spiral over the back of his hand. The touch was light, ceremonial and not; a gesture of the Grove carried into the world.

“For remembering,” she said.

He mirrored the sign over her palm. “For returning.”

The wind rose again, and for a heartbeat the air thinned—one of those delicate moments when the veil sways and the next life might be mistaken for this one. In that sliver of quiet, he saw her face by another fire, in another age, and heard laughter that had not yet been born. The glimpse passed, but the warmth remained.

Footsteps sounded behind them. Odric appeared from the stair's shadow, sea-salt bright on his brow. He inclined his head to Amari'el, then to Kael'Thorin. "Thalan'ar requests you at the Tower. Drenivar's envoys have doubled their visits."

"Tonight?" Kael'Thorin asked.

"Before dawn," Odric said. His gaze slid to the bowl on the rail, then to the sweep of the test beam ghosting the clouds. "The tide is turning in places no eye can see."

Amari'el lifted the bowl and pressed it back into Kael'Thorin's hands. "Take this with you. Soil changes a room."

He managed a half-smile. "So does your presence."

"Then pretend I am in the bowl," she said, and the smile reached her eyes.

Odric did not smile, but his shoulders eased a fraction. "We go by the cliff path." He looked past them into the dark. "Seraphiel is already in the Axis Grove. The wind's uneasy."

Kael'Thorin gathered his cloak, the bowl secure against his chest. He felt the gravity of it again, a center of quiet that would not allow him to be thrown wide.

"Let's move," he said.

They descended into the night together—toward lamps that burned late in the Tower of the First Light, toward pages that waited for
signatures, toward a conversation that would set stones rolling. Above them, unseen, Ka'el traced their path, a patient curve drawn
through shadow, ready to meet the next turn of the Spiral.

The Tower of the First Light never truly slept.

Even in the thin hours before dawn, lamplight stitched the windows, and the spiral stair rang with the soft traffic of scribes and runners.
From the terrace below, Kael'Thorin could feel the tower's pulse—a civic heartbeat, old as the city. Yet tonight another rhythm moved beneath it,
older still. He tightened his hold on the bowl Amari'el had given back to him and began to climb.

Odric led the way, his steps quiet for a man who wore the sea like armor. "Drenivar's second envoy arrived at dusk," he said without looking back.
"His name is Maelion. Polished tongue. Polished boots."

"Polished intent," Kael'Thorin murmured.

At the landing two levels down from the council chamber, Thalan'ar waited in the shadows beside an alcove of tide-marked stone.

The lamplight carved his face into planes. He took in the bowl with a single glance and nodded once, as if an unspoken instruction had been obeyed.

"Seraphiel?" Kael'Thorin asked.

"In the Axis Grove. The wind is listening to Atlantis," Thalan'ar said. Then, lower, "Vaedriel is with us, as far as a chancellor can be.
She will want something to weigh on the scales."

"Weight we brought," Odric said, tipping his chin at the bowl. "Soil changes a room."

They went in together.

The council chamber opened like a shell, its ribs of stone arcing toward a clerestory of night. A handful of elders stood in quiet clusters.
Maelion waited near the far curve, a lean, pale man in a tunic woven with mica threads that caught and held the light.
He smiled without showing teeth.

"Honored Lemurians," he said, voice smooth enough to oil hinges. "Atlantis greets you in friendship."

"Friendship does not arrive before dawn," Odric said, taking his place by the door.

Maelion's smile did not falter. "Sometimes it does, when the sea is calm and the matter is urgent."

Vaedriel stepped forward from the room's center. Her hair, shot with grey, was braided like cable; her eyes belonged to a cliff that had outlasted many storms.
"State your urgency," she said.

"The second lighthouse will be lit at midsun tomorrow," Maelion replied. "Its beam will be measured for harmonics and range. We invite Lemurian observers, so that no rumor need sour cooperation."

A stir moved through the elders. Thalan'ar's gaze flickered to Kael'Thorin and back. This was faster than their worst-case ledger.

Kael'Thorin set the bowl of soil on the council table.

The action was simple. And it changed the chamber.

The fragrance rose—cedar, rain, the ghost of terraces after harvest—and conversations thinned into silence. Even Maelion's eyes flicked to the bowl.
Kael'Thorin rested both palms on the table's edge and said nothing. The room made its own introductions.

Vaedriel understood. She stepped to the bowl and dipped two fingers to the surface, then pressed them lightly to her chest. Her voice, when it came, was not for Maelion alone. "Lemuria will observe. And Lemuria will decide—by our measures, not yours—what safety means to the living sea."

Maelion inclined his head. "We welcome your wisdom." He glanced once at the soil. "As we trust you will welcome ours."

"Wisdom we welcome," Thalan'ar said. "Ownership we do not."

The envoy spread his hands. "Ownership is not our aim. Stewardship is."

"Of our waters?" Odric asked, almost mildly.

"Of shared waters," Maelion corrected. "Your fish do not stop at mid-sea."

"Nor does your beam," Vaedriel said.

The envoy's gaze flickered and steadied. "Which is precisely why we invite you to its lighting." He withdrew a small case from his belt and opened it.
Inside lay a strip of thin crystal, etched with faint sigils—an Atlantean pass-seal. "For three observers. Noon."

The number hung like an insult and a trap. Three witnesses meant three narratives. Three could be contained.

"Six," Thalan'ar said, as if naming the price of salt. "Two from the Groves, two from the Shore, one from the terraces, one from the Tower."

"Four," Maelion countered smoothly. "Two Lemurians, two Atlanteans, paired."

The air shifted. Ka'el—the wind between worlds—moved along the gallery like a thought changing direction.
Kael'Thorin felt the veer and, with it, a faint pressure in his

ribs—the way the Spiral did when a word wanted saying.

He lifted his hand, palm up, no weapon, only soil-fragrance and breath. "Five," he said. "And not paired. We will not be braided into your narrative, nor you into ours.
Five witnesses, each keeping their own account, exchanged at sunset. If harmony is your aim, let it be composed from honest notes."

Silence followed. The elders watched Maelion as one watches the sea for the first sign of a sneaker wave.

At last the envoy's smile returned, barely. "Five." He lifted the crystal. "The pass will accept that number."

"It will because you will tell it to," Vaedriel said. "We are not children at your lens."

"Nor are we thieves at your shore," Maelion replied—too quickly. Then he breathed, calmed the angle of his shoulders, and bowed. "Until noon."

He left with the soundless efficiency of a knife sliding back into its sheath.

The chamber stayed still a beat longer, as if listening for echoes. Then voices rose, not in panic but in that fast, practical cadence that follows reprieve.
Assignments were sketched into air: Odric to choose the shoreline witness; Thalan'ar to sit the Tower's chair; Amari'el to name a singer from the Groves;
Vaedriel to convene a second ring of elders. Seraphiel's absence

was its own task: hold the Axis so that the wind would carry more than rumor.

Kael'Thorin remained by the bowl, palms flat to the table as the council's bustle moved around him. The Encoding's gravity tugged at something within,
aligning him to a direction he had not yet spoken aloud. He did not see the future. He felt the pattern sharpening—Atlantis throwing shape onto sea,
Lemuria answering in root and memory. Two hands on the same vessel.

Amari'el's face rose in his mind for no reason he could name. The spiral she had traced on his skin seemed to glow again, a warmth against the cool of the council stone.
He wondered—without fear—what would be asked of that warmth.

Thalan'ar touched his shoulder. "Walk with me."

They stepped into the outer corridor where the tower's ribs met the cliff and the sea's voice could be heard without doors.
For a moment neither spoke. The eastern sky had begun to pale.

"You moved the number," Thalan'ar said at last.

"The wind moved it," Kael'Thorin answered. "I only said the word."

"Keep letting it." Thalan'ar's gaze angled toward the dim horizon, where Sevrion's beam thinned in the dawn. "By noon, Atlantis will be ready to impress us.

By sunset, we must be ready to remember ourselves."

"Who are the five?"

"You," Thalan'ar said. "Amari'el will choose the Grove's singer. Odric will stand for the Shore. I will sit for the Tower. For the terraces…" He hesitated. "A farmer who has never set foot in a council.
Someone whose measure of safety is rain and harvest. Let Atlantis try to charm that."

Kael'Thorin nodded. "And Seraphiel?"

"Where the wind is." Thalan'ar's mouth quirked. "Which is everywhere."

A bell rang deep within the tower—low, resonant, not alarm but awakening. The day had begun to climb the stair toward noon.

Kael'Thorin lifted the bowl once more and felt its center of quiet find his own. Gravity, Amari'el had said. He understood: not a weight that pinned, but a force that kept orbits true.

"Then we begin," he said.

They turned back toward the chamber to set the witnesses in motion, unaware that on the far side of the seam a second ledger lay open under Maelion's hand.
Beside the neat note *Five accepted*, a smaller line waited, ink poised: *Introduce variance at third measure.*

The vessel had begun to turn.

The sun stood directly overhead, its light refracting in a thousand glints off the polished white stones of Atlantis.
From the highest terrace, the great lighthouse—its base rooted deep into the cliff, its crown carved into a spire of crystal—caught the midday light and threw it seaward in a dazzling sweep. It was not yet lit by flame; this was the hour of stillness before ceremony, when anticipation hovered like a drawn bowstring.

Atlantean crowds pressed into the marble avenues leading toward the lighthouse plaza, their robes a kaleidoscope of dyed silks and fine linens.
Merchants shouted above the murmur, hawking fragrant fruits, copper amulets, and folded maps bearing the city's emblem. Nobles rode past on silver-chained chariots, the polished hooves of their steeds ringing against the stone.

Beyond the plaza's inner ring, on a shaded balcony of black basalt, the Lemurian witnesses stood together, a silent knot among the restless crowd.
Kael'Thorin's gaze tracked the arc of sunlight along the crystal spire, measuring, memorizing. Beside him, Amari'el Shae'Lumae let her attention drift not to the spectacle, but to the invisible lattice of energy flowing between the lighthouse's apex and the ocean's horizon.
She could feel its pulse, deep and old, a rhythm out of place with the revelry around them.

"They've tuned it," Odric murmured, his eyes narrowing toward the crystalline crown. "But not for the sea."
Thalan'ar gave no answer, only a slow, deliberate breath. He could sense it too—the subtle pull not toward navigation or safety, but toward something unseen, perhaps unknown even to

most of the Atlantean citizens.

Seraphiel's voice was quiet, but it cut through the market noise. "Watch the moment the flame is lit. It will tell us more than their words ever could."
A great conch blast split the air, answered by a hundred smaller horns across the plaza.
The crowd surged forward as the High Keeper of the Flame emerged in ceremonial robes of scarlet and gold, his staff crowned with a disc of beaten copper.
Behind him, six acolytes bore an urn of oil that shimmered with a strange inner light.

Kael'Thorin felt Amari'el's hand brush his, not in fear, but in silent solidarity. The Lemurians had crossed half the known world for this moment, and now the air itself seemed to draw taut, the way it does before a storm.
The High Keeper reached the spire's base, lifted his staff toward the sun, and waited for the precise alignment of light and shadow.

The noon flame was about to be born.

Kael'Thorin's gaze lingered upon the receding shimmer of the Atlantean light until it was little more than a ghostly flicker against the horizon. Around him, the murmurs of his companions blended with the sigh of the Lemurian wind. Amari'el stood close, her eyes reflecting both wonder and foreboding, while Thalan'ar's stance had gone taut with the unspoken knowing of change to come.

The sacred rhythm of Lemuria had not yet faltered, but the

threads of something new—something untested—were beginning to weave themselves into the world's loom. And though no decree had been spoken, each heart there felt the quiet oath form within them: to bear witness, to remember, and to be ready.

The twilight circle gathered without announcement. Lamps were hooded; windows cracked to the sea. On the long table of riverwood,
Kael'Thorin set the bowl of dark soil where the lamplight could find it true. The room stilled as if the bowl itself had drawn breath.

Thalan'ar stood to the right, shoulders square to the doorway in quiet defiance. Odric took the threshold, a watch without posture.
Amari'el Shae'Lumae rested her fingers at the table's edge, eyes tracking the sweep of the distant beam with a listener's focus. Seraphiel faced the unlocked window, as though the night were a page she could read by touch.

Across from them, the small ring of guests eased into place. Bren the farmer—hands clean for once, but still nicked with work. Elder Vaedriel with a ledger closed beneath one palm. Two shoreline fishers who could read a tide by breath alone. A Grove singer
Amari'el had chosen for steadiness over fame. No speeches. No ceremony. A room, as Thalan'ar had asked.

Kael'Thorin pressed his palm lightly to the soil, then lifted it—no glow, no sign, just the faint fragrance of cedar and rain released into the chamber. "We asked you here," he said, voice even, "to listen together."

Bren's brow creased. "To what?"

"To what the land remembers about light," Thalan'ar answered. "Not what it fears."

Silence opened, wide and useful. Outside, the Atlantean beam thinned at its edges, then steadied—its sweep a metronome on the skin of the sea. The Grove singer breathed in and out, then began a tone so soft it felt like mist. Amari'el joined a breath later, not harmonizing so much as laying a line beside it—two cords along one path. Seraphiel did not sing, but the wind changed direction at the window, bringing the salt in cleaner.

Kael'Thorin let the Encoding rise. He did not summon it; he allowed it—like loosening a hand from a bridle and trusting the animal to find the way home. Threads answered: soil, water, wind, stone. Not dramatic, not bright. Present. He placed three small crystals at the table's compass points and drew a quiet arc of wave-script between them with his fingertip.

"Say it plain," Odric murmured to Bren. "How does good light sit on a field?"

Bren squinted at the window's narrow strip of sky. "Good light doesn't argue," he said at last. "It shows you where the lines already run. Lets you put seed where seed will take. Bad light pushes. Makes you doubt what you already know." He glanced at the bowl. "Theirs pushes."

Vaedriel opened her ledger, then shut it again, as if understanding that numbers would not be the measure tonight. "If it pushes, can we blunt it?"

"We can soften what it hits," Amari'el said. "Braiding a second pattern under it. Weaving slack into what it would pull tight."

"Cost?" Thalan'ar asked.

"Attention," she said simply. "Not once. Ongoing."

Seraphiel let out a sound barely a laugh. "We were planning to sleep?"

The Grove singer altered the tone—half-step, then whole—and the room seemed to widen. Kael'Thorin felt Ka'el—the wind between worlds—turn
his attention to the lighthouse vanes far across the seam. Not to break. To complicate. The beam hesitated at its apex, recovered, resumed its sweep with a new, almost imperceptible stutter.

Odric smiled without showing teeth. "That's mischief."

"Measured mischief," Seraphiel said. "Enough to keep a story from telling itself."

Kael'Thorin reached for Amari'el's hand. Her fingers were cool, steady. Together they laid their palms close above the soil, not touching it,
and let the Encoding pour through the smallest gesture—breath to breath, pulse to pulse. The crystals at the compass points took a low light;
the arcs of wave-script softened it and sent it back into the bowl, then out into the room, then outward again through stone and street.

"Picture this," Kael'Thorin said quietly to Bren. "Tomorrow a fog rolls in. Not blind, not thick. Kind fog. It takes the shine off the metal
and leaves you the shape of your own work. Can you plant by that?"

Bren's face loosened. "Aye." He lifted his left hand and counted the spiral cord's knots with his thumb. "Aye."

They worked the pattern in silence. No grand spell. No show. A question placed into a living structure and allowed to echo where it would.
Vaedriel added the weight of office—not decree, not threat, simply presence. The fishers contributed the memory of lanterns strung across
night water. Odric stepped once to the door and back, anchoring the room to the world beyond it with the old soldier's craft of walking
a perimeter until it belongs to you.

When the first measure was set, Amari'el released Kael'Thorin's hand and shifted the song. The Grove singer followed, tone thinning to a thread.
Kael'Thorin angled two crystals, then pinched the lamp hooded nearest the window to a narrower crescent. The beam's stutter lengthened by the width
of a breath, then steadied again. Not victory. Room.

Thalan'ar looked to Vaedriel. "You'll need to carry this without naming it."

"I will," she said. "We'll call it prudence in the minutes."

"And in the terraces?" Odric asked Bren.

"We'll call it weather."

A small, ordinary laugh warmed the table. It broke nothing; it eased everything.

Outside, bells rang from the harbor—three, then a pause, then two. The fishers traded a glance. "Boats turned early," one said. "Currents lively."

Seraphiel's eyes unfocused a fraction. "Ka'el says the vanes vibrate when the beam crosses the seam. The engineers hear it and pretend not to."

"Can he keep it up?" Thalan'ar asked.

"For a while." Seraphiel's mouth tipped. "He is the while."

Kael'Thorin gathered the last line of the pattern and settled it into the soil, not to store but to remember—a seed tucked in, not buried.
The bowl's scent deepened, rain after heat. He could feel the city pick it up in small ways: a child tugging a parent's sleeve to look at the moon
instead of the lighthouse; a helmsman easing his course by stars rather than the new glare; a scribe leaving a blank margin where an ordinance
wanted to overreach.

He opened his eyes. "Enough for tonight."

They loosened the circle without breaking it, each leaving a piece of their attention behind like banked coals. Vaedriel took Bren to the outer steps
with a word about dawn. The fishers slipped away in companionable quiet. Odric went last to the door, lingered, and

nodded once—more to the room
than to the people in it.

Amari'el stood beside Kael'Thorin in the hush that followed. "You have a steadiness I didn't see when we began," she said. "The Encoding sits in you differently."

"It sits," he said. "That's the word for it." He found her gaze and held it. "Stay with me in this work."

"I will." No ceremony. The truth of a thing said plain.

From the window, Seraphiel's voice: "Third measure approaches."

They watched without moving. Far across the seam, the Atlantean beam slowed again, as if the night itself had learned to breathe against it.
For one heartbeat the light paused over open water—no lens, no tower, no command—just a bright absence holding still.

Kael'Thorin felt the city lean away from that pause, refusing it, then lean back toward it, considering. The room did the same. So did he.

"Hold," Thalan'ar said.

They held. The light moved on. The question remained.

Dusk gathered like a held breath over the Inner Sea.

From the tower's westward balcony, the city lay below them in tiers of lamplight and shadow. Far across the seam, the Atlantean lighthouse
cut its pale arc—clean, precise, obsessive. Each sweep seemed slower now, as if the great lens were meeting a resistance it could

not name.
To the untrained eye, it was nothing. To those who listened for the world's subtler instruments, it was a stutter in the hand that wished to
steady everything.

Thalan'ar stood with elbows on the stone rail, watching the harbor fires. "Bren says the gulls returned early," he murmured. "They do not care
for the new cadence."

"They are wiser than we are," Amari'el Shae'Lumae said, tying her hair back with a strip of dusk-leaf. Her voice held no bitterness, only respect
for the creatures that read skies the way farmers read soil.

Odric leaned a shoulder to the doorframe. "The shoreline fishers report a back–eddy where there should be none. Nothing to run aground on yet,
but a fool could find a way."

Kael'Thorin listened without interrupting. He could feel the Encoding within him as a warm weight, the bowl's gravity housed now beneath his ribs.
When he angled his attention, the city answered—small lights brightening: a mother choosing lantern over new glare; a helmsman easing his route by
star; a clerk scratching a thin line through a clause that overreached. None of it victory. All of it room.

Behind them, Seraphiel lifted her head slightly, as if hearing a far-off bell. "Ka'el says the vanes shake again at the seam. They've braced the housing, but the tremor travels into the lens." She glanced toward the horizon. "Engineers do not enjoy mystery."

"Nor do priests," Thalan'ar said. "What of Maelion?"

"His ledgers grow neat where the sea grows strange," Odric answered. "He files variance as anomaly, and anomaly as proof of need."

Kael'Thorin stepped away from the rail. "Then we give them what they cannot file. Listening, unpaired. Memory, unbought." He drew a slow breath.
"Tonight we hold the pattern. Tomorrow, we teach it."

A bell rang from the lower streets—first watch. The sound climbed the tower's bones and softened there, as if the stone itself absorbed its urgency.

They descended the internal stair to the round chamber where the twilight circle had been worked. The bowl of soil waited in the center, lamplight
finding the darker richness along its surface. Amari'el set a fresh cloth beneath it—plain, undyed. "So it never has to stand on bare stone,"
she said, half to herself.

Bren arrived with the two shoreline fishers, caps in hand, boots clean but damp. Vaedriel followed, the ledger tucked beneath her arm as always,
though she had not opened it all day. The Grove singer came last, throat raw from teaching children in the terraces, eyes bright anyway.

No ceremony. A room.

Kael'Thorin placed three new crystals at the compass points, smaller than the last and cut less perfectly. "Unpolished holds," he said, and none
asked him to explain. Amari'el drew a thin arc of wave-script with her fingertip and blew across it, a breath that smelled faintly of mint and rain.
Odric walked the perimeter once, then once again more slowly, as if braiding the room to the street outside. Thalan'ar stood at the door with his hands
folded, not as guard but as hinge.

"Say it plain," Kael'Thorin invited, echoing Odric's earlier prompt. "What does tonight feel like on the water?"

"Expectant," one fisher said. "But not for storm."

"For a decision," the other added. "The sea sometimes chooses which story to take forward."

Bren cleared his throat. "You can feel it in the ground, too. Wheat holds deeper when a change comes. Or it lets go." He rubbed his thumb along
the spiral cord Amari'el had given him. "This helps me remember which I'm for."

Seraphiel angled the nearest lamp hood a fraction. The room's shadows shifted; so did the beam on the horizon. The Atlantean light paused a heartbeat,
then resumed with that now-familiar catch near the seam.

"They'll call it atmospheric," Vaedriel said dryly. "And then build taller to reach above the air."

Amari'el began a tone—low, supple, as if singing to the space between stones. The Grove singer joined at the sixth, then slid to the third, and the interference between their notes spun a soft lattice in the room. No glamour, no spell-breaking—only articulation. The Encoding took it up at once, threading the lattice through each breath and returning it to the bowl like tide over rock.

Kael'Thorin held his attention steady. When his mind tried to race ahead—to the council, to the lighthouse, to futures none could guarantee—he brought it back to texture: the porous feel of the riverwood table, the cedar–rain fragrance lifting from the soil, the way Amari'el's shadow curved and softened on the cloth beneath the bowl. The pattern responded to steadiness. It always had.

"Now," Seraphiel whispered.

They felt it together: the third measure. Far across the seam, the beam's cadence altered by a breath, then by another. A pressure arrived—thin, strange, like descending a mountain too quickly. The vanes sang audibly then, a faint metallic cry that astonished the Atlantean onlookers into silence.

Odric's shoulders squared. "Hold."

Amari'el's tone did not waver. The singer's line bent around it like willow around a stream. Thalan'ar turned the door handle a quarter inch and left it there, not to bar, not to open—simply to say to the house: be between. Vaedriel laid one finger on the ledger's closed cover, adding the weight of office to the work, not with law but with attention.

Kael'Thorin lowered his palm until it hovered the width of a hair above the soil. He did not push or pull. He offered. The Encoding moved through his hand as warmth moves through cloth, entering the bowl, then the table, then the stone, then outward through the streets as memory does when a song is sung in one home and caught by another. He felt children on balconies lean into the night; a sailor at mooring glance up at stars; a baker wake early and pause before lighting coals, listening without knowing for what.

The pressure eased. The vanes stilled to their usual tremor. A murmur rolled through the far crowd. The light moved on.

"Again tomorrow," Thalan'ar said, quiet. Not a question.

"Again tomorrow," Kael'Thorin agreed.

The circle loosened without breaking. Bren took up the bowl—careful, reverent—and carried it a few paces as if to test whether the gravity would travel with it. It did. He smiled, the small honest smile of a man who has found a tool that fits well in the hand.

At the threshold, Odric stopped with his palm to the doorframe. His voice was rough with a different kind of knowing. "There's talk along the docks that Maelion has ordered a trial sweep through the fishing lanes at dawn."

"Through the lanes?" Vaedriel's mouth thinned. "He'll call it calibration."

"Or benevolence," Thalan'ar said. "Lighting the way."

Amari'el's gaze moved from face to face. "Then we stand in the lanes first."

"No confrontation," Seraphiel cautioned. "Witness."

"Witness," Kael'Thorin echoed. He lifted the bowl, felt its center align to his own, and nodded once. "At first bell."

They parted into the night—Odric to the harbor, Thalan'ar to the Tower, Vaedriel to the smaller rooms where elders keep memory when halls are closed. The singer touched the door lintel and whispered thanks to the house as Lemurians do. Seraphiel stood a while longer at the window, head cocked, conversing with a wind no one else could hear.

On the balcony, Amari'el and Kael'Thorin paused where the city opened beneath them like a star-map. He turned to her, the bowl safe between his hands.

"You asked me to stay in this work," she said softly. "I will. But remember, Kael'Thorin—" her smile was brief, real "—work is not what we are."

"What are we?" he asked, not to challenge, but to learn the answer anew.

"Belonging," she said. "And the promise to return."

Below, a bell marked second watch. Across the seam, the lighthouse's pale arc swept on, untroubled to any eye that did not listen. Between those two movements—bell and beam—something else moved also: a song too quiet for pride, too stubborn for despair, learning how to be louder without raising its voice.

Kael'Thorin could feel the weight of the air as the gathered assembly grew silent. It was not the silence of uncertainty, nor the absence of sound—but a deliberate, held breath shared by all who stood within the chamber. The crystalline walls, alive with shifting blues and greens, refracted the faint hum of the Source Node at the heart of the room. Each pulse sent a ripple through the water-filled channels that coiled around the dais, catching the light and breaking it into a thousand glimmers.

Amari'el Shae'Lumae stood just beyond him, her gaze fixed upon the converging currents within the node. She did not speak, but the quiet steadiness of her presence settled the tension in his chest. Without looking at her, Kael'Thorin knew that she was listening to more than the surface—her attention reaching through the layers of current, tide, and memory.

Across the circle, Thalan'ar inclined his head toward Seraphiel, and something passed between them—an unspoken recognition of what was to come. Odric stood with arms folded, his shadow stretching long across the floor, the faint flicker of light glancing off the etched lines of his armor. Ka'el, the wind between worlds, was nowhere to be seen, and yet his presence could be felt as a restless stirring along the edges of perception.

The moment before action was always the sharpest. Kael'Thorin drew in a slow breath, letting it anchor him, before stepping forward. His voice, when it came, was calm but carried the weight of the vow they had all taken. 'The path is set,' he said, and the words were less an announcement than an invocation. The chamber seemed to lean toward him, as though the very stones understood the gravity of the moment.

The next step would not be taken lightly—nor could it be undone.

The sea had quieted after the great surge, yet the air still thrummed with an energy that none could name. Kael'Thorin stood upon the basalt outcrop, eyes following the horizon where the last ember glow of Atlantean light had faded. The Lemurian shore breathed in long, deep sighs — the waves folding against the sand in a rhythm as old as the first dawn.

Amari'el Shae'Lumae approached, her steps soundless on the stone. She carried with her a coil of woven kelp rope, still damp from the tides, and laid it upon the ground beside him. "They will not sleep tonight," she said softly, her gaze fixed on the water. "Nor will you."

He turned toward her, the wind lifting the loose strands of her hair. "You see it too," he murmured.

"I feel it," she replied. "The Towers speak to one another, even when the hands that tend them do not. There is a thread between their light and ours, though none have dared to name it aloud."

They stood together in silence, the scent of salt and cedar heavy in the night air. Below, the watch fires along the Lemurian cliffs burned steady — signals of vigilance, but also of restraint. The council had decreed that no Lemurian vessel would cross the midwaters, not yet. Not while the great change still trembled in its infancy.

Kael'Thorin's thoughts drifted back to the first time he had seen the Atlantean fire — years ago, when he was still a boy, pressed against the ship's rail beside his father. The memory returned in fragments: the way the light had lanced the sky, the low hum in the bones, the feeling that something ancient was waking. Now, standing beside Amari'el, he felt that same hum again, but deeper, as though the earth beneath them was holding its breath.

Her voice broke the quiet. "If the day comes when they call to us — truly call — will you answer?"

He looked at her for a long moment before speaking. "Yes," he said simply. "But not before the wind between worlds tells me it is time."

From somewhere far offshore, a single horn sounded — low, mournful, and ancient. Neither moved, but both felt the message within it.

The tide was turning.

The sea was a mirror of molten silver, the horizon painted in the faint lavender blush of twilight. Kael'Thorin stood at the edge of the high western cliffs, the wind weaving through his hair, carrying with it the scent of the deep. Far below, the ocean's surface rippled with an unseen pulse, like the steady heartbeat of Lemuria itself.

Beside him, Amari'el Shae'Lumae remained quiet, her gaze locked

on the horizon where the first star had just awakened in the evening sky.
Her presence was not a stillness of absence, but of depth—like a wellspring hidden beneath still water.
Kael'Thorin found himself listening to her silence, as though it held a language only the heart could hear.

"I have walked these cliffs a thousand times," he said at last, voice low, "but never has the wind tasted the same."

Her eyes, bright yet unshaken, found his. "That is because you have never stood here with the knowing you now carry."

Something in her words anchored him. Not to the stone beneath his feet, but to the truth that his path—every step—was part of a design older than the tides.
He felt the weight of all that had been set in motion: the rift between towers, the shadow on the horizon, the song that even now called to him in his dreams.

"I fear what is coming," he admitted.

"You do not fear the coming," she corrected gently. "You fear the loss that may follow."

Her hand brushed his—barely a touch, yet it carried the heat of fire and the calm of moonlit waters.
It was not a promise of safety. It was an oath of presence.

Kael'Thorin turned back to the horizon, the wind lifting his hair like the banner of some ancient cause.
Somewhere beyond the visible line, Atlantis burned its lights

brighter than the sun, a lighthouse of power that reached across the seas—and yet, the Lemurian heart knew, light could be both guide and blade.

As the last of the daylight surrendered to the indigo veil of night, Kael'Thorin felt it: the threshold.
An invisible edge, crossed not by steps but by the soul itself.

The time to wait was ending.
The time to act was coming.
And in the space between, he stood—anchored not by certainty, but by the silent vow that he and Amari'el would face whatever came, side by side.

The chamber's air hung thick with anticipation. As Kael'Thorin stood before the great crystal array, the hum of its energy coursed through the stone beneath his feet and up into his bones. Around him, the five had taken their places — Thalan'ar at his right, steady and grounding; Seraphiel in the shadows near the rear arch, her eyes half-closed as though already conversing with realms unseen; Odric leaning on the hilt of his ceremonial blade, watching the doors with an unblinking focus; Amari'el Shae'Lumae beside the eastern pillar, her hands weaving the slow spirals of light that anchored the circle; and Ka'el, the wind between worlds, manifest only in the subtle shifting of the torches as though exhaling from beyond the veil.

No words passed between them. They had spoken enough in the hours leading to this — about the risks, the precision required, the gravity of what they were about to bind into the memory of the Earth itself. Now was the moment for action.

The crystal responded to their presence, its facets blooming with inner light. Kael'Thorin stepped forward, placing both hands upon the cool surface. The sensation was immediate — a flood of visions, some sharp and urgent, others slow and vast, flowing into his awareness. He glimpsed cities yet to be born, forests yet to be felled, faces that would one day bear his own echoes. He felt the ache of loss that would ripple through ages, and the triumphs that would rise from it.

Amari'el's voice entered the current of his thoughts like a clear bell in a storm. -*You are not alone in this, Kael'Thorin.*- Her words anchored him as the visions threatened to pull him apart. He turned his mind toward her presence, and in that shared gaze across the circle, they exchanged a depth of understanding that no vow could outmatch.

The encoding began.

Light poured from the crystal into the channels carved into the floor, racing in precise lines toward the five points where his companions stood. Thalan'ar absorbed the first surge, grounding it deep into the stone. Seraphiel wove the second into the unseen lattice that bound worlds together. Odric received the third in a clenched fist, sealing it behind the symbol engraved on his blade. Amari'el drew in the fourth, folding it into a sphere of living light that pulsed between her palms.

The fifth… was not taken, but carried — by Ka'el, invisible, yet felt in the way the air shifted and the light bent. This, Kael'Thorin understood, would be the seed carried beyond Lemuria's fall.

When the last thread of light sank into its keeper, the crystal dimmed, and silence fell. The hum remained, but now it was within them — a resonance they would carry through lifetimes.

Kael'Thorin released the crystal and stepped back. The five met his gaze in turn, and in that unspoken exchange, they all knew: the work was done. The memory was cast.

Beyond the chamber walls, the ocean swelled as if in answer, waves striking the shore in a rhythm that matched the pulse within their chests.

The five did not leave the chamber immediately.

For a long moment, they stood in stillness, listening to the faint reverberation of what had just occurred. It was not only sound they heard, but a sensation—like the lingering vibration after the striking of a bell—that now lived inside them. It bound them together in a way no oath ever could.

Kael'Thorin was the first to move. He approached the archway leading to the terrace, and the others followed. As they emerged into the salt-bright air, the ocean stretched before them in unbroken blue, its surface flashing with shards of sunlight. Below, the people of Lemuria went about their lives, unaware of the great weaving that had just altered the course of their world.

Amari'el came to stand beside him, her hand brushing his briefly. "You feel it too," she murmured. It was not a question.

He nodded. "It is in every breath. Every beat."

They watched as a fishing vessel cut across the bay, its sail catching the wind. Children played along the tide pools, their laughter carrying up to the terrace. Life went on. And yet, beneath it, a new current moved—one that would one day rise into the stories of other ages.

Thalan'ar joined them, his deep voice grounding the moment. "We have done what was needed. But you know this will not be the end of our work."

Seraphiel's gaze was on the horizon, where a thin line of storm clouds was forming. "No. The casting is only the beginning. The patterns we have set in motion will demand tending—through time, through shadow, through loss."

Odric rested his hands on the parapet, eyes scanning the bustling port. "And we will not always be in the same place, or the same time. We will carry this into other lives, other lands. We will meet again, but not always as friends."

At that, Kael'Thorin turned to face them all. "Then we anchor this moment in our hearts. Whatever we become, wherever we walk, let us remember this: we stood here together, and we gave the world a seed it could carry through the dark."

Amari'el's eyes shone, reflecting both sunlight and something older. "And we will see it bloom—whether in this life or another."

The wind shifted, carrying the faint scent of rain. It wrapped around them like the breath of Ka'el, unseen yet undeniably present. For an instant, it seemed to whisper a promise—one none of them could quite put into words, but all understood.

They remained there until the first drops fell, each lost in their own thoughts, yet bound in the same unbroken thread.

Far out to sea, the storm advanced.

The storm reached the harbor by nightfall.

From the high cliffs, Kael'Thorin watched as lightning flared beyond the breakwater, illuminating the black sweep of clouds. The sea roared against the stone, each wave sending a spray of salt into the air that clung to his skin. Behind him, the city's lights flickered in the wind, lanterns straining against their moorings.

He could feel the Encoding within him, resonating more strongly with each gust. It was as though the storm itself recognized the weaving they had done, answering in its own language of wind and wave.

Amari'el joined him again, her cloak drawn tight against the rain. "It's begun," she said softly.

He turned to her, studying the calm in her face despite the fury surrounding them. "What has?"

"The shifting," she replied. "The tides within the world have turned. You may not see its full course in this life, but it will come."

Below, the streets emptied as people sought shelter. But atop the cliff, the five remained—Thalan'ar steady as a rooted tree,

Seraphiel's eyes half-lidded as if listening to voices carried on the gale, Odric with one hand on his blade, measuring the distance to the unseen.

Kael'Thorin took a slow breath, letting the storm's force press against him. He thought of the generations that would inherit this moment without ever knowing it existed. He thought of the battles to come, the friendships that would fracture and heal, the many times they would walk the earth in other names and other bodies.

"Whatever comes," he said, raising his voice above the wind, "we meet it as we have met this day—together, in spirit if not in flesh."

The others gave no reply, but each met his gaze. The promise did not need words.

A final bolt of lightning split the horizon, and in its light, Kael'Thorin thought he saw a figure standing upon the farthest crest of the waves—a shape both familiar and vast, the wind itself given form. Then it was gone, lost to the darkness and the rain.

Ka'el—the wind between worlds—had heard them.

And with that silent acknowledgment, the storm began to ease, leaving the city trembling but unbroken.

The Encoding would hold.

Interlude III: Seraphiel of the Axis Grove

Beneath the wounded heavens, the Axis Grove stood as it always had, yet changed beyond measure. Once, its canopy had been a choir of green, every leaf attuned to the great Song that bound Lemuria. Now its branches shivered with the echoes of loss. The stars above—fractured, veiled by smoke—cast a faltering light, but still the grove shimmered faintly, as though remembering its vow.

It was here that Seraphiel descended.

She came not as fire falling from the sky, nor as thunder upon the earth, but as a breath of radiance. Her wings unfolded like dawn breaking through ash, each feather carrying the pulse of a hidden flame. Her eyes bore both sorrow and unyielding compassion, for she had seen the unraveling. She had witnessed the Circle shatter, the waters rise, the stones break. And yet, she had come—not to mourn, but to witness.

The Axis Grove received her in silence. The trees leaned inward, their trunks scarred but unbroken, as though to form a cathedral around her. The earth beneath glowed faintly, alive with embers that had not yet cooled. Above, the constellations wavered, uncertain in their paths, but Seraphiel's presence drew them into poise. The Grove became once more the spine of Lemuria, its axis humming with memory.

Seraphiel lowered her hand to the soil. It was warm, trembling. 'Not all is lost,' she whispered, though no human stood to hear her. Her words sank into the roots, into the marrow of the land itself. 'The song still waits.'

A hush fell over the grove as Seraphiel rose to her full height, her wings arching outward until they touched the edges of the Axis trees. Light rippled down their trunks, tracing the scars where flame had kissed them and water had torn their roots. It was as if her very presence reminded the grove of what it had once been—a living axis between heaven and earth, body and soul, memory and becoming.

Seraphiel began to speak, though no tongue could name her language. It was not sound but resonance, a harmony that stirred the hidden places within the trees and stones. The air quivered. The soil trembled. From deep within, the grove answered. Branches swayed though no wind moved them, leaves shivered though the night was still. Something ancient was listening.

"Balance has not perished," Seraphiel intoned, her voice carrying both the gentleness of a mother and the severity of flame. "Though the Circle is broken and the song lies wounded, the axis endures. What has fallen can be remembered. What is shattered can be re-woven. But first, the hearts of those who remain must turn toward one another."

As her words settled, a pulse rippled outward from the grove. Survivors wandering the broken lands felt it in their bones, though they could not name its source—a sudden warmth, a quiet urging to lift their heads from despair. For an instant, the heaviness of grief lessened, replaced by the faintest echo of belonging. It was Seraphiel's gift, carried through root and stone, across valley and shore.

Seraphiel closed her eyes, and the grove itself seemed to breathe with her. Each inhalation drew starlight down through the canopy, each exhalation spread a warmth into the soil below. In that rhythm, vision opened.

She saw Lemuria as it had been: radiant, whole, the Circle unbroken. She saw the faces of those who had carried the song faithfully, their voices woven into the marrow of the land. Then the vision shifted—she saw the breaking again, the floods, the fires, the cries. Yet this time, her gaze pierced beyond the surface of ruin. Threads glimmered in the darkness, fine and fragile, but unbroken. They reached out like veins of light, searching for one another.

A voice rose within her, not her own yet resonant with her essence: 'Balance will not return through memory alone. It must be forged through sacrifice. The seed of unity cannot awaken while hearts cling to what is lost.'

Seraphiel bowed her head, wings folding inward. She understood. To heal, something must be surrendered—safety, certainty, the illusion of permanence. Only in letting go could the threads weave anew. Only in giving could the axis be restored.

When her eyes opened again, tears traced fire down her cheeks, glowing briefly before fading. She lifted her face to the shattered heavens. 'So be it,' she whispered. 'If balance requires my flame, I will give it. If the song demands my voice, I will sing until silence takes me.'

The grove answered with a long, low creak, as though the very trees bent in witness to her vow.

From the Axis Grove, Seraphiel's vow unfurled like a wave of unseen fire. It rippled outward, carried on roots and rivers, borne in the whisper of the wind. Though no mortal tongue heard her words, the essence of her promise found its way into the hearts of the scattered survivors.

A mother keeping her children close by a smoldering shoreline felt a sudden courage rise within her, though she could not name its source. A hunter wandering the broken highlands paused, sensing a warmth in his chest that had nothing to do with the sun. In the caves where the wounded rested, an elder dreamed of wings unfurling, and when he awoke, his breath carried a steadiness it had not known since the Fall.

So it was that Seraphiel's vow became more than her own. It was woven into the marrow of the people, a resonance carried silently, awakening small embers of remembrance where despair had sought to take root.

The Axis Grove glowed faintly, its scarred trees standing like pillars of a half-ruined temple. Above, the stars shifted, ever so slightly, as though acknowledging the vow made in their sight. Balance had not yet been restored, but its promise had been sown.

Seraphiel folded her wings and knelt at the grove's center. She placed her hands upon the soil once more, her tears falling to mingle with ash. Though her vow had gone forth, she knew the path ahead would demand more than one voice, more than one flame. The Circle was broken, and only in the gathering of many could the song be renewed.

Her eyes closed, and the Axis Grove held its breath, guarding her vigil through the long night.

The first pale light of dawn crept through the canopy, painting the Axis Grove in hues of silver and ash. Seraphiel remained at its heart, her wings folded, her form still as carved stone. Through the long hours of night she had not moved, keeping vigil over the fractured axis. Her vow burned quietly within her, no longer a flame of fury but a steady ember that would not be extinguished.

Birdsong, tentative and halting, broke the silence. A few small creatures stirred among the roots, sensing that though much had changed, life yet persisted. The grove itself exhaled, its breath faint but present, as though willing itself to remember the song Seraphiel had carried into its depths.

At last she rose, her eyes lifting to the sky. The stars had faded, leaving only the bruised light of morning. Still she spoke, her voice firm though low: "The Circle is broken, but the axis stands. Let this place hold what memory it can, until the threads find one another again."

With that, she unfurled her wings. A quiet blaze of radiance flowed from her feathers, washing over the grove one last time. The scars of fire and flood remained, but the trees seemed straighter, their roots a little firmer, their silence less heavy. Balance had not returned, yet the promise of it lingered.

Seraphiel took to the air, her form vanishing into the brightening sky. The Axis Grove stood alone, scarred yet alive, waiting. Though the Circle was broken, its echo remained, guarded in the roots, the stones, and the memory of the dawn.

Chapter 4: The Fall

The air carried an unfamiliar weight, a kind of stillness that was neither peace nor calm but something waiting to break.
Lemuria's terraces shimmered in twilight, the great crystalline walkways glowing faintly as the last light of the sun kissed their edges.
A hush had fallen over the city—soft, almost reverent—as though every stone, every leaf, every drop of water in the channels knew something was about to shift.

Kael'Thorin stood at the edge of the western ledge, his gaze turned toward the horizon where the ocean met the sky in a molten seam of copper and violet.
He had not found rest since the Encoding. Even in meditation, the memory fields had become turbulent, streaked with impressions of fractures where once there had been endless patterns of harmony.
He pressed his palms together, not in ritual but as if to hold himself steady.

The whispers of the Guides had been quieter of late, as though veiled behind clouds. Only Ka'el—the wind between worlds—spoke with the same constancy, carrying through him a restless current like a tide shifting against a jagged shore.

Amari'el Shae'Lumae's song still lingered within him, a golden memory that wrapped around the core of his being like warmth against the chill.
Yet even her melody was not enough to drown the sense of dread that had begun to coil in the marrow of the people.

They smiled, they laughed, they carried their baskets of fruits and herbs through the market squares, but Kael'Thorin could feel it: the dissonance seeping into the fabric of things unseen.

Seraphiel appeared from the shadow of a high walkway, her robes trailing like streams of midnight ink.
She had always moved as though she belonged to two realms at once—feet on earth, spirit elsewhere—and tonight that quality felt sharper, almost severe.
Her golden eyes caught the light of the fading sun, reflecting a warning Kael'Thorin did not need spoken to know.

"The Axis Grove has grown silent," she said without preamble. "The great trees no longer hum in unison. I felt a thread snap. Small, but real. A single note unraveling."

Kael'Thorin drew in a slow breath, his chest heavy. "It begins, then."

Seraphiel inclined her head. "The spiral strains against itself. What we encoded burns hotter than the earth beneath us can hold."

Her words landed like stone. Kael'Thorin had sensed as much during the rituals, but to hear it from her lips was different—like prophecy sharpened into fact.
He searched her face for some flicker of hope, but found none. She was all clarity and fire, stripped of comfort.

Behind them, the terraces filled with the rituals of ordinary life: children tracing spirals on the stone with chalk, elders lighting lamps carved of river crystal, singers raising soft chants to

accompany the deepening dark.
It might have been beautiful had it not felt like the final act of a people who did not yet know they were closing the curtain on their own story.

Kael'Thorin turned back to the horizon. "Will the others come tonight?"

"They will," Seraphiel said. "Amari'el already sings in the Groves, calling what harmony she can. Odric walks the shore, listening for signs in the tide. Thalan'ar waits in silence, listening to the silence itself."

"And Ka'el?"

Seraphiel's gaze flicked toward the east, where the winds had begun to stir strangely, coiling and snapping in unseen eddies. "Everywhere. Nowhere. Between. Ka'el is restless."

The words lodged in Kael'Thorin's heart. Restless winds, broken threads, groves grown silent—signs enough to foretell what none wanted to admit aloud: the fall of Lemuria had begun, not with flames or tremors but with the smallest fracture, invisible to most, devastating to those who knew.

The great bells tolled from the High Spire, summoning the people to the evening convergence. It was meant as a song of unity, but tonight the tones wavered, bending at the edge of dissonance, as though even the metal itself knew it was being asked to sing against the truth.

Kael'Thorin and Seraphiel walked together toward the gathering,

their steps slow, deliberate.
Between them stretched the unspoken vow of what was to come: to hold memory against forgetting, to stand even as the world beneath their feet prepared to shift and break.

And yet, as they crossed into the great square where thousands were already gathering, Kael'Thorin felt a pang of tenderness—a bittersweet recognition that this would be the last whole night. The last time Lemuria would come together in one voice without the fracture of fear splitting its song.

He whispered, more to himself than to Seraphiel: "Let them sing tonight, even if it is for the last time."

And when the first notes rose into the violet dusk, shimmering like rivers of light across the terraces, it seemed the heavens themselves bent low to listen.

The air hung heavy as the echoes of the great tremor faded into silence. Kael'Thorin stood still, his body taut with the awareness that what had just begun could not be undone. The crystalline walls of the chamber pulsed faintly, their usual luminescence dimmed as though the very heart of Lemuria was straining to breathe.

Around him, the Circle of Elders gathered in fractured unity. Some whispered prayers, others pressed their palms against the glyphs etched into the floor, seeking counsel from the patterns of the spiral. But none could deny the truth swelling between them: the Balance was faltering.

Amari'el Shae'Lumae's voice broke the silence, soft yet carrying the weight of command. "The Seed is stirring. The earth calls to us with both grief and warning. Do you not feel it?" Her eyes, pools of silver light, swept over each of them until they rested on Kael'Thorin.

He did feel it. Every fiber of his being resonated with the fracture, as though his own soul was splitting alongside the land. Yet within that fracture burned a clarity, a vow he had carried long before this lifetime. It pressed now against the edges of his heart, urging him to speak.

"If we do not act," Kael'Thorin said, his voice steady though his spirit trembled, "the spiral will collapse in upon itself. This is no longer a matter of waiting for signs. The Fall is upon us."

Gasps rippled through the chamber. Thalan'ar's golden eyes narrowed, sharp with both caution and knowing. "And what would you propose, Rememberer? To stand against the tide of the Vow itself?"

Kael'Thorin met his gaze without wavering. "Not against it. With it. We must remember what was sown, and we must cast it forward—beyond the ruin that comes."

The words settled into the space like stones dropped into still water, sending ripples through the gathered souls. Seraphiel lowered her gaze, fingers brushing against the staff she carried, the crystal atop it flickering faintly. "To cast forward is to sever ourselves from what we have known," she whispered. "It is to choose exile, even before exile chooses us."

Odric stepped from the shadows at the chamber's edge, the sea's scent clinging to him. "Then exile may be the only way the song survives."

The chamber darkened as though in agreement, the pulse of Lemuria itself dimming another degree. The Fall was no longer a whisper of prophecy. It had begun.

Dawn arrived on a blade's edge—too bright, too clean. The kind of light that pretends it knows what comes next.
The Axis Hall held it without comment. Pillars shone like wet stone; the bowl on the center slab wore a thin skin of brightness that did not belong to fire.
The soil beneath remained dark, patient.

Kael'Thorin had not slept. He did not feel sleep's absence as loss—only as a space where listening had chosen to stay.
Seraphiel stood to his left, hair gathered at her nape, face unadorned and therefore more luminous.
Thalan'ar leaned a shoulder to the threshold stone like a man conferring with an old friend.
Odric came from the shore with salt dried pale along his forearms.
Amari'el arrived last, quiet as the retreating tide, night's chant still faint in her mouth like the aftertaste of honey.

The Chancellor's mantle announced her before she spoke.
Vaedriel crossed the hall without hurry, the carved leafwork along her collarbone catching dawn in small, disciplined glints.
Behind her came elders from the terraces and keepers from the lighthouse, their hands still smelling of oil and linen.
She took her place at the south side of the bowl. "Report," she said—not curt; precise.

Odric set a palm near the rim. "Bells placed. North finger, south stairs, mid-harbor rope hung where children reach first. Watchers at both points through the night. Two bells answered, not struck. The corridor pressed; we did not push back."

Amari'el inclined her head. "Singers in pairs. Few voices. The chant held consent without force.
Where the line thinned, the breath widened. One rupture in the Axis Hall—the crack slept when sung to."

Thalan'ar lifted his hand and let it fall. "Stone feels no fear. But the measure being asked of air is not its native shape."

Seraphiel's gaze slid to the east, where the sea wrote a faint gray punctuation at the horizon. "Three bright points riding the line. They doubled the filament."

Kael'Thorin added the simplest truth. "The bowl's tide withdrew. Not from refusal. To give room."

Vaedriel nodded, once. "The Atlanteans return at first harbor bell to proclaim designation."
She looked not at the Five but at the keepers who had lived with light longer than law.
"Tell me what happens to the noon beam when a line asks it to be constant."

The eldest keeper—Rine, with braid like twisted rope—cleared her throat.
"The beam was meant to be a call, not a leash," she said. "It listens to weather and to heart. It brightens for fog, hushes for

clear water.
When you make it constant, it stops agreeing. It shouts when it should murmur. It becomes a wall to those who know it as a door."

A soft murmur moved through the hall. Vaedriel accepted the keeper's words as ledger, not as anecdote.
"Then the noon beam will not be made constant," she said.

"You may be recorded as refusing safety," Seraphiel observed, not unkindly, simply completing the shape of the day.

"We have refused danger before when it presented itself with manners," Vaedriel replied.
She turned to Kael'Thorin. "Sit with the bowl at proclamation. Listen for what the words do, not only what they say."

"I will," he said.

By the time the city's first bell spoke, the hall had become a corridor of footsteps and decisions.
Messengers loped out toward the terraces: keep your lanterns; keep your rope; let children see you practice.
Singers dispersed to the listening posts. Odric took the south stairs. Thalan'ar stayed with the stone.
Seraphiel and Amari'el flanked the Chancellor as a living balance—edge and song walking beside office.

The harbor looked newly minted under the pale. Nets lay like sleeping handwriting along the quay.
Masts drew incomprehensible music in the air. On the far horizon three small shapes skated the seam between sea and light,

low as gulls and far less alive.
As they came nearer, Kael'Thorin tasted iron again.
Not blood. Ink. Numbers written with a metal pen across water that had never asked to be paper.

The Atlanteans made their entrance in the tone of men doing a favor.
Maelion led, cloak simple as a statement, face composed into the careful brightness of someone rehearsed.
Beside him the cutter officer wore the pale metal chased with symbols that meant law in a city that trusted lines.
Behind them the same clerk bore the narrow case—the one that breathed like a jar—and a second case longer and thinner, as if to cradle a measured reed.

"Friends," Maelion called, smiling with a care that landed like chalk on wet slate.
"Today we mark what has already been proven by experience. We designate lanes for the safety of all who pass your beautiful harbor."

Vaedriel did not smile. "We remember your account," she said. "Our own shows songs returned, lives preserved, rope thrown and caught. We decline the noon beam constant.
We decline to bless a corridor that does not consent to wind."

A stir rippled the Atlantean ranks, then smoothed itself as if an unseen hand had passed over velvet.
The officer stepped forward with the long case. He opened it to reveal three rods nested in felt—silvered tools, each with a small lens set at one end.
"Calibration styluses," he said. "For the lighthouse and the shore

bells. With these, your keepers may bring their instruments to our frequency.
We will record your participation as partnership."

Rine the keeper did not move. "Our bell tones are root, not bloom," she said. "They answer water, not orders."

The officer's lips executed the smallest of tolerances. "We do not order. We correct."

Odric, from the south stairs, laughed once—the sound of a man who had hit his shin on exactly such a word before dawn.
"You can keep your styluses," he called. "We've rope."

Maelion pretended not to hear. "The lanes will reduce variance," he continued, hands open in reason. "Variance kills."

"Sometimes," Seraphiel said. "So does obedience."

He let the comment pass like a cloud he had decided would not rain. He raised his palm for ceremony.
The clerk opened the jar-breath case and produced thin bright sheets—a ledger of lines—and two small plaques chased with narrow script.
Maelion began to read in a voice that expected agreement: "By authority of the Council of Capitals and at the request of certain coastal communities—"

"Not this one," Bren said from behind Kael'Thorin, loud enough to be heard and not so loud as to be removed.
A ripple of fisher laughter moved along the quay like a low tide.
Maelion's smile did not move.

He continued. "—the following lanes are designated for entry, egress, emergency drift, and correction.
At noon, the lighthouse beam will be made constant for testing and alignment."

"No," Vaedriel said.

It was not a shout; it was a key struck true. The harbor heard it and remembered a hundred nights when a woman's single note steadied a boat.

The officer lifted one stylus as if it were a priest's instrument. "If you will not apply these, we will do so and provide instruction," he said. "This is collaboration."

"Consent," Thalan'ar said from the edge of the crowd, "is not the same as instruction."

The first harbor bell answered him, struck by a hand that had not meant to give commentary.
On the horizon the three bright points found their stations—one due west, one a little north, one a little south.
They laid a second filament along the first, then a third, as if braiding a leash out of light.

Kael'Thorin felt the bowl at his sternum lift and settle, lift and settle.
The words went on: clauses, definitions, fines; the sentences stacking like flat stones into a wall.
But underneath the speech he felt the work those words performed—the way they tightened the air in small increments, like fingers polishing wire.

"Do we answer now?" Bren asked Vaedriel in a voice meant for shouldering nets, not law.

"We answer at noon," Vaedriel said. "The corridor wishes to test. We will teach."

"Teach what?" Maelion inquired pleasantly, though something in his gaze had turned to ledger lines no longer taking ink cleanly.

"Number what you like," Seraphiel said. "We will teach air to be more than onc road."

The proclamation concluded to polite silence.
The clerk affixed one thin plaque to the outer pier with resin that smelled like shipwright work done in bad faith.
The second plaque he held as if weighing its usefulness in a place where people used rope.
The officer offered the styluses again. Vaedriel did not reach for them.
Instead she turned to the keepers.

"Keep your lamps. Keep your rope. Keep the bell tones you remember."
Then to the harbor at large, to the children and to the old men with hands like carved driftwood: "And keep looking at the sea more than at words."

The Atlanteans withdrew in good order, which is another way of saying they enjoyed lines even while walking.
The three bright points settled into their hum. The corridor drew itself taut as a rule.

In the space the proclamation left, breath returned. It did not return fully.
The harbor's noise resumed, but softer, as if people had agreed to let their listening take the larger share.

Kael'Thorin stood with the bowl in his hands and watched a skiff slide along a familiar crooked path from net to quay.
A boy leaped to the stone, stumbled, swore in a tone that made the old men smile, and righted a coil with his foot.
This was what he wanted to memorize: not the corridors, not the plaques, not even the bright points singing their thin contentment.
This: the small, competent grace of those who knew water by skin.

Seraphiel's hand found his elbow. "At third bell we gather again," she said. "And then we practice until the corridor finds itself inside a circle it cannot command."

"Can circles fail?" he asked, knowing the answer and needing it spoken to glue his focus to it.

"They can forget," she said. "Which is why we set singers at the terraces."

Amari'el came with a drift of salt air and placed two pebbles into Kael'Thorin's palm: one river-glossed, one unglazed bone-white. "Set these in the bowl at noon when they ask the light to unlearn kindness," she said. "Stone and bone. River and ancestor."

Odric joined them, his jaw set to the idea of work rather than to

the affront of the morning.
"I'll put a third bell at the south stairs," he said. "Low one. If the line presses hard there, the bell will answer without a hand."

Thalan'ar looked up from the plaque as if he had been reading its script into the stone to see if the stone would keep it.
"It will not," he said to himself, then to the others: "But we should not mistake stone's refusal for the harbor's. People can be taught to like straightness when they are tired."

"Then we will help them rest," Seraphiel said simply.

The sun climbed. Fog gathered beyond the breakwater, neither thick nor thin, the kind that tests friends more than instruments. Children ferried water to singers along the terraces. Elders laid rope where rope remembers its work.
Keepers checked lamp-wicks and lenses that had never been asked to shout.

At second bell the Atlantean cutters took their stations more openly, as if modesty had not been part of the morning's plan. On the quay the plaque glinted like a button sewn to a garment that did not fit.
Maelion spoke to the officer in a voice too soft to be ledgered and smiled at passersby with the practiced kindness of a man selling the same thing in different towns.

Inside the Axis Hall, Kael'Thorin sat with the bowl again.
He set Amari'el's two pebbles into the shallow spiral channels—river-stone where the curve widened, bone where it narrowed. The bowl's breath rose to meet them. The first time since midnight the small tide swelled, then settled, as if in agreement.

"Ready?" Seraphiel asked from the door.

"No," he said. "Yes."

She accepted both. "We answer what we can. We refuse what we must. We remember what they will ask us to forget."

The third bell spoke—three measured notes that did not hurry. On the horizon the bright points brightened. On the quay the clerk lifted his stylus toward the lighthouse as if saluting a new officer.
Rine raised a hand for her keepers and received three quiet nods. No one in Lemuria had to be told how to keep time with work.

Noon came on like a held breath finding a chest.

At the lighthouse a wheel turned. Light gathered into the lens and looked for orders.
The corridor sang its thin line and the bright points offered their agreement.
Across the terraces the singers' listening tones rose like water up a beach, not to drown—only to remind.

Kael'Thorin placed his palm above the bowl and chose not to touch.
He felt the beam ready itself to become a wall and watched consent change the shape of his breath from a straight road to an open field.
He did not command. He declared: air is not one road.

On the harbor's skin something unseen braced itself.

The noon beam reached for constant.
The corridor welcomed it the way a ruler welcomes an edge.
Odric's low bell at the south stairs trembled, one note shy of speech.

"Now," Seraphiel whispered, and Kael'Thorin felt the vow rise—the old, golden thread that promised scattering and the remembering of the scattered.

He exhaled, and the bowl exhaled, and in that shared breath the island remembered itself not as obedience but as consent.
The beam struck the lens and began to take the shape it had been offered.

What happened next would tell the making of a fall—or the making of a seed.

The ground trembled beneath the crystal arches of the Great Hall as the tides of discord spilled inward. What had once been the sanctuary of Lemuria's most sacred vows now echoed with voices raised in fear and defiance. The constant—the delicate harmony that bound the island's heart to the currents of the stars—was unraveling.

Kael'Thorin stood at the center, the glyphs at his wrists alive with fire, as though they too felt the fracture. Around him, his companions formed a broken circle. Thalan'ar's eyes were shadowed with sorrow, Seraphiel's wings were half-manifest in a haze of pale light, Amari'el's hands clenched into trembling fists, and Odric's great frame seemed to waver between rage and despair. Each bore the mark of the breaking in their own way.

"This is not the fall of a tower," Seraphiel whispered, her voice sharp with grief. "It is the fall of memory itself."

The dome above them shimmered, fissures spreading like veins of darkness through its once-perfect lattice. Kael'Thorin reached upward, as though he could hold the cracks closed by will alone. But the force that pressed against him was greater than anything he had faced. It was not the malice of an enemy—it was the consequence of Lemuria's own vow stretched too far, a river forced beyond its banks.

Amari'el fell to her knees, the song rising in her throat breaking into a cry. "The spiral is slipping… the threads are scattering…"

"Then we must anchor them," Kael'Thorin answered, his voice steady even as his body trembled. He knew the cost of such anchoring. It would not be their generation who carried the burden of remembrance, but countless lives to come. The vow would not dissolve—it would fracture and seed itself across the ages.

Odric slammed his hand against the crystal floor. "We swore to guard the constant. And now we scatter it like ashes."

"It is not ashes," Thalan'ar said, at last raising his gaze. His voice, though soft, carried the weight of finality. "It is seed. That is the way of the vow. We do not fail—we transform."

The words sank into Kael'Thorin like molten iron. Around him the Great Hall groaned, its luminous walls bowing inward. With a final effort, he raised his arms and spoke the old tongue—not to preserve what was broken, but to guide its breaking toward renewal.

"By the spiral that never ends, by the song that remembers, let this vow fall—not to silence, but to seed."

A shuddering blast of light consumed the hall. The constant was broken. Yet within its ruin, the first echoes of the future vow began to stir.

The sky bore no mercy. Clouds pressed low and heavy against the horizon, smearing gray across the ocean's expanse as though the heavens themselves grieved. Kael'Thorin stood at the cliff's edge, the salt wind tugging at his robes, his chest rising and falling with the rhythm of the storm.

He could feel it—not just in the air, but in his bones: the shattering of a great cycle. The Lemurian song, once steady as a heartbeat, now trembled with dissonance. Voices of the land, the waters, the stones beneath, all wept in unison.

Behind him, Thalan'ar stepped lightly, though even his grace could not soften the heaviness of his presence. The seer's voice, usually clear as bells, carried the weight of foretelling.

"It has begun."

Kael'Thorin closed his eyes, letting the truth settle. He had always known this day would come. Prophecies whispered through generations had spoken of the rending—the unweaving of harmony by hands too eager for dominion. But knowledge did not dull the ache of its arrival.

From the shoreline below, cries rose. Fires crackled where none should burn. The waters of the harbor churned with unease, tides breaking patterns older than memory.

Amari'el Shae'Lumae appeared at Kael'Thorin's side, her hair a cascade of shadow in the wind. Her voice carried not fear, but fire.

"Then we do not stand idle. The Vow was never meant to remain a silent relic."

Seraphiel approached from the grove's edge, her face illumined by a pale, otherworldly glow. She was the stillness in the storm, the unwavering center. She placed a hand upon Amari'el's shoulder.

"Balance is already fracturing. To rush with flame may fracture it further."

Odric came last, his form broad as the trees he had left behind. His brow was furrowed, his heart torn between action and patience. He gazed at Kael'Thorin, as though waiting for the final thread to be pulled.

Kael'Thorin turned at last. His voice was low, yet it carried the strength of oceans.

"We do not stop the Fall. It is the tide already loosed. What we can do is carry the seed forward, across the darkening waters, into the lifetimes yet to come."

The words rang among them, and the truth was bitter. Lemuria would not be preserved by might, nor by ritual alone. Its spirit must scatter—encoded into memory, sung into bloodlines, woven into dreams.

The others bowed their heads, each guide carrying their own grief, yet bound to the same vow.

Thunder rolled, and the earth itself seemed to shudder. The Fall was no longer prophecy. It was here.

The circle was not supposed to break.

Kael'Thorin felt the truth of it ripple through his marrow as if the bones themselves had been inscribed with ancient runes of warning. The chamber, once humming with the resonance of concordant voices, now cracked and faltered like a string pulled too taut.

Amari'el's song faltered first. Her eyes shimmered with silver tears as her voice wove in and out of silence, as if she were already hearing echoes from another world. Seraphiel pressed close, luminous wings trembling, her song steady but fractured, holding too much weight. Odric, stoic, clenched his fists at his side, jaw set in defiance against the tremor he could not control. And Thalan'ar—Thalan'ar bowed his head, the great oak-shadow of his presence dimming, as if even the roots beneath Lemuria had begun to lose their faith.

"The vow cannot hold," whispered Amari'el, her voice like rain scattering into wind.

Kael'Thorin staggered forward, hand stretched as though he

might physically grasp the vow and knot it back together. "It must hold! Without it, we are undone. The Seed will scatter beyond reach, lost to time."

The circle pulsed once more, a dull, hollow beat. The once-golden filament connecting them sparked, frayed, and split into many threads. They rose like fireflies, scattering through the chamber, each one carrying with it the weight of remembrance that none could yet contain.

Ka'el's wind swept through then, sudden and sorrowful, a current that did not belong to this world but to the space between. The others bowed their heads as the unseen being's lament pressed into their hearts.

"This breaking is not the end," Seraphiel said softly, her voice gathering strength despite the ache in it. "The spiral does not collapse—it widens. We must scatter, yes. But scattering is not death—it is the encoding."

Amari'el turned to her, eyes bright with both grief and reverence. "You would let it unravel?"

"No," Seraphiel answered, "I would let it transform."

Kael'Thorin clenched his fists until his nails dug into his palms. His soul ached with the weight of failure, yet beneath it flickered something else: the quiet certainty that this, too, was written into the pattern.

Odric's voice rumbled low, like stone cracking: "Then we scatter the Seed. Across time, across lives, across bloodlines. It will not be lost, only hidden. Until one among us remembers."

A silence followed that was more sacred than any hymn. Even the trembling stones seemed to bow to the vow remade. The circle did not break—it re-spiraled, becoming something both lesser and greater.

Kael'Thorin raised his head. The sorrow did not lift, but a grim resolve settled in its place. "Then let it be so. I will remember, though it take lifetimes. I will walk until the spiral brings us back together."

The others placed their hands across their hearts, sealing the vow anew.

And as the chamber dimmed, the light of Lemuria itself seemed to flicker, as though it, too, understood what had been set into motion.

Kael'Thorin stood at the threshold of the ruined hall, the air filled with the acrid scent of smoke and salt. The chamber where the elders once convened was fractured, its crystalline walls veined with cracks that pulsed faintly, like dying embers of a once-living flame. He could still hear echoes of their voices, not in sound, but in memory—remnants of guidance that now felt impossibly distant.

Amari'el Shae'Lumae moved beside him, her hands trailing along the broken surface of the wall. "The song here is broken," she whispered, her voice strained, "and yet the memory still lingers. It will not let us forget."

Kael'Thorin closed his eyes, feeling the pressure of the vow he had carried since the beginning. The fall of Lemuria was no longer some foretelling—it was unfolding now, around them, through them. The waters that once sang with life were heavy with sorrow. The earth that once carried them with grace trembled beneath their feet.

Seraphiel's wings shimmered faintly as she approached, her presence luminous even in the dimming light. "The axis weakens. If the vow is to endure, it must be scattered now—before all is lost."

Thalan'ar's voice, steady yet weighted, joined hers. "And in scattering, we risk forgetting. Our bonds may be unraveled for lifetimes untold."

Odric stepped forward, his eyes fierce, jaw set. "Better to forget and endure than to remember and perish. The vow must outlive us, even if it takes the shape of strangers who will not know why they ache."

Kael'Thorin turned toward them all—the five who had walked beside him, who had carried him, who had reminded him of who he was. In their faces he saw sorrow, love, and the strange fire of hope that refused to be extinguished. He felt the weight of all they were about to lose, and yet beneath it, the deeper truth: they were not ending, but seeding.

His voice was quiet when it came. "Then let it be so. Scatter the vow. Let it weave itself into the marrow of creation, into the waters, into the stone, into the breath of every child yet to be born. Let it remember itself, even when we do not."

The hall shuddered violently, light cascading from the fractures as if the chamber itself were breaking open into the void. The five gathered close around him, their hands extended, their energies converging in a spiral that burned brighter than the crumbling world around them.

The last note of the vow rose—not as one voice, but as many, layered and eternal. It filled the broken hall, spilled into the trembling earth, and rose into the skies that wept fire and rain. It was a sound that would not die, though none who heard it then would carry it whole.

The vow was scattered. The fall was sealed

The waves did not crash—they pulled, a dragging undertow that seemed to tug at the very roots of the island itself. Kael'Thorin stood at the cliff's edge, his chest rising and falling with the rhythm of a world that was losing its breath. The sky above spiraled in bruised hues of violet and indigo, broken by veins of lightning that forked downward into the sea.

He could feel the weight of the vow etched into his bones—the Encoding was alive within him now, and it pulsed against the collapse as though refusing to yield. Around him, the cries of his kin wove with the keening of the winds. Some prayed, some screamed, others simply stood silent, unable to grasp the enormity of what was unfolding.

Behind him, Amari'el Shae'Lumae placed a hand to his shoulder, steadying, grounding. Her voice was not raised, yet it carried through the storm: "It is not the end. It is the scattering. The seed cannot grow unless it is broken first."

Kael'Thorin turned to her, eyes rimmed with salt and fire. He wanted to believe her, but the sight of the great towers of Lemuria trembling, their crystal spires cracking like glass under strain, made belief feel like a fragile reed in a hurricane.

The waters surged higher, climbing over the shores, devouring villages and temples alike. The light within the earth—the same luminescence that had once sung through every stone and stream—now sputtered, as if drowning.

Still, Kael'Thorin stood, unyielding. If this was the fall, then he would be witness—not as a victim, but as the bearer of memory. His hand clenched around the spiral-mark upon his chest, the glyph burning against his palm. He whispered to the storm, to the guides, to all that listened between the worlds: "Remember."

Kael'Thorin felt the silence in his bones before the sound itself reached him. It was as if the earth drew in a sharp breath and held it, waiting. Then came the low rumble — deep, rolling, and alive, a tremor that began beneath the soles of his feet and climbed the length of his body.

The sky seemed to pale as though its light had been siphoned into the trembling ground. Waters near the shore shivered, their surfaces stippled with invisible hands. Birds took wing in chaotic spirals, their songs lost in the rising resonance.

Around him, the great towers that had for centuries anchored the memory-fields began to moan, their crystalline spires refracting light that no longer danced. It was a sound of mourning, long and hollow, the voice of stone remembering its own fall.

Kael'Thorin's breath caught. This was the unraveling, the long-foretold breaking. Every vow, every thread of memory encoded within Lemuria was being tested, pulled taut against the edges of collapse.

He reached inward for the presence of the Five. Already, Seraphiel's warmth pulsed at the edges of his heart, Amari'el's song quivered like a reed in a rising storm, and Odric's weight anchored his spirit against despair. Thalan'ar and Ka'el lingered just beyond, shadows of light, waiting for his call.

Kael'Thorin opened his mouth to speak, but no words came. For a heartbeat, he was both man and echo, caught in the widening silence before the Fall.

The sky cracked with a brilliance that seared the horizon, a white fire that split the heavens and cast long shadows across the trembling land. Kael'Thorin stood at the ridge of the Axis Plateau, his chest rising and falling with the weight of every vow, every memory, every echo of what had been promised.

Beneath him, the city lights of Lemuria flickered like a constellation collapsing inward. Towers that had once sung with crystalline resonance groaned against the weight of rupturing earth. The songstones shuddered, their tones breaking into discord, voices cracking under the strain of dissolution.

The Five Guides gathered close, their forms luminous against the storm. Seraphiel's eyes glistened with tears that refracted the lightning, her hand pressed over her heart as though holding the very song within it together. Amari'el Shae'Lumae's voice trembled a melody, soft but resolute, weaving protection even as the earth convulsed. Thalan'ar's staff struck the ground, grounding currents of force that threatened to scatter them. Odric braced himself against the gale, his form like an oak standing in a tempest, while Ka'el whispered between the worlds, a wind threading words into Kael'Thorin's ears: *Hold the vow. Hold the thread.*

The ground split. A yawning chasm tore through the gardens of remembrance, devouring fountains, sacred groves, and halls of gathering. Cries rose from the people below, a chorus of fear and prayer. Kael'Thorin's heart broke, but within the breaking came clarity: this was not an end of life, but the fracture of memory. The Song of Lemuria was being scattered into the soul-seed of each who would yet awaken.

Kael'Thorin lifted his hands, palms outstretched. The vow burned through his veins, alive with fire, alive with sorrow and love. He spoke—not in words, but in resonance, his voice becoming chord and flame, a declaration woven into the very marrow of creation:

'Though the land may fall, the vow will not die. Though the seas may rise, memory will endure. Though we be scattered, we will remember.'

The Five Guides encircled him, lending their strength to his vow. The spiral of their combined resonance rose upward, challenging the storm, piercing the veil of fire above. The wind screamed; the earth howled; the seas surged against the distant shores. Yet within that chaos, the vow took root, carried beyond time, beyond ruin.

And still, the Fall deepened.

The air of Lemuria had grown heavy, not with storm alone, but with the burden of what could not be undone. The vow, once a radiant cord stretching between soul and star, now reverberated with a fracture that no hand could mend. Everywhere, the sound of it—like crystal cracking in slow descent—haunted the air, seeping into the marrow of all who lived beneath its echo.

Kael'Thorin stood at the cliffs of the western shore, the sea writhing like a beast unchained. The waves did not crest—they rose like towers, like walls of memory pressing in. Beneath their roar was the sound of weeping: the laments of families watching their sacred homes falter, their songs dissolving into the void. Children clung to mothers, and fathers stood helpless, their tools and weapons useless against the unraveling.

The Five gathered in silence, each a pillar amidst the storm of despair. Seraphiel's eyes glowed with sorrow, her wings folding tightly against her as though to shield her own heart from the cries. Amari'el Shae'Lumae's song trembled, torn between the need to soothe and the knowledge that no melody could restore what had been broken. Thalan'ar's jaw was set, his eyes burning with fire, yet even his warrior's stance seemed a fragile defense against the vastness of the Fall.

Odric bent to the earth, his palm pressed flat to the trembling soil. He whispered in the old tongue, not to hold it back—he knew such a thing was impossible—but to honor it, to remind the land that its sacrifice would not be forgotten. And Ka'el, unseen yet felt, stirred as a wind that moved through the bones of all present, carrying with it the faintest reminder that there was still more beyond the ruin.

Kael'Thorin raised his hand, not in command but in vow renewed. His voice rose above the roar of the sea: "We will carry the memory. We will carry the vow. Though the waters take this land, they shall not take who we are."

The people, broken and trembling, lifted their eyes to him. In that moment, even as the ground split and light fell in sheets from the heavens, a fragment of hope kindled amidst despair. The vow was not gone—it was transmuted, scattered like seeds across the darkened soil of tomorrow.

The sea surged, and the cliffs themselves began to fall. The Five drew close to Kael'Thorin, their presence anchoring him as the world around them came undone. This was no longer about saving Lemuria—it was about remembering Lemuria, so that in some distant age, in some other land, the Song could be sung again.

The tremors beneath the earth grew restless, a warning that the land itself had reached its limit. Kael'Thorin felt the pull of the Spiral deep within his chest, as though the very song of Lemuria was beginning to unravel. Fires licked the horizon where once the towers had stood, their crystalline spires reduced to molten fragments. The waters he loved turned turbulent, rising in waves that smashed against the coastal stone.

Amari'el stood at his side, her voice a hymn of both defiance and surrender. "The seed is not lost," she whispered, her hand upon his. "What falls will rise again. The vow carries us beyond this ruin."

Thalan'ar lifted his staff, the runes along its shaft blazing with memory. "Remember this, Kael'Thorin. When the silence comes, let it not consume you. The Spiral is not an end—it is the turning of worlds."

The cries of the people echoed like thunder across the collapsing city. Mothers clutching children, elders pressing their hands to sacred stones, warriors trying in vain to hold back the flood. And yet, beneath the despair, Kael'Thorin felt the vow burning, a quiet flame that even the storm could not extinguish.

He raised his voice above the chaos, not in command, but in remembrance. "Brothers, sisters—hold to the vow! Even as the land breaks, even as the waters rise, we are not undone. The Spiral carries us onward."

The words rang out across the storm, not halting the fall, but planting a seed in every soul who heard them. A seed that would one day awaken.

The sea forgot its manners.

It rose not in waves but in walls, each heaving face of water holding the memory of a thousand tides and none of their patience. The harbor's ropes went taut as fiddle-strings; bells spoke without hands. Kael'Thorin felt the island pitch beneath him as if a giant had turned in sleep and decided against dreaming.

"High ground!" Odric's voice cut clean through the roar. He was already moving, shoulders squared to the wind, one arm lifting children from stair to stair as if they weighed no more than nets after a poor haul. "Lanterns low! Rope lines on the inner hand!"

Singers on the terraces answered with the steadying tones taught for storms and births. Amari'el's voice threaded them together, not to command but to remind breath of its shape. Each phrase made a little room inside panic—a door propped open for courage to reenter.

A stone tooth of quay sheared off and slammed into the outer wall. The corridor's bright points flared and winked out like insects in a jar shaken too hard. The thin plaque the clerk had fastened that morning peeled away and slapped into the water with all the ceremony of a scolded leaf.

"Thalan'ar!" Kael'Thorin called. "Where does the island want our feet?"

The seer's eyes were half-lidded, listening inward. He pressed his palm to a stair's worn center step, the one smoothed by generations of fishers' heels. "Spiral north," he said, pointing to the narrower path that seemed too humble for flight. "The broad way will break."

Seraphiel lifted both hands and named a silence. It moved like a clear corridor through the clamor, wide enough for three abreast. Those who stepped into it found that their thoughts untangled as if a comb had found them; they did not run faster, but they stumbled less. "Through," she said gently. "Through and up."

Kael'Thorin took the rear where fear collects, passing infants forward, lifting elders, catching the hands of those who had decided to turn back for what could not be carried. "The edge is a promise to stop," he told his body when it wanted to become blade. "Be shore, not spear."

A gull struck the wind and folded, dropping at his feet as if consent had been stripped from the air. He cupped it; its heart rattled like a dice in a cup. Amari'el's palm hovered above, singing in the range only wings remember. The bird's eyes widened, then steadied. It rose, uncertain, then chose a line of sky not owned by corridors.

Behind them the lighthouse lens shattered inward with the sound of a goblet giving up its idea of celebration. A spill of white fire leapt; keepers damped it with blankets that had swaddled infants that morning. Rine, braid like rope, set her boot on the broken rim and turned the wheel by hand. "We will blink for boats," she said to no one and everyone. "Even if we have to throw the light with our arms."

The first wall of water reached the inner steps and failed, broken by the old spiral that had been cut into the rock long before anyone remembered why. Spray slapped faces and tasted of iron and honey. Children laughed without meaning to. Parents cried without wanting to. The island took one slow breath and held.

The breath was not enough.

From beneath the Axis Plateau a sound rose, not like thunder or tearing, but like a great bowl set gently onto stone and finding that the stone had moved. The ground shifted to a new idea of itself. Cracks whispered outward, seeking old conversations in lintels and thresholds, in doorways where lovers had argued and made up, in the stones where elders had warmed their hands in winter.

"Here!" Odric called again, planting a staff where the stair kinked toward the north shoulder. "Hand to rope! Children between!" His tone was a plank laid across a gap—not elegant, but it would hold.

Kael'Thorin felt Ka'el move through the press like a cool draft in a crowded room, carrying the sense of a door somewhere ahead. "Between," the wind said, without tongue. "There is still between." Seraphiel heard it and smiled without teeth. "Of course there is," she answered. "There always is."

They reached the ridge where the old shrine to the tide had been nothing but a circle of stones since before the oldest fisher's oldest story. The circle had cracked. Not badly. Enough to record the day. Kael'Thorin set the bowl from the Axis Hall in the center of the ring and did not touch it. The soil within sat level, unafraid, the tiniest tide consenting to wait.

People gathered in a shoulder of land that felt like the palm of a giant hand, cupped. The high terraces behind them groaned; the low streets below them became a scribble of foam and timber. Those who had climbed carried their grief in both arms and balanced it with small work: tying hair back from faces, passing cups, counting without counting.

Thalan'ar pointed to a stand of young trees bowed by wind. "We lash the little ones there," he said. "Not to bind. To anchor." He moved from trunk to trunk, setting knots that remembered to release. Odric showed the children how to hold the rope with a soft hand that will not burn when it must slide. Amari'el set the oldest among them to humming the simplest night-chant—low, steady, round—so that their teeth would stop knocking and their breath would borrow the chant's shape.

Seraphiel, seeing the way despair eats from the edges, walked the perimeter and gave each watcher a word to hold: this patch, this five paces, this small square of world is your vow. Name it enough, and fear will not take it. The watchers nodded, grateful to be assigned a world they could keep.

The sea surged again and met the island's new idea of itself. For a moment the two wrestled like brothers who mostly love each other and sometimes do not. The island yielded a step, then set its foot. The sea reconsidered and stepped sideways, dragging a street with it. The street did not object; it had always wanted to be in the country.

Kael'Thorin looked down at the bowl. The tide inside had risen a fingernail's height. No one had poured. He exhaled and felt the oath rise with the breath—not as heroism, not as command, but as practice. "Remain," he said to his own chest. "Remain and remember."

A boy with a lantern too large for his hand stood near the ridge's lip, defiant as a candle. Kael'Thorin crouched. "What is your name?"

"Rian," the boy said, as if daring the wind to argue.

"Rian," Kael'Thorin repeated, giving the name a place to sit. "Do you know the rope sign for crooked water?"

The boy nodded, solemn as a three-belled dawn. Kael'Thorin loosened a coil from his own shoulder and put it into Rian's hands. "Then you are our finger of harbor. Two sways if you see a boat that shouldn't trust its eyes. Three if it shouldn't trust its courage."

Rian took the rope as if he'd been waiting all his life to be told what to do and to find it was a thing he could do.

Amari'el slid to Kael'Thorin's side and pressed two pebbles into his palm—a river stone and a small disc of bone. "Set them when you hear the noon that is not noon," she whispered. "Even in breaking, the pattern will ask to be named."

He did not understand and did not need to. He placed river on the bowl's inner curve where the spiral widened and bone where it narrowed. The soil made a small sound not everyone heard, like a jar releasing a day-long held breath.

Below, the lighthouse keepers raised a makeshift shutter and coaxed the ruined lens to blink by hand, a tender, stubborn semaphore. In answer, far out beyond where lanes had been drawn, a scattered clutch of lamps moved like fireflies that had decided to swim. The corridor was gone; the sea was making up its mind again, which is the oldest safety.

"Count them?" Seraphiel asked softly.

"Not yet," Kael'Thorin said. "Remember them first."

A tremor like a yawn rolled underfoot. The shrine's cracked stones adjusted themselves in tiny clicks. Clouds tore, revealing a ragged blue that looked new enough to smell of quarry.

"This ridge will hold," Thalan'ar said, palm flat to rock. "Not forever. Long enough."

"How long is enough?" someone asked, voice pitched just shy of breaking.

"Until you can choose the next step without haste," Seraphiel answered. "Until you can be kind again."

Silence, the good kind, sat down among them. People wiped eyes. Someone laughed at a joke that did not need to be very good. Odric produced bread he'd somehow kept dry and tore it into scandalously uneven pieces. The smallest took the crusts as if they were festival sweets.

Kael'Thorin felt Ka'el brush his cheek, cool as a hand dipped in spring water. Between, the wind said again. Between is still true. He let the word settle into the bowl's breath and into his own. He did not make a speech. He did not lift his hands. He stood, and standing was enough like a vow to count.

"Tonight," Seraphiel said, voice just loud enough to carry to the furthest watcher, "we do not try to keep what cannot be kept. We keep one another. And we remember."

The sea drew back to consider itself. The island, having announced its new shape, waited without apology.

Above the ridge the first stars risked brightness through ragged cloud. Someone pointed. Someone else named them wrongly and was not corrected. The night would not be kind, but it had decided not to be cruel.

Kael'Thorin turned to the Five. "We begin the casting at moonrise," he said. "Not to save what is falling—to carry what must cross."

They nodded, each in the manner of their vow: Thalan'ar with a palm to stone, Odric with a hand to rope, Amari'el touching the bone disc in the bowl, Seraphiel closing her eyes over a silence she had chosen, and Ka'el entering the space between Kael'Thorin's breaths to make room.

The sea sighed. The ridge held. And the night gathered its small mercies for those who had remembered to look for them.

Moonrise found the ridge breathing with the sea. The bowl's small tide rose once more and rested; Rian's rope made two gentle sways to no one in particular, a habit learned into the dark. Around Kael'Thorin the Five stood quiet, their vows cooling like metal set upon stone. Below, the lighthouse blinked by hand—human, patient, imperfect, enough.

Kael'Thorin laid a palm over the spiral at his chest and said nothing. Not prayer, not command—consent. The wind between worlds passed through him, and Seraphiel's silence answered with steadiness. Amari'el's breath became a lullaby the land could keep. Odric's rope hummed; Thalan'ar's touch told the rock: remain.

"We will remember," he thought, and the island returned the thought like a tide returning a shell.

Night gathered its small mercies. Somewhere beyond the breakwater, a scattered clutch of lamps decided together to live.

Interlude IV: Amari'el in the Singing Groves

The Singing Groves lay in the heart of Lemuria, where rivers once braided their silver strands through orchards and flowering trees. Even after the Fall, when so much had been broken, the Groves held an echo of their ancient song. The air there shimmered with memory, as though every branch still hummed with the voices of generations who had gathered beneath their boughs.

It was here that Amari'el Shae'Lumae returned. Her steps were slow, her garments heavy with ash, yet her presence carried a gentleness that even ruin could not diminish. She laid her hand against the trunk of a flowering tree, scarred though it was, and for a moment the grove stirred. Petals loosened and fell like tears, drifting in the faint light of a wounded dawn.

Amari'el closed her eyes. She could still hear them—the songs once woven here by children, elders, lovers, and wanderers. The Groves had been a gathering place, where joy and sorrow alike were given voice. And though silence had now fallen, she knew that silence, too, was part of the song. For every pause carried the promise of a note yet to be sung.

Kneeling, she pressed her ear to the soil. A faint vibration met her, the echo of roots carrying whispers too deep for words. The Groves were not dead. Their song was hidden, wounded, waiting. With a long breath, Amari'el began to hum, her voice low at first, then rising. The sound wove through the trees, fragile but steady, as though coaxing memory itself to awaken.

The sound of Amari'el's humming spread like ripples across still water. The Groves trembled, not with fear, but with remembrance. Branches swayed, releasing petals and leaves that caught the air as though dancing to her melody. The roots below carried her song into the deep, stirring voices long silent.

Her song shifted—no longer a single note, but a weaving. Soft tones of grief, woven with threads of longing, lifted into the canopy. The grove began to answer. A low resonance welled up from the trunks, a harmony born not of joy but of survival. Wounded, yes, but alive. Together they formed a fragile chorus, tree and singer entwined.

Visions stirred in Amari'el's heart as she sang. She saw children playing among the blossoms, their laughter spilling like bells across the meadow. She saw elders tracing songs into the bark, prayers etched into living wood. Lovers pressed hands together under moonlight, their vows woven into the very breath of the grove. All of it returned, flickering through her as memory made song.

Her voice faltered as grief tightened her chest. The visions shifted to the present—branches broken, roots drowned, blossoms burned. Yet still, beneath it all, the song endured. She pressed her palm to the soil again, tears streaking her face. 'Sing with me,' she whispered, not to the grove alone, but to all who still lived. 'Let the silence not be the end.'

The song did not remain within the Groves. Like threads of light carried on unseen currents, it slipped beyond the trees and into the broken lands. Where grief had silenced voices, a stirring began.

On a hillside where a family huddled beside the ashes of their home, a child lifted her head. Though she could not name it, she heard something—faint, lilting, like the echo of laughter she once knew. Without knowing why, she began to hum. Her mother looked down in surprise, then joined her, their voices trembling yet true.

Farther off, a wanderer stopped at the edge of a shattered field. He felt a vibration in his chest, a warmth that urged him to speak. When he opened his mouth, a note emerged—uncertain at first, then steady. Others nearby heard and added their voices, until the field, scarred though it was, carried a fragile harmony.

The Singing Groves swelled in answer. Amari'el felt it—her song was no longer hers alone. It had become a chorus spread across the land, woven by survivors who did not yet know they sang together. Each voice was a thread, reaching, binding, remembering.

She pressed her forehead to the earth, whispering: 'Yes. Remember. Even now, especially now, let the song live.'

As the chorus swelled across the land, the Singing Groves deepened their resonance. The trunks vibrated like vast instruments, their branches trembling with harmonics older than memory. Amari'el knelt in their midst, her body trembling as vision opened within her.

She saw Lemuria not as ruin, but as tapestry—threads torn and frayed, yet glowing still. Where the song touched, the threads quivered, seeking one another. Voices became strands of light, weaving across distance, across sorrow. She saw children's laughter rise like bright threads of gold, elders' chants as deep cords of indigo, the cries of the wounded shimmering silver. All of it wove together, no longer separate, but one living fabric.

And in the center of that weaving stood the Axis Grove, its scarred pillars shining with a light renewed by remembrance. She glimpsed Seraphiel there, wings still spread, her vow now harmonizing with the song. What had begun as flame and balance was now joined by melody and tenderness.

A voice within Amari'el spoke: 'This is the way. Not through power alone, but through remembrance sung together. The Circle is broken, but the song can bind anew.'

Tears streamed down her face. She bowed, not in despair, but in reverence. 'Then I will sing until the end,' she whispered. 'And beyond the end, if that is what is asked of me.'

The grove answered, its branches swaying as though in applause, petals cascading around her like blessings of the ancestors.

Night fell soft upon the Singing Groves, cloaking the blossoms in silver shadow. Amari'el sat among the roots of the ancient trees, her voice worn yet steady. She had sung until her body ached, until her breath was ragged, yet the song did not falter. For it was no longer hers alone—it was the chorus of a people remembering themselves through ruin.

One by one, the trees quieted, their harmonics settling into a low hum, as though carrying her melody into their cores. The earth beneath her pulsed faintly, a heartbeat echoing her vow. The

Groves had heard. The land had heard. Even the broken stars seemed to lean closer, their dim light shimmering in response.

At last, Amari'el lowered her hands to her lap and closed her eyes. A stillness enveloped her, profound and unbroken. She whispered into the silence: "Let this place be sanctuary. Let it hold the memory of our song, until we can gather again."

The petals drifted gently down, veiling her shoulders like a cloak. She leaned back against the scarred trunk of the tree, her tears drying into faint lines of light upon her cheeks. Though her body longed for rest, her spirit glowed with quiet fire. The Singing Groves had answered. They would not forget.

Thus Amari'el kept vigil through the night, the grove itself cradling her as though she were both child and guardian. And when dawn came, the first bird to break the silence sang with a note that carried her melody, a promise that remembrance would outlast even sorrow.

Part III: The Echo of the Seed

Chapter 5: Drift Between Lives

He woke to the sound of water speaking a language he could not yet understand. Not waves, not river—something between, as if the world itself were rinsing its wounds. Kael'Thorin lay still and listened. The breath in his chest felt borrowed, the body around it unfamiliar, as though he had returned from a great distance and not all of him had arrived.

Above him the sky was the color of metal washed thin. The ground smelled of salt and ash. He lifted one hand and found grit in the lines of his palm, like letters he could not read. There were cuts on his knuckles. A bruise bloomed along his ribs. He did not remember how he had received them; he only knew they belonged to the story he had survived.

He rose slowly. The land around him was neither shore nor inland—ruin had blurred the edges. Pools gathered in hollows where gardens once lay. Stone lay in sheaves as if harvested by a blind scythe. In the distance something burned with a patient flame, not devouring, merely insisting on being seen.

When he took his first step, the world tilted—just enough to tell him that he was not entirely in it. A second step steadied him. A third brought a memory: a hand in his, a voice saying his name not as command but as welcome—Kael'Thorin—and a promise he could not yet recall.

He walked toward the sound of the between-water. It led him through spires of broken stone and stands of trees that had shrugged off their leaves. In a clearing he found it: a channel carved by the Fall, neither river nor sea, a seam that glimmered with silted light. He knelt beside it and touched the surface. The water was warm. When it moved around his fingers it felt like memory seeking its own outline.

"If I am alive," he said softly, "then let me live toward what remains." The water did not answer, but it did not refuse him. He cupped his hands and drank. The taste was both salt and soil—the old covenant of earth and ocean meeting in his mouth. He swallowed and felt a thread draw taut inside him, a line cast into the dark. Somewhere, someone had thrown it. Somewhere, he was being pulled.

The water's path wound through the ruins like a silver scar. Kael'Thorin followed it, each step drawing him further into the liminal. The land no longer seemed certain. At times the trees were solid, charred trunks rising from ashen soil. At times they were shadows, fading at the edge of his sight, their branches swaying in a wind he could not feel.

The channel bent sharply and led him to a hollow where stone had split open. Here the water pooled, forming a mirror that trembled with its own light. Kael'Thorin knelt at the edge and stared into it. At first he saw only his reflection—tired eyes, face marked with soot and blood, hair tangled with leaves. But then the water stirred, and another image wove through his own.

He saw a boy running through fields of green, his laughter carrying like birdsong. He saw a warrior lifting his blade not in hatred, but in defense of those he loved. He saw an old man sitting by a hearth, telling stories to children who leaned close to hear the echoes of worlds long gone. Each vision struck him with the weight of recognition. They were not strangers. They were him.

The pool rippled again, and the faces dissolved. In their place he saw a single seed, suspended in the water's depth. It glowed faintly, as though lit from within by the memory of every life it had carried. The sight drew him forward. He reached out, and though his fingers never touched it, a warmth spread through his chest, as if the seed had entered him through breath alone.

Kael'Thorin closed his eyes. The ache in his ribs eased. His heart slowed. He understood: the drift was not only wandering—it was gathering. What had been scattered was searching for itself, and he was its vessel.

Kael'Thorin rose from the pool with the warmth of the seed still alive in his chest. Each breath seemed to carry a subtle glow, as though light had threaded itself into his lungs. He walked on, the path no longer guided by the water alone but by a pull deeper, quieter, as if memory itself had taken his hand.

The land changed around him. The charred trees thinned until they stood like sentinels, silent and skeletal. The stones lifted into arches that bore no mark of mason, yet felt placed by intention. He stepped beneath them and sensed a threshold: the skin between worlds thinning to allow passage. Here the air was still, the kind of stillness that listens.

He slowed, aware he was not alone. Shapes stirred at the edge of sight—first mist, then suggestion, then presence. They did not advance, nor withdraw, but watched. Kael'Thorin felt no fear.

Instead he felt the ache of recognition, the way one remembers a melody after years of silence.

A voice came, not with sound, but as a tremor through his marrow. *You walk between.*

He stopped, lifted his head. "Who speaks?"

The air quivered. Another tremor, distinct, harmonious with the first: *Not who. Many. We are with you.*

Kael'Thorin bowed his head, though he saw no faces. "Then show me what remains to be remembered."

In answer, the mist thickened, and from within it flickered glimpses: a feather burning with light, a hand tracing symbols into bark, a stone lifted silently in offering, a wind coiling through branches. The guides. His guides. Not as full figures, but as impressions—Seraphiel, Amari'el, Odric, Thalan'ar, Ka'el—woven through the drift like threads refusing to be severed.

"I am here," Kael'Thorin whispered. "Find me."

The threshold pulsed once, like a heartbeat, and the presences drew nearer.

The air thickened as the presences drew near, and the arches of stone glowed faintly with their arrival. Kael'Thorin stood still, his heart steady, his breath joined to the rhythm of the unseen gathering.

The first to reach him was Thalan'ar. His presence came as a weight of vision, a clarity that pierced through haze. *Remember,* it said, though no words were spoken. A shard of crystal appeared before Kael'Thorin's inner sight, sharp and luminous. He reached for it and felt the pattern of stars inscribed upon its surface. It was not instruction—it was orientation. The reminder that the sky itself bore memory, and he must learn to read it again.

Then Seraphiel's flame drew close. Her presence was fierce and tender in the same breath. She offered him no image at first, only heat—enough to scorch, enough to comfort. At last the fire shaped itself into wings, vast and radiant, folding around him. In their embrace he felt balance renewed, the vow of flame and compassion that had anchored the Axis Grove. It pressed into him not as burden, but as trust.

Amari'el followed, her song like water drawn through wood, resonant and aching. A single note rang in his bones, then another, weaving until they formed a melody that lifted the heaviness from his chest. She placed in him the memory of the Singing Groves—not whole, not unbroken, but alive. He bowed his head and whispered thanks, though his voice broke beneath the weight of it.

From the edges came Odric, silent as stone. His presence gave no vision, no sound, only stillness. Kael'Thorin felt it settle into his limbs, a gravity that said: endure. He pressed his palm to the ground, and the ground pressed back. His bones understood.

Last came Ka'el, the wind between worlds. A cool breath coiled around him, stirring his hair, whispering across his skin. No image remained—only motion. It tugged at him, beckoning, reminding him that the drift was passage, not end. That his journey did not stop in silence, but moved ever toward becoming.

Kael'Thorin opened his eyes. The threshold shone faintly around him, its pulse steady. He knew then he was not wandering alone. The fragments of vow, of memory, of seed and song—each guide had given him a piece. Together they would carry him through the drift, if he had the courage to walk it.

The presences receded like the tide, leaving Kael'Thorin in the stillness of the threshold. Yet the fragments they had placed within him remained—a crystal's orientation, wings of fire, the echo of song, the weight of stone, the whisper of wind. He touched his chest as if to assure himself they were real, and found his breath steadier than before.

He stepped forward. The ground beneath him shifted, uncertain whether it was soil, sand, or air. At times it felt as though he walked upon the surface of water, each step sinking and then holding. At other times it was like treading upon memory itself—faces rising beneath his feet only to dissolve back into the drift.

Kael'Thorin tested the fragments. He lifted his gaze to the broken constellations, and Thalan'ar's shard of crystal burned in his mind, aligning him. He spread his shoulders and felt Seraphiel's wings brace him, balance holding against the weight of grief. A low hum escaped his throat, tentative, yet Amari'el's melody caught it, weaving it into something more whole. Odric's stillness anchored his stride, even when the path dissolved. And Ka'el's breath was there—always—moving him forward when doubt pressed near.

For the first time since the Fall, he felt less like a man stumbling through ruin and more like a vessel being shaped. The drift was no longer exile. It was passage.

He came to a place where the path widened into an expanse of lightless water. It stretched as far as he could see, a mirror without stars. At its edge he halted, uncertain. The fragments within him pulsed once, as if awaiting his choice.

Kael'Thorin closed his eyes and breathed. "Then let me walk where memory leads." He placed his foot upon the dark surface. It held.

The surface of the water stretched out before him, dark and endless. Kael'Thorin set his second step upon it, then a third. Each held, though the ripples that spread beneath his feet shimmered with strange images—faces, places, fragments of dreams that were not entirely his own.

At first the visions were gentle. He saw a meadow unbroken by fire, children playing with garlands of flowers. He saw a woman's eyes, filled with warmth, watching him across the span of lifetimes. He felt the tug of peace, the desire to stop, to rest within the vision. Yet when he reached toward it, the image fractured, revealing only the black water beneath. His chest tightened with longing, but he did not falter. He stepped on.

The water answered with darker visions. He saw towers collapsing again and again, their stones crushing those who fled. He saw his own body lying upon the ground, eyes wide and unseeing, lips blue with silence. He heard voices crying his name in blame, in grief, in rage. Doubt filled him like smoke, thick and choking. His knees buckled, and for a moment he feared the water would swallow him.

But then a hum rose in his chest, faint but insistent. Amari'el's gift. He clung to it, shaping breath into tone, tone into thread. The visions quivered, shuddered, then broke apart like mist in sunlight. He steadied himself, standing tall once more.

Kael'Thorin drew a long breath. The wings of Seraphiel braced him, Odric's stillness rooted him, Thalan'ar's crystal oriented him, and Ka'el's wind pressed him forward. He whispered into the dark, "You will not keep me. I walk through."

The water rippled in reply, but it did not give way. He stepped again, and the path opened further into the vastness.

The closer Kael'Thorin drew to the shore of light, the more the silence began to change. At first it was only a tremor, faint as the breath of wind across glass. Then it became a murmur, rising and falling in tones too vast to be called words. He slowed his steps, not from fear, but from reverence. The light was speaking.

The whispers deepened, weaving together until they formed a cadence that reminded him of the old chants of Lemuria—sung in the council chambers, in the groves, in the fields at dusk. But this song was older still, vast enough to contain every tongue. It was not telling him what to do. It was telling him what he was: a thread within its fabric.

Kael'Thorin bowed his head. The water at his feet grew luminous, glowing with the reflection of the shore ahead. Each step left behind a brief shimmer before dissolving again into darkness. He realized that his path was not simply given—he was weaving it as he walked.

The voices swelled, and within them he caught fragments that seemed meant for him. A vow spoken in fire. A song carried in grief. A stone's endurance. A wind's passage. And above all, the memory of stars, aligning him to a truth too vast to yet name. Each fragment struck his heart like a bell, and within him the seed pulsed brighter.

He lifted his face toward the horizon. "If I am a thread," he said aloud, his voice steady over the murmuring expanse, "then weave me true."

The shore glimmered in answer, its radiance now shaped like an open hand, waiting.

The radiance grew until it filled his sight, not blinding but enveloping, as though light itself had chosen to become a place. Kael'Thorin reached the edge of the shore, where darkness ended and the glow began. He paused there, breath caught between awe and hesitation.

The water at his feet dissolved into brilliance, and the ground beneath him changed. He stood not on stone, nor on soil, but on woven strands of light—threads that bent and swayed like grass yet held his weight as firmly as earth. Each thread pulsed as if alive, carrying a rhythm that matched the beat of his own heart.

From within the glow, the whispers rose into clarity. They did not become words as he knew them, but harmonies, each carrying meaning beyond speech. Some were deep as the sea's floor, others high as birdsong. Together they wove a chorus that surrounded him, not as command, but as welcome.

Kael'Thorin stepped forward, and the light shifted. Shapes emerged—not fixed forms, but outlines woven of flame, song, stone, wind, and star. The fragments his guides had given him stirred, resonating with these presences. They were not strangers. They were kin. The voices of those who had carried the vow before him, and those who would carry it after.

He fell to one knee, head bowed. "I am only one," he whispered. "Yet I have come."

The chorus answered, vast and tender. The shore brightened until it seemed to breathe, and in its breath Kael'Thorin felt himself gathered—not lost, not broken, but held. The drift was not exile. It was return.

The chorus of light rose and fell, its harmonies circling him like tides of sound. Kael'Thorin closed his eyes, letting it wash through him. Each note seemed to settle in a different place—some in the marrow of his bones, some in the chambers of his heart, some in the silence behind his eyes.

From the weaving of voices, a meaning emerged. The drift was not a punishment, nor a void. It was the place where what had been scattered gathered again, where fragments sought reunion before they could be sown once more. It was womb as much as wilderness.

He felt the seed in his chest pulse, answering the chorus. With each beat of its glow, he understood more. The seed was not his alone—it was Lemuria's vow, carried through him. In its shell lay every memory, every promise, every loss and every hope. His guides had not merely given him fragments; they had awakened the seed so it could carry their gifts forward.

The harmonies converged, focusing into a single thread of sound that pierced his spirit with clarity: -*You are not the end. You are the bearer.*-

Kael'Thorin bowed low, his forehead nearly touching the luminous ground. His voice trembled as he spoke: "Then let me bear it well. Let me be shaped true, even if the shaping breaks me."

The light flared in answer, not to erase his vow, but to seal it. Around him the chorus swelled once more, and in its rise he felt not alone but joined—one voice among countless, each carrying the seed in their time, each walking the drift until remembrance called them home.

Kael'Thorin lifted his head from the radiant ground. The chorus still hummed around him, but its intensity had softened, becoming less a tide and more a current flowing steadily beneath his spirit. The seed in his chest pulsed with quiet certainty, as if it now knew its place within him.

He rose slowly, feeling the threads of light shift beneath his feet. The shore seemed to acknowledge him, its glow leaning inward like an embrace. For a moment he thought it would draw him entirely into its brilliance, dissolving him into its weave. Yet the pulsing of the seed reminded him—his journey was not to remain here, but to return.

The light opened before him, parting like a veil. Beyond it lay not darkness, but a path that curved back toward the broken lands of Lemuria. The water's expanse stretched there still, but now it gleamed faintly, each ripple guiding him forward rather than hindering his steps.

The chorus spoke one last time, not in many voices but in one, vast and tender: *Carry us.*

Kael'Thorin bowed deeply, hands pressed to his heart. "I will."

With that he turned, stepping back onto the dark water. Yet it was changed. Where before it had been fragile, threatening collapse with each step, now it bore him with quiet strength. The drift was no longer trial—it was passage. And as he walked, he knew he did not walk alone. The seed's glow lit his way, and the memory of the shore remained in every breath.

Kael'Thorin's steps carried him back across the vast water, though it no longer seemed endless. The fragments of his guides stirred within him, not as separate gifts but as facets of a whole. Each breath, each stride wove them together: vision, flame, song, stone, and wind. They were no longer merely companions—he was becoming their vessel.

The expanse tested him still, though its trials had changed. Instead of visions of despair, he now faced echoes of himself—moments drawn from his own past. He saw the young acolyte trembling as he spoke the rites for the first time. He saw the warrior gripping his blade, torn between duty and mercy. He saw the man kneeling in the grove, confessing love to Amari'el with a voice unsteady yet true. Each vision rose like a wave, threatening to drown him in regret or longing.

But Kael'Thorin did not turn away. He let the crystal of Thalan'ar align him, the wings of Seraphiel brace him, the melody of Amari'el lift him, the stillness of Odric anchor him, and the breath of Ka'el guide him forward. The visions broke like foam against rock, leaving him clearer than before.

At last the far horizon appeared, dim and fractured, but real—the outline of the broken world. Smoke still clung to its edges, and towers lay bent like weary giants. Yet Kael'Thorin felt no despair. The drift had shaped him, and he carried its shaping within. He walked not as one lost, but as one returning with seed in hand.

The horizon drew nearer, the fractured world emerging like a shadow beyond the glow. Kael'Thorin's steps slowed, not from weakness, but from the weight of crossing. The drift's current began to loosen its hold, threads of light unweaving from his limbs, releasing him back to the mortal path.

He looked down at the water beneath his feet. Where once it had shimmered with visions and trials, now it grew still, dark as obsidian glass. He saw his reflection, and within it the faint pulse of the seed glowing at his chest. The sight steadied him. Whatever awaited on the far shore, he carried within him the memory of the drift and the chorus of light.

The air thickened with the scent of ash. He could hear again the distant groan of broken towers, the moan of wind through ruined groves. Yet what once would have filled him with despair now stirred something else: resolve. He had crossed through the womb of the drift, and he returned not as the man who had fallen, but as one remade in remembrance.

At the edge of the water, where light gave way fully to soil and stone, Kael'Thorin paused. He turned once, gazing back at the expanse. There was no shore of radiance now, no chorus singing. Only silence and the memory of what had been given. He pressed his palm to his heart in salute, whispering: "I will not forget."

Then, with steady breath, he stepped onto the broken earth of Lemuria once more.

The soil of Lemuria felt brittle beneath Kael'Thorin's feet, crumbling like ash yet firm enough to hold him. He inhaled deeply, and the air carried the scars of the Fall—the sharp tang of stone cracked open, the bitter trace of smoke, the faint sweetness of sap bled from wounded groves. All of it mingled, a reminder of what had been lost and of what endured.

The seed glowed softly at his chest, and with each pulse he felt the fragments of his guides stir. Thalan'ar's clarity sharpened his gaze upon the ruins; Seraphiel's fire warmed his resolve; Amari'el's song hummed faintly in his breath; Odric's gravity steadied his stride; Ka'el's wind brushed across his skin, urging him onward. He was not returning empty. He was carrying them all.

He passed the first of the broken trees, its trunk split and blackened, yet a green shoot curled at its base. Kael'Thorin knelt, brushing the tender sprout with his fingertips. It trembled but did not break. "You remember," he whispered, as though speaking to the land itself. "Then so shall I."

As he rose, he felt the land answer in silence—not restoration, not yet, but recognition. The soil beneath his feet grew firmer, the air less acrid. Even in ruin, Lemuria listened.

Kael'Thorin tightened his cloak around his shoulders and began walking toward the shadowed outline of the groves, each step an oath renewed. The drift had given him passage; now the broken world awaited his bearing.

Kael'Thorin entered the shadow of the groves, though they were not as he remembered. Great trunks that once stretched skyward like pillars of song now lay split and blackened, their crowns shattered into ash. Branches jutted like broken spears, and the air carried the lingering ache of silence where once a thousand voices had sung.

Yet within the ruin there were stirrings of life. Here and there small shoots pressed through the ash, pale leaves trembling as if unsure of their right to exist. The seed within Kael'Thorin pulsed in answer, a steady rhythm that seemed to reach outward. Wherever its light touched, the faintest shimmer stirred in the wounded bark, as though memory itself leaned toward healing.

He laid his palm upon a fallen trunk, charred nearly to stone. Beneath his hand, the pulse of the seed merged with the faintest echo still lingering in the wood. For a moment he felt the tree's last song—the crack of its fall, the cry of its roots torn from the earth, the silence that followed. He bowed his head in grief, but also in vow. "You are not forgotten," he whispered. "Your song remains in me."

As he rose, the faint shimmer deepened, a thread of green coursing through the char. It was not restoration, but it was remembrance, and remembrance was the beginning of renewal.

Kael'Thorin walked deeper into the grove, each step guided by the seed's glow. Though ruin lay heavy, he felt no despair. He was not merely witnessing what had been lost—he was carrying the memory of what still could be.

Kael'Thorin lingered in the silence of the ruined grove, his hand still faintly trembling from the torrent of memory. The seed had quieted, yet it did not return to stillness. Instead, its rhythm shifted, becoming not only pulse but direction, as though it sought to lead him onward. He closed his eyes, listening inward, and felt the tug—a gentle but unmistakable draw to the east.

He rose, brushing the ash from his hands. The grove stretched around him in ruin, yet the faint shimmer of remembrance lingered wherever his steps had passed. Though the devastation weighed heavy, it no longer felt final. The memory of song was still alive, and the seed bore its echo forward.

As he walked, fragments of his guides stirred within him, responding to the seed's pull. Thalan'ar's clarity sharpened his vision, revealing faint paths where none seemed to exist. Seraphiel's fire warmed him against the chill of silence. Amari'el's melody lifted in his breath, soft but steady. Odric's stillness anchored his stride. Ka'el's wind whispered against his skin, urging his steps toward the unseen horizon.

The grove began to thin, giving way to a barren stretch where the soil was cracked and dry. Yet even here, faint traces of green curled upward—small shoots daring to reach for light. Kael'Thorin paused to kneel by one, touching it gently. The seed pulsed in answer, and for a heartbeat he felt the sapling's fragile will to endure. He whispered, "Grow," before rising once more.

The pull toward the east grew stronger, as though the drift itself had not released him entirely, but was guiding him still—toward what lay beyond the grove, toward what the seed must next encounter.

The grove gave way to open land, a vast expanse of soil cracked like old pottery, its fissures glowing faintly with the memory of fire. Kael'Thorin paused at its edge, the seed thrumming within his chest. The pull eastward grew insistent, like the tide's call to the moon. He drew his cloak tighter and stepped forward.

The land resisted him at first. Each step sank slightly, the soil shifting beneath his weight as though reluctant to bear him. Yet the seed's glow steadied his stride, and the resistance softened. Soon the fissures themselves began to shimmer faintly as he passed, like veins of light awakening at his presence.

Above him the sky remained clouded, ash drifting in slow spirals. But a break appeared upon the horizon, a faint line of pale gold. It was not the brilliance of the drift's shore, but something subtler—fragile, yet undeniably alive. The seed pulsed sharply at the sight, and Kael'Thorin felt its rhythm align with the distant glow.

He quickened his pace. The cracked earth stretched far, but no longer felt barren. With each step, he realized, the seed was not only carrying memory—it was awakening it in the land itself.

Small shoots broke the surface behind him, curling green against the ruin. They were fragile, but they were proof. Renewal had begun.

Kael'Thorin set his gaze firmly upon the horizon, the pull of the seed guiding him. Whatever awaited beyond the broken plain, he knew it was part of the vow he now bore.

As Kael'Thorin pressed onward, the pale horizon grew sharper, its glow no longer a distant blur but a thread of light running across the broken plain. The seed within his chest thrummed faster, its rhythm quickening like a heart approaching reunion. Each step brought with it a sense of expectancy, as though the land itself held its breath.

Shadows moved at the edge of the glow. At first Kael'Thorin thought them tricks of the ash-laden air, shapes born of longing. But as he drew nearer, the shadows steadied. They were figures—indistinct, woven more of presence than form, yet unmistakably waiting. The seed pulsed sharply, and Kael'Thorin felt its rhythm align with theirs, as if answering a summons older than himself.

He slowed, his breath deepening. The figures did not advance, nor did they retreat. They stood as guardians of the threshold, woven from memory and vow. Their outlines shifted—sometimes bright as flame, sometimes still as stone, sometimes vast as wind. They were not of the drift, nor of the broken land, but of the passage between.

Kael'Thorin placed a hand over the seed and whispered, "If you are of this vow, then show me how to walk it."

The figures stirred, and the glow of the horizon widened slightly, as if in invitation. The seed flared in answer, and Kael'Thorin knew he had come to the next gate of remembrance.

Kael'Thorin stepped forward, the ash beneath his boots giving way to the faint shimmer of the horizon's glow. The figures ahead wavered like heat rising from stone, yet the closer he drew, the more defined they became. They were not of flesh, nor wholly of spirit—they were woven from remembrance itself, strands of vow given shape.

One leaned upon a staff of crystal, its form tall and austere. Another bore wings that shimmered with fire's hue. A third seemed to hum with melody, its outline rippling as though of song. The fourth stood as still as stone, vast and unmoving. The last moved like wind, impossible to fix yet ever present. Kael'Thorin's heart leapt as he recognized them—not the guides themselves, but reflections of the fragments they had given him.

The seed pulsed with fierce brightness, and the figures stirred in answer. They raised their hands, not in warning but in acknowledgment, as if to say: you are known here.

Kael'Thorin bowed deeply. "I carry your gifts," he said, his voice steady though reverent. "But I do not yet know how to bear them fully."

The figures did not speak, yet the horizon's glow widened further, its brilliance spilling like a path laid open. The seed's rhythm steadied, its pulse aligning with the radiant line. Kael'Thorin understood—this threshold was not to test him, but to reveal that the vow he bore was already alive within him.

He lifted his gaze and stepped into the widening glow. The figures dissolved into light, their presence merging with his own. The horizon blazed, and Kael'Thorin crossed into what lay beyond.

The blaze of the horizon enveloped him, warm and searing all at once. Kael'Thorin closed his eyes, yet even with lids shut the radiance poured through, filling every corner of his being. He braced for the weight of the drift or the sorrow of the broken land, but what came was neither. It was a stillness—a vast, suspended breath between worlds.

When the light dimmed enough for him to see, he stood in a place unlike any he had known. The ground was neither soil nor sea but a luminous expanse, shifting as though woven from threads of dawn. Above him stretched a sky that held no sun, no stars, yet glowed with its own living light. It was a place between, a threshold carved out of remembrance.

Kael'Thorin turned slowly, the seed within him beating steady. He felt no opposition here, no demand, only presence. And in that presence he sensed others—not figures as before, but currents, streams of essence that moved around him like unseen rivers. Each bore the weight of vows long kept, some broken, some fulfilled, all feeding into the flow of this place.

He realized then what this realm was: the Crossing. Neither drift nor earth, but the passage where bearers of the seed were gathered before being returned. It was here that vows were measured, not by judgment, but by remembrance itself.

Kael'Thorin placed a hand over his chest, the seed burning gently beneath his palm. "Then let my vow be remembered," he whispered.

The currents stirred, encircling him like a silent choir, as though the Crossing had heard.

The Crossing stirred around him, the unseen currents drawing tighter, their movement less like rivers and more like voices threading into one another. At first they were faint, indistinct, like whispers heard through stone. But as Kael'Thorin stilled his breath and listened, they began to take shape.

They were not the voices of gods or guides, nor of the chorus he had heard upon the radiant shore. They were human, familiar, intimate. Some were strong, spoken with certainty. Others trembled, half-broken, yet carried the same weight of vow. Each belonged to one who had borne the seed before him. Their words were not commands, but fragments of devotion: "I carried it through fire."
"I bore it into silence."
"I planted it in the dark, where none could see."

Kael'Thorin felt the whispers brush across his skin, enter his chest, settle into the rhythm of the seed. It was not that they lived in him, but that the seed was a vessel for all who had borne it. Every vow uttered in love or grief was remembered here, woven into a tapestry beyond time.

For a moment he faltered, bowing his head beneath the weight. How could he, one man, bear what countless others had borne and broken? Yet even as the thought rose, another voice whispered, clear and unwavering: "You are not alone."

Kael'Thorin lifted his head, tears stinging his eyes. The currents no longer felt vast and distant—they felt like kin. He was part of a lineage of remembrance, and the seed was their bond.

"Then I will walk with you," he whispered. "And you with me."

The whispers surged in answer, not as command, but as embrace.

The voices in the Crossing did not fade. They swelled, weaving together like threads drawn into a single cloth. What had been whispers became harmony, a song not of triumph but of endurance. It carried no single language, yet Kael'Thorin understood every word. It was the memory of vows spoken across ages, joined now as one.

The seed within his chest answered, glowing brighter with each refrain. Its rhythm aligned with the song, until Kael'Thorin could no longer tell whether the seed carried the harmony, or whether the harmony carried him. He felt himself woven into it, no longer a lone bearer, but part of a lineage vast as the sea.

The song bent then, curving toward him, shaping itself into meaning: *The vow you bear is not yours alone. It belongs to all, and through you it will be carried forward.*

Kael'Thorin trembled. He thought of the broken groves, of the ash that still clung to Lemuria's soil. He thought of Amari'el, her voice a flame that would not yield to silence. He thought of the countless faces he had seen and lost. And in the harmony he heard them all—not vanished, but remembered.

He fell to his knees, pressing both hands to his chest. "Then let me be faithful," he whispered. "Let me carry you into what comes."

The harmony surged, not as thunder but as a rising tide, lifting him back to his feet. The currents around him shimmered, and the Crossing seemed to open—a path unfolding ahead, woven from the very song itself.

Kael'Thorin stepped onto the path of harmony, its light weaving beneath his feet as though each note became stone to bear his weight. The song did not fade as he walked; it deepened, gathering strength, as though every step drew forth more of its hidden refrain. The currents of the Crossing flowed alongside him, no longer distant but close, like companions walking unseen.

With each stride, Kael'Thorin felt his own vow stretching, intertwining with the countless others carried in the song. His voice joined theirs—not aloud, but from the marrow of his being. He did not speak words, but intention: *I will bear this seed into the broken land. I will remember, and I will plant remembrance where silence reigns.*

The harmony swelled in answer, and the path widened, unfolding into a great expanse. At its far end glimmered an arch of light, simple yet radiant, like the first dawn after endless night. It was no longer the pale horizon, nor the blaze of the drift's edge. It was something else—an opening carved by vow itself.

Kael'Thorin paused, standing before the arch. He felt the seed burn warmly in his chest, steady and sure. The voices hushed, not disappearing, but settling into quiet expectancy, as though the Crossing itself awaited his choice.

He lowered his head and whispered, "I will not turn back." Then, lifting his gaze, he stepped toward the arch of light.

As Kael'Thorin crossed the threshold of the arch, light poured over him like water, searing yet gentle, stripping away the last remnants of the drift's silence. He staggered, not from weakness but from the sheer immensity of what pressed against him. The seed within his chest blazed, and for a moment he thought it might consume him utterly.

But instead of burning, it opened. Light unfurled from him in waves, not only upward but outward, touching the expanse of the Crossing. In that instant he was not Kael'Thorin alone. He was every bearer who had ever carried the seed, every vow spoken across generations. He felt their strength, their failures, their longings, all gathered into the pulse that now coursed through him.

The arch of light bent around him, shaping itself to the rhythm of the seed. It was no longer merely a passage, but a mirror, showing him what he had become: a vessel of remembrance, bound not by his own strength, but by the lineage he carried. He saw himself walking the broken land, planting seeds of light where ash still reigned. He saw groves rising again, not as they once were, but as they could be. And within the vision he saw faces—Amari'el, his guides, those he had lost—all watching, not with sorrow, but with trust.

The vision dimmed, and he found himself once more at the heart of the light. The seed pulsed steadily, no longer painful, no longer uncertain. It had been shaped, and so had he.

The arch opened further, revealing beyond it the faint outline of Lemuria's scarred horizon. The time of return had come.

Kael'Thorin stepped forward, and the light of the arch folded around him, seamless and whole. For a heartbeat he felt himself suspended between all worlds—the drift, the Crossing, the scarred soil of Lemuria—each pressing upon him like layers of breath. Then, with a final pulse of the seed, the Crossing dissolved.

The air struck him first, cool and sharp, carrying with it the bitter tang of ash and the faint sweetness of green struggling to rise. His boots touched soil—real, solid soil—though it was fractured, cracked, and weary. He staggered, not from weakness, but from the sheer weight of return.

Behind him there was no arch, no radiant horizon. Only the hushed wind of Lemuria's scarred plain. The Crossing had sealed, leaving him once more upon the living earth. Yet its memory clung to him, not fading as dreams did, but etched into the marrow of his being.

Kael'Thorin pressed a hand to his chest. The seed burned steady, no longer trembling as it once had. Its rhythm was sure, and within it he felt the harmony of the bearers, their whispers now woven into his own breath. He was not merely returned—he was entrusted.

The horizon before him stretched wide, broken yet waiting.

Smoke curled faintly in the distance, and beyond it the silhouettes of mountains lay shrouded. He exhaled, a breath that carried both grief and resolve. The vow had crossed with him. Now it must take root.

Kael'Thorin set his steps upon the scarred plain, the soil crumbling faintly beneath his boots. Each step felt both alien and familiar—this was Lemuria, yet not the land he had once known. The air held memory of fire, but also the faintest promise of renewal, as though the earth itself waited to see what he would bring.

The seed guided him, not with force but with a steady rhythm that tugged gently eastward. He obeyed, walking through the stillness of the plain. Around him lay remnants of ruin—shards of crystal half-buried in ash, bones of trees twisted into blackened forms, rivulets of stone melted and frozen mid-flow. Yet here and there, he saw signs of defiance: a blade of grass piercing through cracks, a blossom trembling in the wind, the faint shimmer of dew clinging to broken stone.

Kael'Thorin paused often, laying his palm upon these small signs of life. Each time, the seed pulsed in recognition, and a faint warmth spread outward. The grass stood taller, the blossom's color deepened, the dew shimmered brighter. They were not grand restorations, but subtle affirmations—the earth remembering itself through him.

As he pressed onward, the horizon began to change. What at first had been only barren land now hinted at something more. A low rise lifted in the distance, and beyond it faint shapes stirred, too distant to discern. The seed quickened, urging his pace. Whatever awaited there, it was bound to his vow.

At the crest of the low rise, the land fell away into a shallow basin ringed by broken stone. Not an amphitheater—too rough for that—but a natural hollow where the earth seemed to lean inward as if to listen. Half-buried pillars jutted from the rim, their faces scored by fire and time. At the basin's heart lay a scatter of shattered crystal, dull with ash yet glimmering faintly beneath it, as if the light had not entirely left.

The seed throbbed in Kael'Thorin's chest, firm and insistent. He descended, boots sliding in loose grit, and came to rest beside the crystals. When he knelt, warmth rose through his knees, a pulse from the earth that matched his own. He spread his palms upon the ground. For a breath nothing moved. Then—very softly—the ash parted, and a thread of water surfaced, no wider than a reed. It curled like a silver vein through the dust, catching what little light the sky allowed.

Kael'Thorin bowed his head. He did not command; he consented. Thalan'ar's clarity aligned him to the quiet geometry of the basin, Seraphiel's balance steadied his breath, Amari'el's melody rose in the hum that formed at the back of his throat, Odric's stillness held his body like stone, and Ka'el's wind stirred the ash from the glimmering shards. The hum became a low chant, simple and spare. The thread of water strengthened, winding toward the crystals until it pooled among them with a sound like a remembered name.

He lifted a single shard and set it where the trickle gathered, a keystone for a new remembering. Light moved within the crystal—not bright, but alive. Around the basin's rim the broken pillars seemed to take a fraction more of their own weight. The place had not been restored, but it had been claimed: a first sanctuary for those who would come.

Kael'Thorin rose and looked back across the plain. Far off, the shapes he had glimpsed earlier wavered again—no longer rumor, but possibility. He set a small cairn at the basin's edge, three stones balanced upon one another, and whispered, "Here, remember." Then he turned toward the distant figures and began to walk.

Kael'Thorin descended from the basin with steady steps, the cairn and the shimmer of water behind him, the horizon ahead. The figures he had glimpsed now resolved more clearly, no longer mirages but forms moving with intent. They were not spirits, nor bearers of the seed, but men and women—Lemurians—scarred and weary, their garments streaked with ash. Some leaned upon staffs, others carried children upon their backs. Their eyes held the weight of survival, yet also the faint, unyielding spark of hope.

As Kael'Thorin drew nearer, the seed pulsed, and the people paused as though sensing it. A murmur rose among them, not of fear, but of recognition—as if they had been waiting for this moment without knowing why. One child slipped free of her mother's grasp and took a hesitant step forward. Her gaze fixed upon Kael'Thorin's chest where the glow of the seed faintly shone. She whispered a word too soft to catch, but it carried, and the others echoed it: *Remember.*

Kael'Thorin knelt before the child, lowering himself so his eyes met hers. He placed a hand upon the soil between them, and the seed flared. A tremor rippled outward, subtle but undeniable—the earth acknowledging both vow and witness. The child smiled faintly, and the murmur among the people deepened into a low chant. They did not sing as the bearers in the Crossing had, but their voices were no less sacred. It was the beginning of a people reclaiming their own song.

He rose slowly and looked back toward the basin, where water pooled among the crystals. Then forward, toward the gathering of survivors. The vow had carried him through drift and Crossing. Now it was rooted in earth once more, entrusted to the living.

Kael'Thorin exhaled, steady and sure. The first sanctuary had been born, and with it the first steps toward remembrance. The path was only beginning.

Interlude V: Odric at the Shore

The western shore bore the weight of the broken world. Waves shouldered themselves against the black stone, withdrew, and struck again, each return a measure of persistence. Foam clung to the rock like pale breath and then was gone.

Odric came alone. He moved as the cliffs did—without hurry, without ornament. Salt stung the cuts on his hands, and sand ground beneath his bare feet as if the earth itself were reminding him of its nearness. He welcomed the ache. It made him real.

He laid one palm upon the basalt and closed his eyes. Beneath skin and callus, he felt the slow conversation of stone: the deep patience, the memory of pressure, the long story of heat and cooling. The shore remembered the making of the island, and it remembered the Fall. It held both without complaint.

"I will hold as you hold," he murmured—not to claim strength, but to borrow its posture. The wind pushed hard against him. He did not sway.

Far offshore, a shattered pillar broke the surface, a remnant of something once tall and certain. Odric watched it take the waves—head bowed, body unmoving, each strike a lesson. Endurance was not refusal; it was consent to remain. The sea did not hate the stone, and the stone did not resist the sea. Between them, a covenant older than memory endured: give, receive, return.

Odric lowered to one knee and pressed his forehead to the rock. In that contact, the noise fell away. The cliff breathed its cold breath into his bones, and the bones answered. He would keep this place. He would listen until the land told him where the living might stand.

The tide fell with the sun. Shadows stretched across the shore, drawing long fingers over stone and sand. Odric did not move. The rhythm of the sea had become his own: the inward pull, the outward release, the steady cycle of return. Breath was tide, heart was tide, silence was tide.

When night gathered its cloak around the horizon, the waters gleamed with broken starlight. Odric raised his eyes and saw how the sea mirrored the heavens—fractured, dimmed, yet enduring in its reflection. Above and below, the same truth held: that even in ruin, pattern remained.

He gathered a stone from the beach, smooth from years of waves grinding it against its kin. Turning it in his palm, he considered its story. Once jagged, once torn from cliff or mountain, it had been reshaped not by resistance, but by yielding. Patient surrender had made it whole again.

Odric placed the stone upon his chest and lay back against the earth. He let the sky and sea wash over his sight until they became one vast expanse. No vision came, no voice broke the silence. Only the certainty of presence—the knowledge that to remain, to endure, was its own vow.

As the tide crept back toward him, lapping at his feet, he whispered: "I will be as you are." And the waves, indifferent and eternal, accepted his promise.

The night deepened, and with it the sea's voice grew more insistent. Waves surged higher, casting spray over Odric's face and chest. Still he did not move. His breath held to their rhythm, his body unmoved by their force. It was not defiance but recognition: the sea would do as it must, and he would remain as he was.

In the silence between breakers, he began to hear it—the communion that stone and tide carried in their endless dialogue. Not words, not visions, but a weight of knowing pressed into his marrow. The cliffs spoke of ages endured, of pressure and fracture, of the long patience that made mountains rise and fall. The sea spoke of journeys without end, of carrying and returning, of dissolving what would not yield.

Together they impressed upon him a single truth: nothing is truly lost that consents to be remade. The land had broken, yes, but in its breaking lay the shape of new shores. The Circle had shattered, yes, but its fragments might still find place in a wider ring.

Odric bowed his head. He pressed his palm flat against the wet stone beside him and let the sea wash over it. His voice, when it came, was low and steady: "Then I will stand with what endures. I will carry what cannot be carried, until others come to lift with me."

The tide rolled back, as if in assent, leaving his hand marked with salt and grit—an anointing not of oil, but of earth and water.

Dawn came thin and gray, a quiet blade parting night from day. Odric rose with it. Salt had dried upon his skin in pale traces, and sand clung to his palms like fine ash. He did not brush it away. He welcomed the marks—signs that the shore had taken him in.

He walked the tideline until he found a break in the cliff where the rock stepped down into the surf. There, he began to lift stones. Not the largest—the sea would simply claim them—but those that fit the hand, each shaped by years of yielding. One by one he stacked them, balancing curve upon flat, weight upon patience, until a small cairn stood at the meeting of earth and water.

It was not a monument. It was a marker—a place to say: here the living may gather; here the shore keeps faith. He set his palm upon the topmost stone and felt the whole column take his weight without complaint. The water reached for it, tested it, then withdrew.

Odric looked along the coast and saw other places where such cairns might stand. He would build them as far as his strength allowed, each a quiet promise that endurance could be shared. If others came, they would know where to stand. If no one came, the cairns would still speak to the sea on their behalf.

He turned his face to the wind and closed his eyes. No prayer formed on his tongue, yet the vow within him settled deeper, like a stone sinking to the bed of the world. When he opened his eyes again, the light had strengthened. The shore received it without flourish. So did he.

By midday the sky had cleared, a pale blue stretching far over the restless waters. Odric sat upon the black stone, his back straight, his hands resting upon his knees. He had spoken little, yet his silence was a language the shore understood.

The cairn he had raised stood firm against the tide's return. Wave after wave struck, foamed, and fell away. Each impact was a question, and each survival was an answer. Odric watched and learned, letting the rhythm press itself deeper into him.

As the sun leaned westward, he gathered another stone. This one he did not place upon the cairn but carried into the surf. He waded knee-deep, the water tugging at him with each pull. Lifting the stone high, he cast it far into the waves. It vanished beneath the surface, leaving only ripples. He stood still until they faded.

"Take it," he said at last, his voice carrying no demand, only release. "Make of it what you will."

The sea received the offering, untroubled, unbound. Odric returned to the cairn, touched the topmost stone, and inclined his head. The vow was sealed—not in fire, nor in song, but in endurance. The shore would hold, and so would he.

When the evening shadows lengthened, he remained where earth met water, the stone-keeper at his post. Alone, yet not forsaken. Silent, yet speaking in the oldest tongue. The waves broke and broke again, but he endured, anchoring the promise of Lemuria to the steadfastness of the shore.

Chapter 6: The Watcher's Return

The air was heavy with stillness as Kael'Thorin walked the scarred plain. Each step pressed into soil that bore both ruin and renewal—the faint shimmer of green threading upward through cracks, the lingering scent of ash carried by the wind. He had learned to listen to the land, to hear in its silence the faint rhythm of memory still alive. Yet this silence was different. It was not the quiet of rest, but of expectancy, as though the very breath of the world had paused.

He halted and lifted his gaze. The sky, once a dull shroud of gray, had begun to shift. At first it was subtle—a deepening of shadow, a tremor of light between the clouds. Then the pattern grew clear: stars not yet visible by nightfall pressed faintly through the veil, aligning themselves in geometries that had no place in the natural course of heaven. The constellations bent, folding into new forms. Kael'Thorin felt the seed in his chest quicken, its glow pulsing in answer.

A memory stirred—words once spoken by Thalan'ar: *When the sky no longer belongs to itself, the Watchers will return.*

The air thickened. Not with storm, not with fire, but with presence. Kael'Thorin's breath slowed as the horizon itself seemed to lean inward, a vastness pressing against the edges of the world. Though no form yet appeared, he knew: he was no longer alone.

From the horizon, the presence deepened. What at first had been only a pressure upon the air now gathered into form—not solid, not flesh, but vast outlines that bent the fabric of the world.

Kael'Thorin narrowed his eyes, though sight could not fully contain them. It was less seeing and more recognition, as if his bones remembered what his eyes could not grasp.

The sky itself seemed to arc downward, its constellations folding into pillars of light and shadow. From these pillars the Watchers emerged, colossal yet indistinct, their edges dissolving into horizon, their centers vast as silence. Each bore a shape, though not a shape fixed by mortal understanding: wings that stretched wider than mountains, crowns of flame that burned without smoke, eyes like orbs of dusk and dawn merged into one. Their forms shifted even as he watched, reminding him that what they were could not be bound to one visage.

The seed in his chest pulsed hard, not with fear but with recognition. He felt its glow respond as though the Watchers themselves had reached into him, testing the vow he bore. His breath slowed. He did not flee. For though their presence unsettled the air and made the soil tremble, Kael'Thorin knew they were not storm nor ruin. They were witness.

The plain bent beneath their arrival. Wind scoured in sudden bursts, carrying with it voices without sound. Kael'Thorin bowed his head, not in submission, but in acknowledgment. For the Watchers had returned, and in their return the weight of Lemuria's vow was being measured.

Their gaze fell upon him, though no eyes in the mortal sense could be discerned. It was not a look but a weight, an immeasurable attention that pressed into the marrow of his bones. Kael'Thorin felt his breath catch as the silence deepened, thick as stone, vast as the gulf between stars. The Watchers did not speak. They did not need to. Their very being asked the question: *What do you bear?*

The seed within him responded before his lips could. It flared, light pulsing against his chest, spilling faintly through the fabric that covered him. Its rhythm matched the unseen cadence of the Watchers' presence, a call and answer between bearer and witness. He felt exposed, not in shame, but in truth. Every choice, every hesitation, every vow whispered in solitude seemed to stand unveiled beneath their regard.

Kael'Thorin lowered to one knee, not in submission but in acknowledgment of the immensity that surrounded him. His voice was steady when he spoke: "I carry what was entrusted. I bear the vow."

The air did not shift, yet something within it did. A tremor moved across the plain, subtle yet undeniable, as though the land itself had heard and bore record of his words. The Watchers remained unmoving, their vast forms inscrutable. Yet Kael'Thorin sensed the first measure had been taken, and the weighing of Lemuria's promise had begun.

The silence that followed stretched until it felt like a living thing, vast and deliberate. Kael'Thorin knelt in it, steady though his heart thundered. He knew the Watchers did not ask for words in the way mortals did. They sought resonance, the alignment of vow with essence. What he bore must answer, not only his tongue.

From the Watchers came no sound, yet a low vibration filled the air, seeping into soil and bone alike. It was not voice but resonance, a testing of harmony. The seed within Kael'Thorin throbbed in reply, its glow rising until it pushed through fabric and skin alike, casting a faint light across the scarred plain. The rhythm of his vow joined with the rhythm of the Watchers' resonance, and for a moment it was as though two choirs—one human, one eternal—sought to find their common pitch.

The strain was immense. His body shook as the resonance pressed deeper, seeking cracks, searching for fracture. Memories surged unbidden: the grove aflame, Amari'el's voice in sorrow, Odric's silent vigil at the shore. Each memory was weighed. Each vow tested. Kael'Thorin felt his spirit stretch to breaking, yet he did not let go.

At last the vibration eased, leaving the plain in quiet once more. Kael'Thorin's breath came ragged, his body trembling, but the seed glowed steady at his chest. The Watchers had pressed against him with their full weight, and still the vow endured.

Though they spoke no words, Kael'Thorin understood: the first proof had been given.

Kael'Thorin steadied himself, his breath still uneven as he pushed against the weight that lingered in the air. The Watchers did not vanish, nor did they advance. They remained vast upon the horizon, their outlines bending sky and soil alike, inscrutable as the tides of eternity. Yet something in their presence had shifted. He was not crushed beneath them. He was permitted to rise.

He drew himself to his feet, the seed glowing faintly but firmly at his chest. Each pulse of its light seemed to echo into the vastness, and the vastness returned it, a rhythm of recognition.

Kael'Thorin understood then: the vow was not only being weighed—it was being heard.

The silence broke, not into words but into vision. Around the Watchers' forms the air rippled, and Kael'Thorin's sight filled with images not his own. He saw mountains split open by storms of fire, seas surging high enough to swallow whole coasts, stars themselves shifting in their courses. He saw cities rise in splendor, then fall into ruin, their songs silenced in dust. He saw people—countless faces—bearing seeds of vow in every age, carrying them like hidden lanterns through shadow and forgetting.

The images came not as prophecy but as truth: this was what the Watchers had seen, what they remembered. They were not bound to one world or one time. They were the witnesses of cycles, the keepers of consequence. And now their gaze measured whether Lemuria's vow would stand in that long procession.

Kael'Thorin clenched his fists, not in defiance but in resolve. Whatever they required, he would meet it. He would not let the vow be found wanting.

The strain deepened. Kael'Thorin's body quivered beneath the immensity pressing in from all sides. The visions had not ceased, but now they came layered, folded upon one another—ruins dissolving into birth, birth collapsing into death, vows spoken in joy echoing against vows whispered in despair. The torrent blurred the boundary of time, and Kael'Thorin felt his spirit pulled thin across the ages.

His breath faltered. The seed blazed against his chest, but even its glow seemed fragile against the weight of what the Watchers bore into him. A human vessel was never meant to hold such breadth. His knees weakened, and he staggered, one hand pressing against the scarred earth to remain upright.

Yet in the breaking came clarity. For in the fragments that rushed through him—faces, places, battles, births—there was one thread constant: the vow. Though carried by countless voices, though spoken in different tongues and etched into differing hearts, it was the same vow, luminous and unbroken. Not triumph, not perfection, but remembrance, passed hand to hand like a flame that refused extinction.

Kael'Thorin closed his eyes. He let go of the strain, not resisting the flood but yielding to it. His body trembled, but his spirit found a stillness deep within, the place where the vow rested untouched. The Watchers' weight pressed harder, testing his surrender, and still he did not break.

When at last he opened his eyes, the horizon shimmered with a faint radiance, as if even the vastness had acknowledged his endurance. The Watchers remained unmoving, but their silence had shifted. They no longer pressed to crush. They pressed to refine.

The pressure shifted. It no longer pressed upon Kael'Thorin's limbs or mind, but turned inward, seeking the glow lodged beneath his breastbone. The seed answered as if recognizing a forgotten kinship. Its light drew in, then unfurled, as a shell might open to the sea.

Kael'Thorin felt himself recede to the edges of his own body.

The Watchers were not weighing his strength now. They bent their vast attention toward the seed—not to claim it, but to read it, as if its pulse were a script written before stone learned to keep its shape. What rose was not image but pattern: a lattice of harmonies, the first vow braided through them like gold wire, the early names of balance sounding once and then again in descending echoes. Axis and flame. Water and wind. Stone accepting weight so song could rise. The vow was older than Lemuria and younger than breath; it had only borrowed Lemuria's tongue.

The seed brightened, and the patterns deepened. Kael'Thorin sensed a lineage of custodians—hands that had held and released, hearts that had promised and fallen and promised again. He felt their nearness as a warmth behind the ribs, a choir at the threshold of speech. The Watchers' attention moved through that lineage without judgment, tracing continuities, noting fractures, gathering each thread back to the single, unbroken line of return.

For a breath he was afraid he would vanish—erased by the immensity unfolding within him. He let the fear pass like wind through grass. "I do not own it," he whispered. "I carry." The seed answered with a steadying pulse, as if confirming the word.

Something eased. The resonance of the Watchers drew back a fraction, not in withdrawal but in acknowledgment, like a tide that has reached its mark. The plain sighed—he could hear it, a soft settling of ash and grit. Above, the distorted constellations held their impossible alignments, waiting.

Kael'Thorin straightened. The seed's light remained, quieter now, but sure. Whatever came next would not be only a test upon him, but a charge given through him. He lifted his gaze to the vast figures on the horizon and steadied his breath for what they would reveal.

The Watchers did not release their gaze, though it no longer pressed as before. Instead, it stretched outward, widening until it encompassed not only Kael'Thorin but the land itself. The scarred plain seemed to quiver under the weight of their regard. Stones shifted as though stirred by tides unseen, and the faint shoots that had dared to push through ash bent toward the horizon as if acknowledging their return.

Kael'Thorin felt the seed within him respond again, pulsing not in isolation but in communion. Its rhythm expanded into the soil beneath his feet, threading through root and crystal alike, weaving itself into the fabric of Lemuria. He gasped softly as he realized: the Watchers were not only measuring him, but reawakening the land's memory.

Visions flooded him once more, but this time they were not of distant ages. They were here—immediate, intimate. He saw the Singing Groves before the fire, their branches alive with resonance. He saw the Axis Grove standing tall, its pillars unbroken, the vow held in flame and balance. He saw children laughing, their small hands tracing patterns into soil that glowed beneath their touch. It was not fantasy. It was memory, pulled forth from the land itself.

The weight of it nearly broke him anew, for to witness what was lost is a sharper blade than to endure what is broken. His chest ached with longing. Yet the seed held firm, steady as Odric's stone, reminding him that remembrance was not given to wound, but to anchor.

The Watchers' forms shimmered, vast silhouettes bending sky and soil. Kael'Thorin felt their silence deepen once more, and within it an unspoken truth unfurled: if Lemuria's land remembered, then so could its people. The vow was not yet extinguished.

The visions ebbed, leaving Kael'Thorin standing in the charged silence of the plain. His chest rose and fell, the seed within him steady but heavy, as though its glow carried the weight of all that had just been unveiled. Around him, the Watchers loomed, their vast presences neither closer nor farther, but changed—as if they had turned from questioning to expectation.

The sky trembled. Lines of light traced across the heavens, faint at first, then sharp, converging into a sigil vast enough to encompass the horizon. Its shape was unfamiliar, yet it stirred recognition deep within his marrow. The vow had symbols beyond language, marks woven into the architecture of being itself. This was one of them, revealed now by the Watchers as both reminder and command.

Kael'Thorin lifted his head to behold it. The sigil pulsed, and with each pulse the seed within his chest echoed. His breath aligned with its rhythm until he was no longer drawing air of his own, but sharing in the breath of vow itself. In that rhythm he felt joined not only to the Watchers, but to all who had carried the vow before him. He was not one against the vastness. He was one within it.

A great wind swept the plain, bending shoots and scattering ash.

It carried no destruction—only announcement. The Watchers had set their mark. The vow was recognized. Now it must be lived.

The wind that swept the plain dwindled into stillness, yet its echo lingered in Kael'Thorin's chest. The sigil above remained etched across the heavens, its vast lines burning faint but unyielding, a mark of vow inscribed into the firmament itself. He stood beneath it in awe, knowing that such a sign was not mere vision. It was record. It was remembrance made visible.

The Watchers had not spoken, yet their silence pressed with greater force than any words. Kael'Thorin felt as though he stood in a vast chamber, its walls formed not of stone but of attention, immeasurable and absolute. He could not escape their regard, nor did he wish to. For in their gaze he felt the ancient truth: that the vow was larger than Lemuria, larger than himself, larger even than the Watchers who bore witness. It was thread, woven through the first breath of creation, and his role was not to possess it, but to carry it onward.

The seed glowed steadily at his chest, pulsing in rhythm with the sigil above. Kael'Thorin lowered his head, whispering words that came unbidden: "I will walk until my steps are no more. I will carry until I am carried."

The words rose like sparks, taken up by the wind though no breeze stirred. They vanished into the Watchers' silence, and for the briefest instant, Kael'Thorin thought he heard a response—not sound, not speech, but resonance, like a chord struck upon the world itself, affirming what had been spoken.

The Watchers did not vanish. They remained, vast and inscrutable, waiting for him to take the next step.

The silence thickened once more, no longer the stillness of testing, but of threshold. Kael'Thorin felt as though he stood on the lip of a chasm, with only the faint glow of the seed to steady his steps. The Watchers did not move, yet their presence deepened, enfolding him like vast tides unseen. It was not his body they weighed now, nor even his spirit, but the vow itself—its strength to endure, its will to bind across time.

Above, the sigil shifted, its lines elongating and folding inward, becoming a spiral of light and shadow that turned slowly across the heavens. Kael'Thorin's breath caught, for the spiral was more than symbol. It was the path itself, the eternal return of memory into form, form into memory. The vow was not static—it moved, as all living things must. And in its motion, it demanded to be carried.

The seed burned hotter in his chest, pressing outward as if it wished to leave him, to leap into the sky and take its place within the turning. Kael'Thorin dropped to both knees, clutching his breast. His cry was soft, yet it echoed across the plain: "I cannot contain it alone."

The Watchers did not intervene. They did not lessen the weight. But within the spiral above, a line of light reached downward, a filament as thin as breath. It brushed against him—not to take the seed, but to tether it, as if to remind him that no bearer walks in solitude. The vow is never held by one, but by all.

Relief mingled with awe as Kael'Thorin lowered his head. He

understood then: the Watchers were not here to claim the vow, but to ensure it was woven beyond him, anchored to a tapestry greater than any single soul.

The filament of light held, fine as breath, and Kael'Thorin felt the tremor in his chest ease. The seed's pressure did not lessen; it steadied, as if a vast hand had cupped a flame to keep it from the wind. The spiral above turned with unhurried certainty, and in its measured revolutions he sensed intention—neither judgment nor comfort, but charge.

The Watchers' silence changed timbre. It rang now like a bell struck somewhere outside of time, and meaning unfurled without words. Images rose—not prophecies he could barter with, but instructions traced in resonance. He saw the basin he had claimed in the scarred plain, water finding crystal and naming it sanctuary. He saw two other places called forth from the land's deep memory: a ridge of black stone where wind carved runes no hand could write, and a hollow where ash lay rich as soil awaiting seed. Upon each place a pattern appeared—circles interlaced, threefold and whole.

Kael'Thorin understood. The vow could not be borne in one body alone. It must be grounded in the world, set as signs that the land and the living might remember together. Three sanctuaries: water with crystal, wind with stone, ash with seed. Not temples of triumph, but thresholds of return.

The spiral brightened at his assent. The filament brushed his sternum and vanished, leaving the seed's glow his only lamp. He bowed his head, speaking softly into the charged air: "I will set the circles. I will call the people to them—not to witness me, but to remember what we are."

A movement like the slow drawing of a tide rippled across the plain. The Watchers did not approach, yet their vast regard inclined, as if to say that the charge was heard. Above, the constellations held their impossible alignments a moment longer, then relaxed by a fraction—enough to remind him that time still moved, and so must he.

Kael'Thorin rose slowly, the echo of the charge still reverberating in his bones. The Watchers loomed vast and unyielding, yet their presence no longer pressed to crush. It steadied him, as though their silence had become a pillar against which he might lean. The vow was not his burden alone; it was a current flowing through him, demanding not possession, but passage.

The spiral above turned once more before fading into the vastness of the night. The constellations unbent themselves, resuming their familiar courses, yet he knew the heavens would never look the same again. He had seen them open. He had seen them align. The memory of that geometry would never leave him.

Kael'Thorin pressed a hand to his chest where the seed pulsed, no longer straining to escape, but firm, resolute. He thought of the sanctuaries shown to him—the basin, the ridge, the hollow of ash—and felt their pull upon his spirit. They were not dreams. They awaited him in the living world, places where vow and land might clasp hands once more.

The plain around him had grown quiet. Even the wind seemed to wait. He turned his eyes back to the horizon, to the broken line of mountains that stretched dark against the stars. Somewhere beyond lay those sanctuaries, and somewhere closer still the remnants of Lemuria's people, wandering, searching, waiting for a sign.

He whispered into the silence, uncertain if the Watchers still lingered: "I will not falter. I will set the circles."

No answer came, yet the soil beneath his feet felt steadier, and the night air gentler, as though the vow itself had heard and held him to his word.

Kael'Thorin set his first steps toward the east, where memory tugged at him with steady insistence. The seed pulsed in rhythm with his stride, a lantern within, guiding him not with maps but with resonance. Each beat of its glow whispered of the places shown in vision: water mingling with crystal, wind carving runes into stone, ash cradling seed. The sanctuaries were not merely destinations; they were promises waiting to be embodied.

The plain stretched wide and empty, yet he did not feel alone. The Watchers' presence no longer loomed, but lingered—like constellations unseen in daylight, their weight pressed into the memory of the sky. He carried their silence with him, and in that silence was both charge and witness.

As he walked, fragments of song stirred at the edges of his hearing. At first he thought them echoes of Amari'el, but soon he understood: it was the land itself, responding faintly to the vow quickening within him. A hum vibrated beneath the soil, weaving through stone and root. It was not loud, not triumphant, but it was alive. Each step drew it forth, coaxing it from beneath the ash like water rising to the surface.

Kael'Thorin lowered his head and whispered, "Then walk with me." The words disappeared into the night, yet the hum deepened, and he knew the land had heard.

The further Kael'Thorin walked, the more the hum of the land deepened. What began as a faint resonance beneath the soil grew into a rhythm that matched his stride, as though each step awakened echoes long asleep. Stones seemed to quiver as he passed, not shifting visibly, yet carrying the sense of alignment, of listening. Even the wind turned gentler, no longer carrying the sting of ash, but a coolness that brushed against his skin like acknowledgment.

He knew then that the land was not dead. It remembered. Beneath its scars lay memory unbroken, waiting only for vow to stir it into breath again. The basin, the ridge, the hollow—they were not chosen at random. They were places where remembrance had pooled, hidden yet waiting, like seeds lying dormant through the long winter.

As the resonance grew stronger, Kael'Thorin felt the seed within him respond in kind. Its glow flared brighter, threads of light pressing faintly through his flesh. He quickened his pace, guided not by sight but by the pull of vow itself. His body was weary, yet his spirit moved as if borne on unseen currents.

At the crest of a low rise, he paused to look ahead. The land fell into shadow, broken and quiet, but through the darkness he sensed the first sanctuary drawing near. It was not visible to the eye, but the seed thrummed with recognition, whispering to him that the place awaited.

Kael'Thorin descended the slope, each step met with a deepening resonance. The hum beneath the earth grew richer, like a chord gaining depth as new notes joined. The soil itself seemed to breathe, faint threads of warmth rising with the night air. He pressed his palm against the ground as he walked, and each time he did, a soft vibration pulsed in reply, a recognition passing between bearer and land.

The plain narrowed into a shallow vale, its edges framed by broken stone. Though ruin marked the place—splintered trunks, scorched soil—he felt no despair. The vow's memory lingered here, woven into the roots and veins of the earth. What was broken had not been erased. It had only been waiting.

At the vale's center, he halted. The seed within his chest thrummed with steady insistence, brighter than it had burned since the drift. His breath caught as he realized: this was the first sanctuary shown in vision. The basin awaited.

He lowered himself to one knee, pressing both palms to the soil. Closing his eyes, he let the rhythm of the seed flow outward, aligning with the pulse that stirred in the land. Together they wove, bearer and earth, vow and memory, until the silence was filled with a quiet resonance that seemed to stretch beyond hearing. Though no water yet rose, though no crystal yet gleamed, Kael'Thorin knew the sanctuary had awakened.

Kael'Thorin placed his hands firmly upon the soil, steadying his breath as the seed thrummed within him. The resonance of the land rose to meet it, and together they formed a rhythm like two voices learning to sing in harmony. He felt the plain lean inward, the silence deepening, as though the very air waited for him to speak.

He whispered the words not of command, but of remembrance: "As water finds stone, as flame seeks air, as seed roots in earth—so let vow find place."

The soil beneath his palms warmed, and from its fissures a thin trickle of water emerged, clear against the ash. It wound its way toward a scatter of half-buried crystals, veins dulled by time yet quickened now by the touch of living current. The water pooled among them, and light stirred faintly within their fractured faces, a shimmer like memory returning.

Kael'Thorin bowed his head lower, his voice steady: "Here be the first circle. Not temple, not throne, but sanctuary of remembrance. Let all who come know they walk not alone, but within the vow carried across ages."

The seed pulsed brightly, its glow flowing into the soil until the basin shimmered with a soft radiance. The broken stones steadied, and the faint hum of the land grew clearer, a tone that lingered even in silence. The sanctuary was not yet whole, but it was awake, its memory rejoined to the vow.

Kael'Thorin exhaled, rising slowly to his feet. The night wind passed gently over him, carrying with it the sense that the Watchers still observed, unseen but near. The first charge had been met.

Kael'Thorin lingered at the basin, his gaze resting upon the shimmer of water winding through crystal. It was not grandeur that stirred him, but the simplicity—the proof that remembrance did not require vast temples or unyielding towers. A trickle of water, a pulse of light, a hum deep within the soil: these were enough to root the vow into earth once more.

He knelt and touched the water's surface. The ripples spread outward, delicate rings glimmering faintly as though carrying his touch into the stones themselves. The seed in his chest pulsed in answer, a single beat of affirmation. This sanctuary would endure. Not through strength, but through the constancy of memory.

As he rose, Kael'Thorin turned slowly, scanning the plain around him. The night air was cool, the stars returned to their familiar courses, yet he sensed the Watchers still. Not looming now, but distant—observing, waiting. Their silence pressed lightly at the edges of his perception, a reminder that though the first circle had been set, two remained, and the vow demanded completion.

He adjusted his cloak and began walking toward the ridge glimpsed in vision. Each step carried a new steadiness, as though the land itself now bore part of his burden. Behind him, the basin shimmered softly in the dark, a quiet beacon for those who would come after. Ahead lay shadow, but also promise.

Kael'Thorin whispered into the night: "One circle awakens. Two yet sleep. I will find you."

The night pressed close as Kael'Thorin walked eastward, the first sanctuary fading behind him. Though its shimmer no longer filled his sight, he felt its presence still—woven into the earth, a steady note within the great chord of vow. The land itself seemed lighter for it, the soil breathing more freely, as if some long-clenched hand had eased its grip.

Ahead, the ridge rose darker against the starlit sky. Its flanks were jagged, carved by ages of wind that had left their etchings upon the stone. Even from afar he sensed its weight—a place where air and earth had contended for dominion until both surrendered into harmony. This was no mere rise of rock. It was the second sanctuary.

The seed within his chest pulsed with growing intensity, guiding him as surely as any star. Each beat aligned with the rhythm of the plain, as if unseen footsteps walked beside him, echoing his vow in silence. He thought of the Watchers, vast and inscrutable, whose gaze still lingered upon his path. Their silence was no longer testing but witnessing, an attention that carried both gravity and charge.

Kael'Thorin drew a long breath and whispered into the night: "I come as one, but I carry the many."

The wind shifted in answer, sweeping down from the ridge with a low murmur, carrying the taste of stone and the sharpness of air. It was not voice, but it was welcome. The sanctuary was near, and it had already begun to stir.

As Kael'Thorin neared the ridge, the wind rose in slow exhalations, curling through fissures in the stone with a sound like hollow flutes. It was not the roar of storm nor the whisper of calm, but a voice in between—measured, deliberate, as though the ridge itself had waited for his arrival.

The seed quickened in his chest, its rhythm aligning with the gusts. Each pulse sent a tremor through the air, and in answer faint markings stirred upon the stone. Lines barely visible began to glow with a pale shimmer, winding upward in patterns that curved and intersected. They were not carved by hand, but by time and breath—runes etched by the ceaseless work of wind upon rock, hidden until the vow called them awake.

Kael'Thorin pressed his palm against the nearest surface. The stone was cool, yet alive, vibrating faintly as the seed's glow passed through him into the ridge. The markings brightened, revealing circles within circles, a language not spoken but breathed. He did not need to decipher them. He felt their meaning: sanctuary, threshold, remembrance.

The wind surged, carrying with it dust and ash, yet instead of blinding him it cleared his sight. The whole ridge shimmered, runes unfolding in vast spirals across its face. It was not a wall to be scaled, but a scripture written by the world itself, declaring that the vow had reached its second resting place.

Kael'Thorin bowed his head. "Here be the second circle," he whispered. "Written not by my hand, but by yours."

The wind fell still for a heartbeat, then swept once more, as though sealing his words into stone.

Kael'Thorin stood within the circle of runes, the wind curling about him in steady rhythms, neither violent nor still. It breathed as though alive, a presence that pressed close yet never bound. He spread his arms wide, letting the seed's glow spill through him and into the stone.

The runes brightened. Each mark upon the ridge pulsed with

faint light, not constant, but timed to the inhalation and exhalation of the wind. It was a living rhythm, an ancient harmony between air and stone that had always been present, waiting only for vow to call it awake.

Kael'Thorin closed his eyes. He spoke words not crafted but received, carried to his lips by the breath that wove through him: "By wind that moves and stone that endures, by vow that breathes and vow that binds, let this place awaken. Let it be circle, not of conquest, but of return."

The ridge answered. A gust surged downward, wrapping him in its current. The seed within his chest flared, threads of light spiraling outward into the runes. The stone vibrated under his palms, and the markings expanded, unfurling across the ridge like banners lifted by unseen hands. From fissures in the rock, dust and ash poured free, revealing veins of crystal gleaming faintly in the starlight.

The wind roared once, then steadied, carrying the vow across the plain in invisible currents. The second sanctuary was awake. Its memory, long hidden, now sang again in stone and air.

Kael'Thorin lowered his arms, breath steady though his body trembled from the force that had passed through him. He bowed his head, whispering into the charged air: "Here is the second circle. Here the vow breathes with the earth once more."

Kael'Thorin remained within the circle, his palms still pressed against the stone as the final resonance of the vow faded into the ridge. The wind no longer surged, but moved in long, steady breaths, carrying the scent of earth freshly opened. The runes continued to glow, faint but enduring, like embers that would never truly extinguish. The second sanctuary was alive.

He drew back a step and let his hand fall to his side. Silence settled, yet it was no longer the silence of ruin. It was the quiet of a hall newly consecrated, a place waiting for footsteps yet to come. He could almost hear them: the voices of Lemuria's scattered children, finding their way here, touching the stone, feeling the breath of the vow flow through them as it flowed through him.

Kael'Thorin turned his gaze outward. The plain stretched wide below, dark and broken, yet no longer barren. He felt the ridge send its song outward, carried by the wind, reaching across soil and ash, calling to what still lived. The vow had been rooted here. It would not remain hidden.

Lifting his head, he whispered, "Two circles stand. One remains." His voice carried farther than it should have, borne by the breath of the ridge. It returned to him as an echo, not hollow, but full, as though the land itself had repeated his words in assent.

He lingered a moment longer, letting the strength of the place settle into him. Then he adjusted his cloak and began his descent, the seed pulsing steady within his chest, guiding him toward the last sanctuary where ash awaited seed.

Kael'Thorin left the ridge behind, its glowing runes fading into the night, though their resonance lingered like a steady breath at his back. The seed within his chest pulsed with calm strength, no longer straining as it had in the Crossing, but guiding him with the certainty of rooted flame. Each step felt aligned, carried by the vow that now hummed through sanctuaries both of water and of wind. Yet the path ahead pressed heavier, for he knew the third circle would demand more than awakening—it would demand planting.

The land sloped downward into a long hollow. Even from a distance he felt its difference. The soil here was darker, rich with ash that clung to his boots and rose in faint puffs with each step. It smelled of endings—fire spent, wood consumed, groves turned to cinder. Yet beneath the bitterness was another note, faint but undeniable: fertility. Ash was death, but it was also beginning.

Kael'Thorin paused at the hollow's edge, gazing across the expanse. No crystal gleamed here, no runes shone, no water stirred. Only silence, thick and expectant, as though the land itself awaited the moment when seed would touch soil. The seed within him pulsed harder, a rhythm that shook his chest. He pressed his hand against it, whispering, "Yes. I know."

A chill wind passed through the hollow, scattering the ash. In its wake he saw faint impressions—small depressions in the soil, like furrows ready for planting. It was not his imagination. The land had prepared itself, waiting for this union of vow and earth.

He stepped forward, heart steady, breath deep. The time had come for the final circle to be set.

Kael'Thorin knelt within the hollow, his knees sinking into the dark ash. The air hung heavy, carrying the scent of char and old flame, yet beneath it he sensed the hidden promise of renewal. He spread his hands across the soil, feeling the fine grains slip between his fingers, soft as dust, weighty as memory. The seed within his chest flared in response, a rhythm strong and insistent, pressing outward as though eager to join with the earth.

He bowed low, pressing his brow to the ground. The words came not from thought but from vow itself: "By ash that remembers fire, by soil that waits for seed, let what is broken bear fruit again. Not as it was, but as it must be."

The earth stirred. Beneath his palms the ash shifted, forming shallow furrows like lines traced by unseen hands. He felt the pull of life coiled deep, hidden yet unspent, awaiting the touch of vow to call it forth. The seed in his chest pulsed harder, its glow flooding his arms until his hands shone faintly against the soil.

With a long exhale, Kael'Thorin pressed his hands into the furrows. Light spilled outward, threads of radiance sinking into the ash. For a moment there was only silence, the hush of expectancy. Then, slowly, tender shoots pierced upward—fragile yet certain, green against gray. They rose in quiet defiance, drinking from the memory of flame to become life once more.

Kael'Thorin's eyes burned with tears. He whispered hoarsely, "Here be the third circle. Born not from what was spared, but from what was consumed."

The hollow glowed faintly as the shoots spread, weaving together into a living ring. The vow had taken root. The final sanctuary was awake.

Kael'Thorin rose slowly from the hollow, his body weary but his spirit carried by the steady rhythm of the vow now rooted in earth. The tender shoots swayed in the ash behind him, their glow faint yet enduring, a circle alive with promise. He turned eastward, toward the plains where shadows stretched long, and the thought of Lemuria's scattered people pressed upon him. He could see their faces in memory: the weary, the grieving, the children whose eyes searched for light.

The seed pulsed, no longer straining, but guiding. He felt its rhythm urging him forward—not to wander alone, but to gather, to call, to weave the living into the sanctuaries. For the vow was not only land remembered, but people restored.

He lifted his hand to the night sky where the constellations had flared and faded. Though the Watchers had withdrawn, their silence lingered, a vast reminder. They would not carry this work for him. They had set the charge, sealed the vow, and entrusted its walking to him—and to all who would remember.

Kael'Thorin drew a long breath, his voice low but resolute: "I will gather them. I will call them home to the circles."

The wind stirred, soft and sure, curling around him like an unseen companion. It carried his words outward into the plain, into the scattered night, into the waiting world.

With steady steps, Kael'Thorin began his journey anew, no longer seeking only for himself. Behind him the sanctuaries glowed in silence, ahead the people awaited. The vow had been rooted in earth. Now it must be sown in hearts.

Interlude VI: Ka'el Between Worlds

There is no waking for Ka'el, for he has never slept. He does not emerge from silence so much as reveal that he has been moving through it all along, unseen and unmeasured. In the spaces between heartbeats, in the pause between one vow and the next, he stirs. He is motion without form, passage without destination, the exhale that binds one world to another.

The drift has not forgotten him, nor has the earth. Both know him, though neither can hold him. For he is the breath that crosses thresholds, the whisper of becoming that carries fragments of vow from the dying into the unborn. Where Kael'Thorin walked the waters of the drift, Ka'el moved also, curling unseen through his hair, brushing across his skin, urging him forward when despair pressed near.

Now Ka'el moves freely through the liminal. The Crossing is behind Kael'Thorin, the broken land ahead, and between them lies Ka'el, weaving unseen paths. He is not tethered to stone or flame, not bound by root or song. His nature is the in-between, the reminder that what cannot be grasped still shapes the world.

No one calls his name aloud, yet all breathe him. No one sees his face, yet all feel the stir of his presence when silence breaks into motion. He is the unseen companion, the current that ensures the seed does not linger in stillness, but moves, always moves, toward its next becoming.

Ka'el moves where boundaries blur. He coils through the remnants of the Crossing, circling the arches of light that still hum faintly with the vows of countless bearers. He does not remain—he never remains—but each current of his passing stirs the memory of those who walked there. Their whispers cling to him, not as weight but as threads, and he carries them onward without effort.

He drifts then across the scarred plain of Lemuria. No eyes see him, no hand can reach for him, yet his passage is marked in subtler ways: a curl of ash lifting from the soil, a blade of grass trembling though no foot has passed, a weary heart drawing breath when despair threatened to silence it. He does not heal directly, but he moves what must move, urging life toward its next rhythm.

Ka'el has no face, yet if he did it would change with every moment. To the grieving he is a sigh that loosens the chest. To the watchful he is a whisper warning that change is near. To the children who cry in the night he is the gentlest breeze, carrying the promise that they are not alone. Always unseen, always between.

Though he cannot be bound, Ka'el is no wanderer without purpose. His path is vow itself, the movement that ensures remembrance does not stagnate. Where the seed lies, he circles; where the vow stirs, he exhales; where silence threatens to seal, he opens a way. He is not the song, nor the stone, nor the flame, nor the vision—but without him, none of these would cross into becoming.

The voices find him. Not because he seeks them, but because all that drifts must ride the wind. Ka'el gathers them as easily as breath, threads of vow trailing from the Crossing into his unseen currents. They cling to him, yet never weigh him down. He is not keeper, but carrier, moving their tones from silence into the wide spaces between worlds.

Some voices are strong, ringing with clarity: vows spoken by those who bore the seed through fire. Others are faint, fragile as reeds—half-broken, yet still breathing remembrance into the dark. Ka'el does not measure their strength. He carries them all, weaving them into his passage until their distinctions blur. Together they form a resonance, a low hum that follows him wherever he flows.

At times, fragments of story brush across him. A warrior's last breath as he whispered a promise into the soil. A mother's song as she laid her child upon the roots of a sacred tree. The laughter of children who carried nothing but still embodied remembrance by the purity of their joy. Ka'el gathers each fragment without judgment, scattering them again like seeds on the wind, ensuring that nothing entrusted to the vow is ever entirely lost.

In this way he becomes archive, though he writes nothing. The currents of his movement are the scroll, the sky his parchment, the breath of mortals his ink. The vow endures not only because of what is remembered, but because Ka'el refuses to let forgetting have the final silence.

Ka'el has no memory of beginnings, nor expectation of endings. He is not bound by the rise and fall of ages, nor the boundaries of flesh and soil. He is the interval, the unseen passage, the current that threads what was into what will be. Where others anchor themselves to root, stone, or flame, Ka'el remains unmoored, for his power lies not in permanence but in motion.

Yet motion is not absence. Ka'el is not the void, nor is he a wandering without aim. His nature is purpose shaped by transience: to move what must move, to stir what must not remain still. Without him, even memory would stagnate, clinging too tightly to grief, to ruin, to what can no longer be. Ka'el loosens the grip of sorrow, carrying its weight into the open sky until it becomes breath again.

In rare moments, he contemplates his own essence. If he could speak, his words would be questions. What is wind, if not the reminder that nothing truly belongs to itself? What is passage, if not the proof that every threshold is meant to be crossed? He is both everywhere and nowhere, a force without face, and yet those who walk the vow know him. They feel his presence in the stirring of leaves, in the shiver across skin, in the unlooked-for courage that comes in the moment of despair.

Ka'el does not envy those who walk in flesh. Nor does he long for their permanence. He knows his gift is liminality itself—the between, the mystery. And mystery, too, is sacred. Without it, the vow would have no space to breathe.

Chapter 7: The Covenant of the Circles

Dawn broke gently over the hollow, the first pale light spilling across the ash where tender shoots had begun to rise. Kael'Thorin stood at the circle's edge, his cloak heavy with the dust of long journeying, his breath slow and steady in the cool air. Behind him the three sanctuaries pulsed faintly in memory—the basin of water and crystal, the ridge where runes breathed with wind, and the hollow where life had stirred from ash. Each was awake, each alive, yet their purpose was not fulfilled. For the vow could not remain bound to earth alone. It must live in those who walked upon it.

He gazed eastward, toward the broken plains and scattered remnants of Lemuria's people. He could almost see them: wanderers carrying grief heavy as stone, children whose eyes searched for what had been lost, elders who whispered fragments of songs though their voices trembled with forgetting. They were not gone. They waited. And the vow now burned within him to gather them.

The seed pulsed firmly beneath his chest, no longer straining but guiding, its rhythm as steady as a heartbeat. He pressed his hand against it and spoke softly into the morning air: "The circles are awake. Now the people must be called."

The words drifted outward, carried on the wind. He did not shout, nor did he need to. The vow itself bore them, weaving through the plain like a current of unseen fire. Those with ears to hear would feel it. Those with hearts still open would know: remembrance was stirring, and it called them home.

Far across the plain, a woman stirred from uneasy sleep. Her dreams had been filled with water and light, with voices that whispered of circles she had never seen. She woke with tears upon her cheeks and a fire in her chest that she could not explain. Without a word, she gathered her cloak and took her child by the hand. The boy did not question her. His eyes shone with the same strange knowing, as though he too had heard the call.

Elsewhere, a wanderer paused upon a ridge of broken stone. He had walked alone for many days, his provisions nearly gone, yet when the wind turned he felt something stir deep within his bones. It was not hunger, nor weariness, but memory—something older than his own life, something that had once been sung to him by a voice long forgotten. He turned east, his feet moving before his mind could catch them, carrying him toward the hollow.

Across the fractured land, others felt it too. Some woke from dreams of fire that had not consumed, but refined. Others heard echoes of songs they thought lost, rising faintly in their ears. Still others felt only a stirring in the chest, a pressure that was not pain, but calling. One by one, scattered and broken, they began to walk. None knew exactly where their steps would lead. Yet all felt the same truth: something was waiting, and they must go to meet it.

The vow was moving, and the people were moving with it.

By the time the sun had lifted above the horizon, Kael'Thorin felt the first stirrings at the edges of the hollow. Shapes moved against the light—figures weary from travel, yet steady in their steps. He turned and beheld them: men and women, children and elders, scattered souls drawn together by threads unseen. They carried no banners, no weapons, only the remnants of their lives—bundles of cloth, tools of wood and stone, small tokens salvaged from ruin. But their faces bore the same expression: the quiet awe of those who had been summoned by something greater than themselves.

The first to arrive was the woman and her child. She paused at the rim of the hollow, her eyes widening as she beheld the circle of tender shoots stirring in ash. Her son tugged at her hand, pointing with wonder. Without hesitation she descended, her gaze meeting Kael'Thorin's as though she had known him always. She did not speak, but her silence was full of assent.

Others followed. The wanderer from the ridge. A pair of youths who had walked three days without rest. An elder leaning on a staff carved by his own hand. They came not in throngs, but in a slow, steady stream, each arrival echoing the vow's call as surely as the sanctuaries themselves. And with each new presence, Kael'Thorin felt the air thicken, the hollow becoming not only a place of gathering, but of covenant.

The vow was no longer his alone. It was already beginning to take root in the hearts of the people.

Kael'Thorin stepped forward, the seed's glow steady beneath his chest, casting a faint radiance into the morning light. The gathered survivors fell silent, their eyes upon him not with fear, but with expectancy—the stillness of those who sensed they had reached the edge of something greater than themselves.

He lifted his hands, not high as a ruler would, but outward, open, as one who offered. His voice was low, yet it carried across the hollow with a weight beyond sound: "You were not summoned by me. You were summoned by remembrance."

The words sank into the air, and the seed pulsed in rhythm, affirming them. He continued: "The circles stand awake—the waters that mirror, the stones that breathe, the ash that bears new life. But they are not enough. Earth remembers, yes, but earth alone cannot keep vow. It must be spoken in flesh, carried in breath, lived in heart."

He looked upon them—faces weary, eyes dimmed by loss yet kindled now with faint light. "The vow does not belong to me. It belongs to us. To you, to your children, to all who will walk after. I carry it for a time, as others have before me. But it is not mine to keep. It is ours to become."

The silence deepened. The people stood still, yet Kael'Thorin felt the hollow tremble faintly, as though the earth itself awaited their assent. And in their eyes he saw it: the first flicker of covenant, fragile but real, awakening in the hearts of the remnant.

At first there was only silence. The gathered survivors stood as though rooted, their faces etched with weariness and wonder alike. Then a sound broke the stillness—not a word, but the soft weeping of the woman who had come with her child. She pressed her hand against the boy's back, and when he looked up at her, his small voice rose into the air: "We will remember."

The words trembled, fragile as the shoots in the ash, yet they carried with them the weight of promise. Others shifted, moved by the boy's declaration. The elder leaning on his staff struck the ground once, the hollow knock of wood on stone ringing like a vow renewed. A pair of youths clasped hands and bowed their heads. The wanderer from the ridge lifted his arms to the sky, eyes closed, lips moving in silent assent.

One by one, gestures and voices joined. Some spoke words aloud—snatches of old songs, fragments of vows half-remembered. Others said nothing, but their bodies bent forward, their eyes shone, their spirits pressed outward into the circle. Together they became a chorus of assent, uneven yet undeniable.

Kael'Thorin felt the seed blaze warmly, its light spilling farther than before. It pulsed in rhythm with the people's response, weaving their voices into its glow. The vow was no longer solitary. It had taken its first root in the hearts of the remnant.

The murmur of assent grew, no longer scattered voices but a rising chorus woven from many tones. Some sang softly, recalling fragments of songs once taught beside hearth-fires. Others spoke words of vow handed down through families, phrases half-forgotten yet rekindled now with living fire. Children mimicked their elders, their high voices lifting the echoes into something pure. The hollow itself seemed to vibrate, its air charged with memory reawakening.

Kael'Thorin stood among them, his hands lowered, his face bowed. He did not guide their words, nor command their voices. He let them rise of their own accord, trusting that the vow needed no master—only vessels willing to carry it. The seed within his chest pulsed in time with their voices, and he felt its light weave outward, stitching unseen threads between each person gathered.

The elder raised his staff once more, this time tapping it three times against the stone. The sound echoed deep, like the beat of a drum. Others began to add their rhythms—hands clapping, feet striking earth, stones lifted and brought down in measured cadence. Soon the hollow resounded with a great weaving of sound and motion, a covenant not spoken alone, but enacted together.

Kael'Thorin lifted his gaze. Around him, the people no longer appeared as wanderers or remnants. They stood as a circle, bound not by blood or name, but by vow. He felt the air thrum with their unity, and he knew the sanctuaries had not only awakened the land—they had awakened its people.

The rhythm of the people's voices and movements grew steadier, weaving into a pattern that carried the strength of something greater than ritual. Kael'Thorin felt it surge through the hollow like a tide, washing away the dust of despair, replacing it with breath renewed. Each voice, each gesture, seemed to knit itself into the whole, no longer separate strands but one living fabric.

A child stepped forward, placing a small stone upon the ground at the center of the circle. Others followed—tokens of wood, shards of crystal, simple belongings once kept in silence. They were not offerings of loss, but signs of presence: proofs that they still lived, that they still remembered. A young man cut a lock of his hair and laid it beside the stone, while an elder unstrapped a carved charm from her wrist and set it gently upon the earth. Soon the circle's center glimmered with fragments of their lives, woven together as covenant.

Kael'Thorin felt the seed in his chest flare warmly. He placed his hand over it and spoke softly, not to command, but to affirm: "These are not sacrifices. They are signs. The vow is not in what we lose, but in what we join."

The people murmured in assent, their eyes alight. The hollow's air thickened with a presence that was not only earth and sky, but something greater—the Watchers' silence pressing at the edges, as though they too bore witness to this weaving of lives into vow.

As the people's voices and offerings settled into the hollow, Kael'Thorin felt the ground tremble faintly beneath his feet. It was not the quiver of weakness, but of resonance, as though the sanctuaries themselves had stirred in answer. The basin of water and crystal shimmered in his mind's eye, its light rippling outward; the ridge with its breathing runes seemed to pulse with the rhythm of the wind; and here, the shoots in the ash bent gently as if nodding in recognition. Three circles, three voices, one vow.

The seed within his chest blazed, not in strain but in joy, its glow spilling into the air until the hollow itself seemed lit from within. The survivors gasped softly, some reaching out their hands as the warmth touched them. It was not fire, not flame to burn, but the gentle radiance of belonging. For the first time since ruin had fallen, they felt the land receive them not as exiles, but as children returned.

Kael'Thorin lifted his gaze. "The earth has heard," he said quietly. "The circles breathe with us. What is spoken here is not lost."

The air deepened, charged with presence. Though the Watchers did not appear, Kael'Thorin felt their vast silence pressing close, bearing witness to the covenant. The people looked to one another, their faces shining with the dawning awareness that they were no longer wanderers. They were keepers.

Kael'Thorin stepped closer to the gathered circle, his voice steady though his chest ached with the weight of the moment. "The vow is not mine alone," he said. "It is yours to speak, yours to carry. Let each voice rise, not as echo, but as covenant."

The people shifted, uncertain at first. Then the elder struck his staff once more, the sound ringing like a summons. Slowly, hesitantly, a woman lifted her voice: "I will remember." Another followed: "I will not turn away." A youth whispered, "I will carry for those yet to come."

The words grew. One by one, voices rose from the hollow, speaking not in unison but in harmony, each vow distinct yet woven together. Some promised to teach, others to guard, others to sow. A mother swore to sing each night to her children. A wanderer vowed to guide strangers as brothers. A child, clutching a stone in both hands, cried, "I will keep it safe."

Kael'Thorin's eyes burned. The seed within his chest flared warmly, pulsing in rhythm with the vows. It was no longer a solitary glow but a constellation, reflected in the hearts around him. The hollow trembled faintly, as if the land itself recorded their words.

When at last the voices quieted, silence returned—but it was no longer empty. It was full, alive, heavy with promise.

The vows lingered in the hollow like incense, rising unseen yet permeating all. Kael'Thorin stood among them, his breath slow, the seed within his chest steady and strong. He felt its rhythm expand outward, as though the sanctuaries themselves were echoing the people's promises. The basin shimmered in the distance, the ridge thrummed with wind, and the tender shoots in the ash bent gently as if in blessing.

Kael'Thorin raised his voice once more: "So it begins. The vow is no longer hidden. It walks with us, breathes with us, grows with us. These circles are not places to be guarded alone—they are thresholds for all who will remember."

He turned, extending his hand to the woman with the child, then to the elder with his staff, then to the wanderer who had come from the ridge. "You are the keepers now. Not of stone, nor of relic, but of vow. Carry it in your steps, in your words, in the way you lift one another when the night presses near. Carry it, and it will not fail."

The people bowed their heads, not in subservience, but in agreement. A quiet hum filled the hollow, rising not from earth alone but from the gathered hearts. Kael'Thorin closed his eyes, listening. The covenant was sealed—not in grand ceremony, but in the simple assent of the remnant, bound to earth, to sky, and to one another.

When the vows had settled into silence, Kael'Thorin stepped back, allowing the people to hold the moment for themselves. He knew the covenant could not be sealed by his voice alone. It must live in theirs, in the weight of their choices, in the breath of their days to come. The hollow was no longer a gathering place only. It had become a living circle of memory.

A young girl broke the silence. She held a sprig of ash in her hand, blackened but unbroken, which she must have carried since the burning of the groves. She knelt and pressed it into the soil beside the shoots, and her clear voice rang out: "Grow again."

The people stirred. Others stepped forward, bringing tokens not asked of them: seeds wrapped in cloth, bowls of water carried through long travel, stones polished by hand. They placed them gently within the circle, adding their presence to the vow. No one commanded them, yet the movement spread until all had given something—not as offering, but as joining.

Kael'Thorin felt the seed within him resonate, its light flickering outward to embrace each act. He lifted his gaze to the people, his voice quiet but firm: "These are the beginnings of covenant. Not mine, not yours alone, but ours, rooted in earth and carried in heart. What we place here will outlast us."

The people bowed their heads, and the hollow thrummed with the strength of what had been set in motion.

As the people placed their tokens within the circle, a low hum rose through the hollow. It was not their voices, but the land itself answering. The shoots trembled in the ash, their green brightening, and the faint trickle of water could be heard from beneath the soil. Far off, Kael'Thorin sensed the basin stir, its crystals glimmering as though reflecting the light of a dawn not yet seen. The ridge too responded, wind sweeping across its runes in rhythmic breath. Three sanctuaries, joined now not only to him, but to the people.

The survivors gasped, their eyes widening as the air thickened with presence. Some reached for one another's hands, others bowed low, others simply stood still, trembling in awe. The vow was no longer abstract, no longer hidden in one bearer's chest. It was alive, moving between them, weaving earth, air, and water into their own breath.

Kael'Thorin raised his voice, speaking into the resonance: "The circles are not stone alone. They are us, joined with earth, joined with sky, joined with flame. So long as we walk in remembrance, they will not fail."

A murmur of assent rippled through the people, and Kael'Thorin felt the seed within him grow lighter, as though its weight had been divided among many hearts. For the first time since the fall, he did not feel alone in his charge. The vow was carried, and it was carried together.

From the murmurs of assent rose a melody, faint at first, as though carried on the edges of memory. An elder began it—her voice cracked with age, yet steady in tone. It was a fragment of an ancient hymn, once sung beside waters now long vanished. Others joined, hesitant, filling the gaps with sounds rather than words, until the broken song became whole again, reshaped by many voices. What had been nearly forgotten returned, not as it once was, but as it must be now.

Children added their voices, light and unburdened, weaving brightness into the song. Youths sang strong, their tones carrying defiance and hope. The wanderer who had walked alone sang as though he had always carried harmony within him, waiting for this circle to call it forth. The melody grew into a living covenant, binding them not by oath alone, but by song.

Kael'Thorin closed his eyes, letting the sound wash over him. The seed within his chest pulsed with the rhythm, not leading, not commanding, but blending, becoming one with the chorus. He had spoken vows, he had carried weight, but this—this was what the vow had always awaited: the moment it became song in the mouths of the people.

The hollow itself seemed to echo, the stone walls vibrating softly, the shoots trembling in time with the melody. It was as if the land remembered the tune, and welcomed its return.

The song swelled, filling the hollow until it seemed to pour beyond its stone edges, carried outward into the plains. Kael'Thorin opened his eyes, and in the glow of the people's faces, he saw what he had not dared to hope: the vow alive, not as burden, but as belonging. Each voice was distinct, yet together they formed a harmony that was more than song. It was covenant made audible.

As the melody deepened, Kael'Thorin felt the air shift. A vastness pressed against the circle, subtle yet undeniable—the Watchers. They did not descend as before, but their presence brushed the edges of the gathering like a tide touching shore. The people shivered, some bowing, others clutching their neighbors' hands, for though the Watchers spoke no word, their silence was immense. It bore witness.

Kael'Thorin pressed his hand to his chest, steadying his breath as the seed pulsed in recognition. He lifted his gaze and spoke into the song: "They hear us. The vow is not hidden. It has been seen."

The people's song did not falter. If anything, it grew stronger, emboldened by the unseen presence. Voices rose higher, carrying tones that wove through the air like threads of light. The shoots in the ash bent again, the ridge hummed faintly in the distance, and the basin shimmered with quiet ripples. Earth, air, and water bore witness alongside the Watchers. The vow was sealed in many worlds at once.

The covenant-song climbed higher, weaving into harmonies that no single voice could have carried alone. It was as if the sound itself had taken on life, rising above them like a canopy of light. Kael'Thorin felt the ground steady beneath his feet, the soil no longer brittle with ruin but vibrant with promise. Every note seemed to root deeper, binding not only the people to one another, but the sanctuaries to the living memory they now shared.

Children laughed as they sang, their voices bright threads cutting through the solemn weight of the hymn. Elders added depth, their tones low and grounding, as if anchoring the covenant across generations. The youth, strong in breath and conviction, carried the melody forward with vigor. The song became a tapestry of all ages, woven into one fabric of vow.

Kael'Thorin closed his eyes and let himself be carried by it. The seed within him pulsed not as a solitary flame, but as part of a constellation, its light mirrored in the hearts around him. For the first time since the Watchers' return, he felt the vow no longer as a burden pressing upon him, but as a bond carried together.

When the song reached its peak, the hollow thrummed with resonance. The shoots in the ash swayed, the ridge exhaled in long breaths of wind, the basin rippled with light. The Watchers' silence deepened, not heavy now, but vast and steady, as though affirming what had been set. The vow was not only sealed. It was alive.

Slowly, the covenant-song began to soften, not fading into silence but settling like embers after flame. Voices lowered, yet the resonance remained, a steady thrum that seemed to breathe through earth and body alike. The people's eyes shone, some wet with tears, others alight with a quiet strength newly kindled. They looked at one another not as wanderers bound only by loss, but as kin gathered in remembrance.

Kael'Thorin lifted his head, feeling the seed's glow pulsing calm within his chest. He stepped into the circle's center, his cloak brushing the tender shoots that had risen from ash. The people parted to let him pass, though their presence pressed close around him like a living wall. He raised his hands slightly—not commanding, but inviting.

"The vow lives," he said, his voice steady yet low. "It breathes in you, in the circles, in the earth itself. What was lost has not vanished—it has taken root anew. But a root must grow, and for growth, it must be tended."

He looked across the circle—at the woman with her child, at the elder with his staff, at the youths whose voices had carried strength into the song. "This is not the end of our gathering. It is its beginning. Each of you carries a spark now, and sparks must be shared, or they fade. From this day, you are not only survivors. You are keepers."

The people stirred, a murmur of assent rising. The covenant had taken shape. Now it awaited its tending.

The murmur of assent quieted as Kael'Thorin lowered his hands, his eyes moving slowly across the faces gathered in the circle. He saw not only weariness, but a new steadiness kindling within them. The vow had found root, but roots must spread. He felt the seed in his chest guiding him, its pulse steady as he spoke.

"The circles are more than signs," he said. "They are wells from which we must drink, fires from which we must carry flame. One heart cannot hold them alone, nor one voice, nor one family. They belong to all. And so the keeping of them belongs to all."

The people listened, leaning forward, their eyes intent. Kael'Thorin gestured to the hollow, where shoots swayed gently in ash. "This is the third circle, born of fire and death, now living again. It must not be left untended. As with the basin and the ridge, it must be visited, sung to, kept in breath and memory. Will you walk to them? Will you tend them together?"

The elder lifted his staff in response, striking the ground once in firm assent. The woman with the child pressed her son's hand to her heart, her eyes shining. A chorus of agreement followed—low voices, young voices, trembling voices—all binding themselves to the task. Kael'Thorin felt the vow expand outward, no longer carried only by the sanctuaries, but by the people's promise to tend them.

In their assent, the covenant began to take form in practice, rooted in earth and guarded in living hearts.

The people stirred as Kael'Thorin's words settled, and from among them rose the first responses. A youth lifted his voice, strong and eager: "We will carry songs to the circles. When we gather, we will sing so the earth does not forget." His words drew nods, and an elder added, "And we will tell the stories, not only to our children, but to any who come among us, so that the vow is never hidden."

Others spoke in turn. A woman promised to tend the shoots with water drawn from distant springs. A wanderer vowed to mark the paths to each sanctuary, so that none who sought them would be lost. A child lifted a stone high, declaring in his small but fierce voice: "I will carry this each time, so the circles know me."

Kael'Thorin listened, his heart swelling as the covenant began to take shape in the people's own voices. They were not commanded, they were not bound by fear, yet one by one they offered what they could, weaving practice into promise. The vow was no longer an abstract bond of heaven and earth—it was becoming a living rhythm of their days.

The seed within him pulsed in steady harmony with their words. For the first time, Kael'Thorin felt not only the burden of vow, but its joy—the joy of seeing it borne in many hearts, each carrying their part, each voice adding to the whole.

The people did not wait for another command. Their words of promise turned into action, flowing naturally as water from a spring. The youth who had spoken of song began to hum, then lifted his voice into a melody. Others joined him, weaving tones old and new until the hollow thrummed with their covenant once more. The woman who had pledged water drew a small clay vessel from her satchel, pouring its clear contents over the tender shoots. They glistened as the drops touched them, their green brightening as if drinking directly from her vow.

The wanderer who had promised to mark paths took stones from his pouch, placing them carefully at the circle's edge. He traced patterns with his fingers, not runes of power but marks of direction, signs that would guide others to this place. Even the child who had spoken laid his stone reverently at the circle's heart, patting it with both hands as if sealing his small covenant with the earth itself.

Kael'Thorin watched, his chest tightening with a depth of feeling he had not known in many days. This was not ritual imposed. It was remembrance born anew, arising of its own will, shaped by the people into forms the land could receive. He felt the seed glow warmly, joining their gestures into one living bond.

The vow was no longer vision alone. It was being walked into the world.

When the hush had settled, Kael'Thorin stood at the circle's edge, gazing at the faces of those gathered. He saw strength where once there had been only weariness, and light in eyes that had been dimmed by grief. The covenant had begun to take form—not in one act, but in the weaving of many hearts.

He lifted his voice, calm but resolute: "What we have set here is not for this moment alone. It must walk with you into the days ahead. The vow is not bound to this hollow, nor to me, nor even to the sanctuaries. It is bound to you—your steps, your words, your tending of one another. Where you walk, let the circles walk also."

A woman raised her hand, her voice trembling but strong: "And when we falter?"

Kael'Thorin's gaze softened. "Then you rise. The vow is not broken by failing—it endures by returning. Each time you remember, each time you lift another, each time you choose to walk again, the vow lives. It was never meant for perfection, but for faithfulness."

The words sank deep, and he felt the circle steady. Shoulders lifted, faces grew firm, and the silence became rich, filled with resolve.

The people remained silent for a long moment, breathing in Kael'Thorin's words as though drinking water after drought. Then one of the youths spoke: "If the vow must walk with us, then let us choose how it shall be kept." His suggestion stirred the circle, and voices began to rise, not in debate, but in offering.

A mother lifted her child into her arms. "Each dawn, we will speak the vow aloud, so that the day begins with remembrance." An elder followed: "At dusk, we will tell the stories, so that the night carries memory into dream." Another added: "When one falls into sorrow, let two walk beside them until their strength is restored."

The people nodded, each idea welcomed as though it had always belonged. Soon a pattern took shape: songs at the sanctuaries, stories told by firelight, shared tending of earth and water, care for the weak and grieving. These were not laws carved into stone, but living practices—threads woven into daily life, strong enough to endure the turning of seasons.

Kael'Thorin listened, his heart swelling. He had carried the vow through fire and silence, across plain and ridge, but here it was becoming what it was always meant to be: a covenant alive in the rhythm of the people's days.

As the people's voices wove their practices into shape, they did not wait for a distant day to begin. At the elder's urging, some gathered dry wood and struck flint until a small flame flickered to life. Around it, they sat and told fragments of stories—of groves that once sang, of rivers that glowed at night, of names nearly lost but now remembered. The mother who had spoken lifted her child, whispering the vow into his ear, and others followed, speaking it aloud so that the circle itself seemed to breathe with their words.

A pair of youths fetched water from a nearby spring, pouring it gently over the shoots until the ash grew damp and the small leaves brightened. The wanderer placed more stones at the circle's edge, marking the path so that others would know where to find it. Even those who had nothing material to give offered their presence—singing, holding hands, or sitting quietly with eyes closed, their breath steady, their hearts joined.

Kael'Thorin stood in silence, his chest burning with quiet fire. This was the vow made visible: not in grand gestures or decrees, but in the daily acts of a people choosing to remember. He pressed his palm to the seed and whispered, "This is how it lives."

The air trembled faintly, and he felt the Watchers' silence lean close once more, as if affirming the truth of what was unfolding.

Night drew its veil across the plains, yet the hollow did not fall into silence. The small fire crackled at the circle's heart, its smoke curling into the dark sky. The people gathered close, their faces lit by its glow, their voices low but steady. Songs rose again—fragments of old hymns, lullabies whispered to children, chants that spoke of vow and return. Between verses, they shared food in simple bowls, passing them from hand to hand, each gesture sealing fellowship.

The shoots in the ash gleamed faintly, their green reflecting the firelight. The stones placed by the wanderer marked the hollow's edge like sentinels, while the water poured earlier still dampened the soil, giving the circle the scent of life renewed. Everything around them spoke of covenant taking root—not tomorrow, not in some distant vision, but here, this night.

Kael'Thorin remained among them, not apart. He listened as children asked questions of the elders, and the elders answered with stories once feared forgotten. He watched as youths kept the fire fed, their laughter mingling with the solemnity of vow. He felt the seed glow within him, lighter now than ever before, as though it too rejoiced in being shared.

Above, the constellations shimmered faintly out of alignment, bending once more into patterns unseen by common eyes. The Watchers leaned close, their vast silence bearing witness to the first night of the people's keeping.

The night stretched long, yet none within the hollow felt its weight as burden. Around the fire, they kept their first vigil together, their voices weaving between silence and song. Some rested with heads upon one another's shoulders, others whispered stories to children until sleep claimed them, but all remained within the circle, unwilling to step beyond the covenant that had begun to take shape.

Kael'Thorin walked among them, his presence quiet, offering no command but sharing in their watch. At times he knelt to listen as elders spoke of days before the fall, their words carrying not only sorrow but wisdom hard-earned. At other times he sat with the youths, who asked questions of what might come, their eyes bright with unbroken hope. He gave no prophecy, only reminded them that the vow was not in knowing the path, but in walking it faithfully together.

The seed within his chest pulsed in gentle rhythm, steady as the crackling of the fire. He felt its weight spread through the circle, no longer centered in him alone but shared. Each person carried a portion now, their breaths woven into the same living current. The vow had ceased to be solitary; it had become communal.

When the first light of dawn touched the horizon, the people stirred with quiet joy. Their vigil had not been empty. It had been the beginning of a life lived in covenant.

With dawn's light spilling over the hollow, the people rose from their vigil. The fire burned low, but its embers glowed steady, as if echoing the covenant that now lived within them. Children rubbed sleep from their eyes, yet even their play seemed touched by new reverence as they traced small circles in the ash with their fingers. Elders leaned on staffs, but their steps carried fresh strength, as though the night had restored what despair had taken.

Kael'Thorin stood among them, watching as they stirred, as water was shared, as voices lifted in gentle song to greet the day. No one told them to sing, no one told them to pour the water, yet these acts flowed naturally, as though the vow itself now guided their rhythm. The sanctuaries lived in their hearts already.

He raised his voice, low but clear: "This is the first morning of the covenant. Let it be remembered not because of what I speak, but because of how you live. Carry this day into all that follows, and the vow will not wither."

The people nodded, their faces solemn yet bright. The woman with her child lifted him high so that he could see the shoots gleaming in the soil. The youths clasped hands, their laughter carrying promise. The elder struck his staff once, and the sound echoed like a seal upon the dawn.

It was not an ending, but a beginning—the vow stepping beyond circle and sanctuary into the living breath of a people restored.

As the sun lifted higher, the people began to ready themselves to leave the hollow. Bundles were gathered, staffs lifted, children drawn close. Yet there was no haste, only a quiet reverence in each movement, as though they knew they were carrying more than provisions. They carried the vow itself, living now in their hands and feet.

Before they departed, Kael'Thorin walked once more to the

center of the shoots. He knelt, pressing his palm to the soil where ash had given way to life. The seed within his chest pulsed, answering the rhythm of the earth. He spoke softly: "This circle will not be abandoned. It will be tended, and through it, we will remember."

The people gathered close, adding their assent in voices and gestures alike. Some touched the soil, others lifted hands skyward, others simply closed their eyes and breathed deeply. Together they marked the moment, sealing it as covenant before taking their first steps outward.

The wanderer who had laid stones at the circle's edge added one more, setting it firmly into place. The elder struck his staff three times, the sound echoing like a drumbeat across the hollow. The woman with her child whispered the vow aloud, the boy repeating it with solemn gravity. Their voices rose into the morning air, a final blessing upon the place.

Kael'Thorin stood, lifting his gaze toward the horizon. "Now," he said, his voice calm but strong, "let the vow walk."

The circle stirred into motion, its people beginning their first steps beyond the hollow. The path outward wound between the stones the wanderer had set, guiding their feet as though marking the boundary between old life and new. Children ran ahead, laughing, while elders followed with measured steps, their staffs steady upon the earth. The youths walked at the edges, watchful and strong, carrying themselves as though the vow had already shaped their shoulders.

Kael'Thorin remained at the rear, his gaze sweeping across the hollow one last time. The shoots swayed gently in the morning light, their green vibrant against the black soil of ash. The fire's embers still glowed faintly, and the stones marked a clear path inward for those who would come later. It was not abandonment—it was entrusting. The circle had been awakened, and now it would live through the steps of those who carried it outward.

As they walked, songs rose again—soft at first, then stronger as voices joined. They were not the grand hymns of old temples, but simple melodies, born of firelight and vigil, woven from the promise they now bore. The plains received their sound, carrying it farther than their feet could travel. The covenant had begun to move.

Kael'Thorin's chest burned with quiet pride. The vow was no longer bound to him. It had become the breath of a people, and through their walking, the land itself would remember.

As the people walked outward across the plain, Kael'Thorin lingered at the rear, watching the slow weaving of their steps into the land. Each footprint seemed to echo, not as solitary mark, but as part of a larger pattern taking shape. He felt it as surely as breath—the covenant was no longer contained in the hollow, but moving, expanding, alive.

The songs carried on the wind, drifting far beyond their small procession. He imagined them reaching others still scattered across the land—souls wandering in grief or silence, pausing as faint melody touched their hearts, stirring memory. The vow was calling not only those here, but those yet to arrive.

Kael'Thorin pressed his hand to the seed within his chest. Its glow had softened, no longer burning with solitary fire, but pulsing gently, a part of the greater rhythm carried by many hearts. He whispered into the morning air: "It begins."

Lifting his gaze, he watched the horizon. The path stretched long, shadow and light braided together, yet for the first time since the fall he felt no dread in its length. The vow was not a burden upon one soul—it was a covenant shared. And in that sharing, it would endure.

The plain opened wide before them, its scarred expanse bathed in morning light. The people's steps left no grand trail, yet Kael'Thorin knew the land remembered. Each footprint was taken into the soil as covenant, joining the circles that now thrummed with life. What had once been only ruin began to feel like promise—a canvas upon which remembrance would be written anew.

As they walked, voices lifted again, not in unison but in harmony. Some sang the hymn that had been reborn the night before. Others wove simple chants, naming water, wind, and ash as living companions. Children added their laughter, skipping between adults, their joy a testimony that the vow was no longer only solemn but alive with hope. Every sound became part of the covenant, woven into air and earth alike.

Kael'Thorin's gaze swept across them, and he felt a deep stirring. This was the vision the Watchers had pressed upon him—the vow not bound to temples or monuments, but carried in living hearts, walked into the world step by step. He whispered, almost to himself: "The covenant breathes."

The wind shifted, cool and steady, brushing across the company as if to affirm the words. The path stretched on, long and uncertain, yet filled now with a rhythm strong enough to carry them forward.

As the company pressed farther into the plain, Kael'Thorin felt a shift beyond what his eyes could see. The covenant, carried now in their songs and steps, was rippling outward. It moved not only with them, but beyond them—like roots spreading unseen beneath soil, reaching places yet untouched. Somewhere, he knew, others would pause in their wandering, sensing the faint echo of the vow upon the wind. Some would hear it in dream, others in memory, others in the sudden quickening of their hearts. The covenant was already seeking them.

He slowed his pace, allowing himself to feel the breadth of it. The Watchers' presence brushed the edge of his awareness—not looming now, but steady, as though marking that what had been charged to him was truly underway. They did not speak, but their silence bore weight, affirming what he already knew: this work was no longer his alone.

Ahead, the people's voices rose in laughter and song. Children darted between lines of travelers, their joy carried far across the morning air. Kael'Thorin smiled faintly, a rare softness settling across his face. For the first time since the vow had burned within him, he felt the beginning of rest. Not because the burden had lightened, but because it was now shared.

The covenant was alive, and it was multiplying.

By midday, the plain stretched wide before them, its horizon shimmering in the heat of the rising sun. Yet Kael'Thorin felt they were not alone. The covenant's call had traveled ahead of them, and now the land bore signs of its reach.

They came upon a stream that had once run shallow and choked with ash. Now its waters flowed clearer, small rivulets cutting fresh channels through the soil. Children rushed to its edge, splashing with laughter, while elders dipped hands reverently, whispering prayers of thanks. The people marveled, for they knew no hand among them had done this. It was the vow, weaving itself into the veins of the land.

Further along, they found a cairn of stones newly raised. It was simple, unadorned, yet its shape was unmistakable: a circle within a circle, the sign of remembrance. Someone had passed this way before them, drawn by the same unseen summons. Hope stirred in the people's eyes, their voices buzzing with excitement. They were not the only ones answering the call.

Kael'Thorin knelt at the cairn, placing his hand upon the warm stone. The seed within his chest pulsed in harmony, confirming what he already knew: the covenant was spreading, awakening hearts across the broken land. Their circle was no longer solitary—it was part of a widening chorus.

The discovery of the cairn filled the people with renewed strength, and their steps carried them forward with greater certainty. Kael'Thorin felt it too—a steady current pulling them onward, not as wanderers but as participants in something larger than themselves. The covenant was no longer confined to their circle; it was drawing others into its weave.

As they walked, the land seemed to speak in small signs. Birds returned to the air above, their wings catching light as they wheeled in loose spirals, a sight long absent since the fall. Grasses sprouted in patches where once there had been only ash. Even the wind bore a different weight, cool and carrying, as though it had become a messenger of the vow.

The people began to speak of those they might meet—friends lost to scattering, kin carried far, neighbors thought gone. Each voice carried not only longing but new hope, the belief that the covenant's call would gather them again. Kael'Thorin listened in silence, his heart warmed by their faith. The seed within his chest pulsed in affirmation, reminding him that the vow was not meant to remain small. It would spread, as water fills rivers, as fire leaps from spark to spark, until the remnant became a people once more.

And as they crested a rise, they saw faint figures in the distance—travelers walking toward them, drawn by the same unseen call.

The figures in the distance grew clearer as the company descended from the rise. At first they appeared cautious, their steps slow, their shapes weary with long travel. Yet as the two groups drew nearer, a spark of recognition flickered in their eyes—not of faces known, but of the call that had drawn them both. The covenant had already spoken in their hearts, and now it carried them into one another's presence.

The people quickened their pace, children running forward with laughter, elders leaning eagerly on their staffs. Soon the two circles met in the open plain. There were no words at first, only silence heavy with awe. Then one of the new travelers, a woman with braids streaked silver, lifted her voice: "We dreamed of light in the ash. It led us here."

A murmur of recognition passed through Kael'Thorin's company. The woman with her child stepped forward, her hand pressed over her heart. "We too were called. The vow lives in us."

The two groups mingled, exchanging names, tokens, and fragments of story. Some wept openly, not for sorrow, but for relief—that they were no longer alone. Their circles had become one.

Kael'Thorin stood among them, his chest burning with quiet fire. The seed pulsed in steady rhythm, affirming what unfolded before his eyes. The covenant was no longer bound to a single gathering. It was multiplying, weaving the scattered into a people reborn.

The mingling of the two groups flowed naturally into covenant. A youth from the new company stepped forward, carrying a bundle of dried herbs. He laid them gently upon the ground between the circles, saying, "These are all we carried from our hearth. Let them burn here, so that our fire joins yours."

The elder from Kael'Thorin's company nodded, striking his staff once as assent. Together they kindled the herbs, their smoke curling skyward, fragrant and strong. Children from both groups gathered close, adding small twigs and leaves until the flame rose steady. Their laughter mingled, bright against the solemn air.

Others followed. A woman poured clear water into the soil where the shoots might one day rise again. Two men carried stones, placing them side by side as markers. A child traced a circle in the ash with her finger, then clasped hands with another she had only just met. Each act was simple, but together they became covenant—a weaving of lives into vow.

Kael'Thorin stood in silence, his heart stirred. He saw in these gestures the promise that the covenant was no longer fragile. It was resilient, growing stronger with each meeting, each joining. The seed pulsed within him, steady and calm, no longer a burden to bear, but a fire shared.

When the fire of the joined herbs burned steady, Kael'Thorin stepped forward. The two groups quieted, their eyes lifting to him not as strangers to a leader, but as kin awaiting the weaving of their shared vow. He raised his hands gently, palms outward, and his voice carried with calm strength.

"You have walked from different places, through grief, through silence, through loss. Yet the vow has drawn you here—not to one hollow, not to one circle, but to one another. This covenant is not bound to soil alone. It is bound to hearts, to hands, to the steps we take together."

He looked across their faces, lingering on children clasping hands, elders leaning on staffs, youths carrying stones. "The Watchers do not measure us by what we have lost, but by what we choose to carry. And now, we carry remembrance together."

A murmur of assent rippled through the gathered. Some bowed heads, others raised hands, others pressed palms to earth. The fire crackled, and the smoke carried their agreement skyward.

Kael'Thorin lowered his voice, yet it reached all who listened: "From this day, we are not two groups. We are one people. One vow. One covenant."

The seed within his chest pulsed in affirmation, and the air trembled faintly—as though the sanctuaries themselves echoed the truth of his words.

In the silence that followed Kael'Thorin's words, the people seemed to stand taller. A sense of kinship wove through them—no longer two gatherings bound by chance, but one people joined by vow. The fire at their center crackled steadily, its smoke carrying the fragrance of the herbs skyward as if offering their covenant to the unseen.

Then, without prompting, an elder from the new company stepped forward. She drew water from a leather vessel and poured it slowly onto the earth beside the flame. The soil hissed faintly, the mingling of elements sealing the moment. A youth from Kael'Thorin's company followed, placing a crystal shard he had carried since before the fall into the damp soil. Others came in turn—stones, seeds, songs lifted into the air. Each act simple, yet woven together they became a rite: the covenant embodied in fire, water, earth, and voice.

Kael'Thorin watched, his heart stirred to quiet awe. This was no ritual crafted by decree; it was remembrance rising naturally from the people, shaping itself around their unity. The seed within him pulsed softly, steady as a heartbeat, affirming that this was the vow alive in its truest form.

When the last token was placed, the people clasped hands in a wide circle around the fire, their joined voices speaking as one: "We remember."

As the people's voices faded into silence, a stillness fell over the plain. The fire's glow burned steady, the dampened soil gave off a faint scent of renewal, and the circle of joined hands pulsed with quiet strength. Kael'Thorin felt it before he saw it—the Watchers' presence descending once more. Not with the weight of judgment, but with the vast solemnity of witness.

The constellations above wavered, bending faintly out of their courses, aligning into patterns unseen by common eyes. Their light poured down upon the gathering, weaving with the firelight and the shimmer of the people's tokens until the hollowed plain itself seemed to glow. Children gasped, elders bowed their heads, youths stood wide-eyed in awe. The Watchers did not take form, but their silence pressed close, immense and tender all at once.

Kael'Thorin bowed low, pressing his palm to the earth. The seed within his chest pulsed in rhythm with the stars, affirming the unity now sealed. He whispered, "Bear witness. Not to me, but to us."

The silence deepened, and though no voice answered, the people felt it—an unseen assent, vast and unshakable. Their covenant had been seen. It was now part of the greater remembrance, carried not only in earth and flesh, but marked in the heavens themselves.

The silence of the Watchers lingered like a mantle, settling over the gathered people with weight and wonder. For a long moment no one spoke, yet all felt the vastness pressing close, affirming what had been born among them. Then, as though moved by one breath, the circle tightened, hands clasping more firmly, voices rising once more—not in fear, but in affirmation.

The elder lifted his staff, striking it once against the earth. "We are one circle," he declared. The youths echoed, "We are one people." The women and children added their voices: "We are one vow." Together, the words wove upward, joining fire and stars alike.

Kael'Thorin felt the seed blaze within him, not as solitary flame but as part of the living constellation that surrounded him. The people's voices were not only sound—they were power, threading themselves into earth, air, and sky. The sanctuaries stirred in response, faint glimmers reaching across distance as though answering their cry.

He lifted his voice above the chorus: "So let it be carried. Not in stone, nor in temple, but in every step, in every breath. The vow lives because we live it."

The people roared in answer, their cry rolling across the plain. The covenant was no longer fragile. It was strong, rooted in many hearts, sealed by earth and witnessed by heaven.

With their cry still echoing across the plain, the people began to move as one. The fire was tended until only steady embers remained, the water poured reverently into the soil, the stones set in firm circles to mark their meeting place. Nothing was left abandoned; everything was left as covenant.

Kael'Thorin walked among them as they prepared to journey onward. He saw no longer the weary remnants of ruin, but a company carrying light. Children clutched stones and tokens, elders leaned on staffs with renewed strength, youths walked tall with eyes bright. Their steps were not scattered but woven, each stride part of a greater rhythm.

As they set forth, voices lifted once more—not in the high swell of ceremony, but in the cadence of travel: simple chants, call-and-response, the rhythm of feet striking soil. The covenant was no longer only spoken at sanctuaries. It was being carried into the world.

Kael'Thorin lingered at the rear, his hand pressed to the seed in his chest. It pulsed calmly, no longer demanding, no longer burning, but steady as breath. He looked to the horizon and whispered, "Let remembrance walk."

The wind rose, cool and sure, sweeping before them as if clearing the path. The covenant's journey had begun in earnest.

The company pressed deeper into the land, their steps steady, their voices carrying snatches of song and vow across the plain. The sun rose high, casting long light over the broken earth, yet the people no longer moved as wanderers. They moved as a covenantal company, their rhythm sure, their path shared.

At intervals they paused, not from weariness but from choice. At one resting place, children gathered stones into a small ring, and elders blessed it with words of remembrance. At another, youths carved simple marks into wood, signs that spoke of unity and return. These acts were not commanded; they rose naturally, as if the vow itself guided their hands.

Kael'Thorin walked among them, his presence no longer solitary at the center but woven into the life of the people. He spoke little, offering only brief words of encouragement, for he saw that the covenant was strong enough to sustain itself. The seed within his chest pulsed lightly, like a steady drumbeat in harmony with the company's steps.

As dusk began to gather on the horizon, Kael'Thorin lifted his gaze to the sky. The constellations shimmered faintly, already bending as though preparing to bear witness again. The path of remembrance was only beginning, but its strength was undeniable.

As dusk settled, the people chose a gentle rise upon which to make their camp. They gathered stones into a ring, rekindling fire at its heart, and placed their tokens—stones, herbs, and bowls of water—around it. The rhythm of covenant had already become instinct, shaping their rest as surely as it guided their steps.

Children played in the fading light, tracing circles in the soil, their laughter ringing like bells. Elders began to tell stories once more, their voices carrying fragments of memory that stretched back to days of Lemuria's glory. The youths, strong in voice and eager in spirit, lifted songs into the darkening sky. The plain filled with sound and presence, a living testament that the vow was no longer fragile—it was enduring.

Kael'Thorin sat among them, his cloak spread upon the earth. He listened, not as bearer apart, but as brother within. The seed glowed faintly in his chest, steady and calm, as though it too rested in the company's keeping. For the first time since the sanctuaries had awakened, he felt no weight pressing upon him, only the quiet strength of shared remembrance.

As stars emerged overhead, bending faintly out of their courses, the people lifted their voices together in vow. Fire, song, and story braided with the silence of the Watchers, who once more leaned close. The covenant's second night began, strong and sure.

The second night deepened, and with it the covenant grew firmer, like roots pressing deeper into soil. Around the fire, the people settled into rhythms that felt both new and ancient. Children curled against their parents, lulled to sleep by stories and song. Elders spoke of cycles long past, when covenants had been tended in other ages, reminding all that what they now lived was not invention, but continuation.

Kael'Thorin sat close to the flame, watching sparks rise into the star-strewn sky. The seed pulsed lightly, steady as the embers' glow. He felt its warmth shared among those gathered, no longer a burden, no longer solitary. The vow had become communal fire, warming all within its circle.

In the stillness between songs, the people's breaths aligned, a collective rhythm that seemed to merge with the night itself. Above, the constellations bent faintly again, as if affirming each heartbeat. The Watchers' silence pressed near, vast and sure, not demanding but bearing witness. It was a silence that steadied, anchoring the covenant into the turning of time.

Kael'Thorin closed his eyes, breathing with them, and whispered inwardly: "It is alive."

The night passed not as waiting for dawn, but as dwelling in presence. By the fire's light, the covenant rooted itself more deeply into the lives of a people reborn.

Dawn broke softly over the encampment, washing the plain in hues of rose and gold. The fire had burned down to embers, yet its glow remained steady, a quiet witness to the covenant that had carried them through the night. The people stirred slowly, their movements unhurried, shaped already by new rhythm. Children rubbed sleep from their eyes and immediately traced circles in the soil with their fingers, as though instinct had taken hold. Elders greeted the day with words of remembrance, voices low but resolute, while youths lifted their arms to the rising sun in song.

Kael'Thorin rose with them, the seed within his chest pulsing in harmony with the dawn. He raised his voice, not as command but as affirmation: "The covenant is kept in waking, as it is in resting. Let this day be lived as vow."

The people answered with gestures and words alike—bowed heads, clasped hands, voices rising in chorus. Water was poured upon the soil, stones were laid in fresh circles, and fragments of story were spoken aloud to greet the morning. These acts, simple yet steady, became their liturgy: the covenant made visible in the turning of the day.

Kael'Thorin watched with quiet awe. This was not ceremony for its own sake. It was life woven into vow, a rhythm that would endure as long as breath itself. The second morning of their covenant had begun, and with it, a people's remembrance grew deeper roots.

The company descended from the rise, their eyes fixed upon the smoke in the distance. With each step the air seemed to thrum with quiet expectancy, as though the covenant itself urged them forward. Children tugged at their parents' hands, their laughter mingling with the hush of awe, while elders whispered prayers under their breath.

As they drew nearer, the shapes of another gathering came into view. Figures moved about a fire ringed with stones, their gestures deliberate, their voices lifted in song. It was not the same hymn Kael'Thorin's people had carried, yet its cadence bore the same spirit. It was remembrance given new form.

The two circles beheld one another across the plain, silence falling heavy for a moment. Then a man from the distant company raised his hand in greeting, his voice carrying: "We too have been called."

A murmur of joy rippled through Kael'Thorin's company. The woman with her child stepped forward, her son clutching his stone tightly. "The vow lives in us as well," she answered, her voice strong. Slowly, the two groups closed the distance between them until they stood as one circle around two fires.

Kael'Thorin felt the seed blaze warmly within his chest. The covenant was not spreading by decree or command, but by awakening—hearts stirred, lives drawn together. Here, before his eyes, remembrance was multiplying.

The two circles stood together, the air between them charged with expectancy. For a breath there was only silence, then the elder of the new company stepped forward. He carried a vessel of water wrapped in cloth, its surface shimmering faintly with the light of dawn. Lifting it high, he declared: "We pour this to remember."

He tipped the vessel, and clear water spilled onto the earth, seeping into the soil between the two fires. The act was simple, yet it bridged the distance between the gatherings. Moved by the gesture, the elder of Kael'Thorin's company struck his staff upon the ground, the echo ringing like assent. Others followed—children laying stones, youths lifting their voices in song, women sharing food drawn from their satchels. Soon the space between the circles was no longer boundary, but bond.

Kael'Thorin watched in quiet awe. These were not rituals handed down in rigid form, but living expressions of vow, rising unbidden from the people themselves. Every gesture was remembrance taking shape, every voice another strand in the covenant's weave.

When the two circles clasped hands at last, encircling both fires, Kael'Thorin felt the seed flare with warmth. The vow was not only multiplying. It was uniting.

That night, the two circles became one. The fires were drawn together, their flames licking upward until they merged into a single blaze. Around it, the people sat shoulder to shoulder, sharing food, song, and story. Children from both gatherings played beside the firelight, tracing circles in the dust and teaching each other fragments of songs they had carried. Elders spoke in turn, weaving memory into the night—some recalling visions that had called them forth, others telling of sanctuaries glimpsed from afar.

The youths kept watch at the circle's edges, their voices rising in chants that echoed against the plain. Women passed bowls of water hand to hand, pouring it onto the soil in blessing, while men set stones at the fire's boundary, firm markers of their shared vow. Every gesture, every voice became covenant, weaving two strands into one fabric.

Kael'Thorin sat among them, silent, his heart full. The seed pulsed steady warmth within him, but it no longer felt central. Its light had spread outward, reflected now in every face around the flame. The vow had ceased to be solitary—it was alive in a people reborn.

As the stars wheeled above, bending faintly in their courses, the Watchers' silence pressed near once more. The people lifted their voices in unison: "We remember." And the night received their vow as witness.

As the night deepened and the fire burned low, Kael'Thorin withdrew slightly from the circle, watching in silence as the people continued their vigil. Children slept in their mothers' arms, youths kept the embers alive, and elders murmured fragments of story, their voices blending with the steady rhythm of breath and song. The covenant had taken form, not in a single act, but in the simple weaving of lives together.

Kael'Thorin pressed his palm to the seed within his chest. Its glow was soft now, no longer blazing with burden, but steady, a quiet flame joined to many others. He realized with a depth of certainty that the vow was no longer his charge alone. It lived now in them—in the people who carried it, who spoke it, who tended it day by day. The sanctuaries had awakened, but it was here, in these circles of flesh and breath, that remembrance truly endured.

Above, the constellations bent faintly once more, the Watchers bearing witness in their silence. Their presence did not weigh heavily as before, but steadied, vast and sure, as though affirming that what had been planted would not be lost. Kael'Thorin bowed his head, whispering into the night: "It is kept."

The words were not his alone. They belonged to the people, to the covenant, to the memory that now pulsed in living rhythm. The vow was alive, and it would remain.

When dawn touched the horizon once more, the two circles—now one—rose as a single people. The fire's embers glowed faintly, stones and tokens lay firm in the soil, and the memory of song lingered in the air. Children stirred first, laughing as they traced fresh circles in the dust, their small hands sealing what elders had spoken. Youth lifted their arms to greet the light, while elders blessed the day with words that carried both past and promise.

Kael'Thorin stood at the edge of the company, his cloak brushed with morning wind. He pressed his palm to the seed within his chest, feeling it pulse not as solitary flame, but as echo, woven with countless other heartbeats. The vow had been carried, shared, multiplied. It was no longer his burden, nor even his gift. It was theirs—the covenant of a people reborn.

He lifted his gaze to the rising sun. The Watchers' silence pressed faintly at the edge of his awareness, vast yet gentle, as though bearing witness to the closing of one chapter and the opening of another. Kael'Thorin bowed his head, speaking words that belonged to all: "It begins anew."

With steady steps, the people turned toward the horizon, their voices lifting once more in song. The land received them, the sky bore witness, and the covenant walked into the world.

Chapter 8: The Stone Beneath the Skin

Kael'Thorin did not look back once he had crossed the first ridge. The voices of the people grew faint behind him, replaced by the low murmur of wind sweeping across the plain. He felt their song lingering still in the air, yet it was no longer his to tend. The covenant was alive in them, steady and strong. His task was different now—hidden, solitary, written not in chorus but in silence.

The land stretched barren before him, a sea of stone and ash. Each step pressed into the soil as though carving a mark deeper than his own weight. His chest throbbed with the pulse of the seed, the rhythm both steady and demanding. At times it felt like a second heartbeat, at others like a stone lodged beneath his ribs. The further he walked, the heavier it became.

By dusk he reached a wide expanse broken only by scattered boulders, their surfaces scarred with fissures. He paused there, resting his hand against the rock, feeling its coldness seep into his palm. The stone did not answer, yet he sensed a kinship—enduring, silent, unyielding. He whispered into the still air: "If I must become you, let me not break."

The wind carried no reply. Only the stars above, bending faintly from their courses, gave sign that he was not alone.

Through the long hours of night, Kael'Thorin pressed onward. The plain was stripped of all softness, nothing but blackened earth and jagged stone. His steps fell heavy, each one a negotiation between will and weariness. The seed within his chest had grown restless—its glow no longer gentle, but sharp, like a shard pressing outward from beneath the skin.

By moonlight he saw no clear path, only the fractured ground stretching endlessly ahead. The silence was immense, broken only by the rasp of his breath and the low hum of the seed. At times the sound seemed to rise outside of him, vibrating faintly in the stones beneath his feet. The vow was not only within him—it was threading itself into the earth.

Near midnight he staggered, dropping to one knee. Pain tore through his chest, and for a moment he thought the seed might rend him apart. He pressed his hand against the ground, gasping, and felt the cold solidity of the stone beneath. Its stillness steadied him, a reminder that endurance was not loud, but patient. He whispered through clenched teeth: "Make me strong as you are. Let me endure."

The stars wheeled slowly overhead, their faint bending a silent reply. Kael'Thorin rose again, trembling, and continued deeper into the wilderness.

By dawn, Kael'Thorin's steps had grown unsteady. Each breath came with sharp edges, as though the seed within him pressed against bone and sinew, seeking to carve its way outward. His body trembled under its weight, but still he walked, compelled by a force deeper than weariness. He knew this path was not meant for return. It was meant for transformation.

The wilderness stretched silent around him, vast and merciless. Yet in that silence, he felt a presence—distant at first, then nearer, pressing against the edges of his awareness. The Watchers had drawn close once more. Their gaze did not descend in thunder or flame, but lingered like the weight of unseen constellations bending above him. They did not speak, yet their silence was thick, immense, as though the stars themselves leaned to see what he would become.

Kael'Thorin lifted his face to the sky, sweat beading along his brow. "If I must be broken," he whispered, "let it be for remembrance. Let it be for them."

His words fell into the air like sparks into endless dark. For a heartbeat the seed within his chest pulsed so strongly that his vision blurred, and he staggered forward into the waiting plain, his trial only just beginning.

By midday Kael'Thorin reached a hollow where the land dipped into a bowl of stone. Black cliffs rose in jagged arcs around it, their faces etched with scars from fire and time. At the hollow's center stood a circle of weathered pillars, their surfaces rough and fractured, as though they had borne witness to ages of silence. Here the wind fell still, leaving only the low hum of the seed within his chest.

Kael'Thorin staggered into the circle, his breath ragged, his legs trembling. The stones loomed tall above him, yet their presence was not hostile. They waited, ancient and unyielding, as if they had been placed for this moment. He pressed his palm against one of the pillars, feeling its cold surface beneath his skin. The stone did not give, but its stillness seeped into him, lending him a steadiness his body could not provide.

He sank to his knees in the center of the hollow. The seed burned so brightly that he thought his ribs might split. His chest rose and fell in shallow gasps, each breath a struggle between life and collapse. Yet in the heart of that circle he felt a strange certainty: this was the place of his trial, the crucible in which the vow would carve itself into being.

Closing his eyes, Kael'Thorin whispered, "Let it be done."

The hollow lay silent around him, the cliffs rising like guardians of stone. Kael'Thorin sat with his back straight despite the trembling of his limbs, his breath shallow, his chest alive with fire. The seed no longer pulsed gently; it flared in uneven surges, as though testing the limits of flesh. Each wave left him shuddering, yet still he remained, rooted in the circle's heart.

The pillars seemed to lean closer in the stillness. Shadows shifted across their scarred surfaces, taking on shapes that whispered of memory—faces of those he had known, fragments of the fallen city, echoes of the companions who had walked beside him. Seraphiel's calm presence hovered at the edge of sight; Amari'el's voice rose faintly like a song carried on wind; Odric's steady strength pressed against his back; Thalan'ar's fierce gaze lingered; Ka'el's breath stirred as unseen wind across his skin. They did not appear in full form, yet their essences wove around him, unseen threads holding him upright.

Pain carved deeper through his body, each surge threatening to tear him apart. His hands pressed against the stone beneath him, fingers digging into its rough surface as though anchoring himself. "If I am to be broken," he whispered hoarsely, "let the breaking carve remembrance into me. Let me not fall empty."

The cliffs gave no reply, but the silence itself seemed to seal his words. And within that silence, the seed grew brighter still.

As the hours passed, the fire within Kael'Thorin grew unbearable. Each breath seared his lungs, each heartbeat struck like a hammer against stone. The seed no longer felt contained—it pressed outward, searching, as though it sought to carve itself beyond the fragile bounds of flesh. He closed his eyes, unable to endure the glare of day, and slipped into a realm between waking and dream.

Visions rose unbidden. He saw the towers of Lemuria before the fall, radiant and whole, their crystalline spires gleaming in sunlight. He saw the faces of those who had perished, their eyes full of trust, their voices calling his name. The weight of their memory pressed upon him, yet with it came their strength. They had not entrusted the vow to him in vain.

Then came his companions—Seraphiel, Odric, Amari'el, Thalan'ar, and Ka'el. Not in flesh, but in essence: Seraphiel's calm steadiness, Odric's grounding force, Amari'el's song like water over stone, Thalan'ar's fire of resolve, and Ka'el's whisper like wind between worlds. They circled him in silence, their presence luminous, each one a fragment of the vow that bound them all.

"I am not alone," he murmured, tears burning his eyes. The seed pulsed in answer, its glow fusing with the shapes of his companions until he could not tell where they ended and he began.

The visions thickened until Kael'Thorin could no longer tell whether he knelt among the stones or drifted in some vast expanse beyond them. The voices of his companions wove around him, their presences both near and far, sustaining him even as his body shuddered under the strain. The seed pulsed like a second heart, each beat sharp as a chisel striking from within.

Pain racked him, fierce enough to drive a cry from his throat. His hands clawed at the ground, fingers digging grooves into the stone floor of the hollow. He felt his body nearing its limit, every muscle trembling, ribs aching as if about to split. Flesh was too fragile to contain what burned inside him.

Yet even in the breaking he felt clarity. The vow was not meant to rest upon his shoulders like burden. It was meant to become him—bone, sinew, breath, soul. It would not destroy him, but neither would it leave him unchanged. He must yield to its carving.

Through blurred vision he saw a glimmer of light etch itself across his chest, lines of fire tracing the shape of a sigil he did not recognize. The mark burned, searing through skin and muscle, yet with the pain came certainty: the vow was no longer around him, nor above him, but within. The stone was setting beneath his skin.

The mark seared deeper, and Kael'Thorin's body convulsed with its fire. His breath came ragged, tearing through his lungs as though the seed consumed air itself to feed its glow. He fell forward onto his hands, trembling, sweat mingling with dust until the ground beneath him darkened. Every fiber of flesh screamed against the weight of remembrance now being carved within him.

For a moment, blackness surged at the edges of his vision. He thought he might surrender to it, slip into death and let the vow pass on without him. But even in that brink of collapse, something held him—threads unseen, woven of all who had trusted him, all who had spoken vow into his keeping. Their memory anchored him like roots gripping soil. He could not let go.

The Watchers' presence thickened above the hollow, constellations bending into forms unseen by ordinary eyes. Their silence pressed close, immense yet steady, as if to remind him: this was the hour appointed. Flesh would break, but remembrance would endure.

With a hoarse cry, Kael'Thorin slammed his palm against his chest. He felt the seed shift, hardening, embedding itself into bone. The pain was blinding, but within its blaze came revelation: the vow was not burden nor flame—it was stone, eternal and immovable, set beneath his very skin.

Darkness closed in, not as ending, but as threshold. He collapsed onto the stone floor, surrendering to the transformation that had claimed him.

Unconscious upon the stone floor of the hollow, Kael'Thorin drifted into a vast expanse where neither sky nor ground could be discerned. There was only light, shifting like water, and the echo of voices long forgotten yet deeply known. The pain of flesh fell away, replaced by a strange clarity. It was as though the breaking of his body had opened a gate into the marrow of remembrance.

Visions stirred before him. He saw the crystalline spires of Lemuria, whole once more, shimmering with a light that was not of sun but of soul. From their heights flowed rivers of song, and within those rivers he glimpsed his companions—Seraphiel,

Odric, Amari'el, Thalan'ar, and Ka'el—woven into the current, eternal and radiant. Their eyes met his, and he felt no burden in their gaze, only affirmation: the vow had taken root.

The vision shifted. Towers of crystal dissolved into other forms: columns of stone rising from the sea, a temple half-submerged, voices chanting in cadence with waves. A city unlike Lemuria stood before him—one he had never seen, yet recognized in the marrow of his soul. The name whispered on the wind was Atlantis.

Kael'Thorin reached for it, his hand trembling in the vision's light, as though touching the thread of what he would one day become.

The vision of Atlantis grew sharper until Kael'Thorin felt as though he stood upon its very shores. The air shimmered with currents of power, drawn from crystals towering like mountains, their surfaces alive with inner fire. Bridges of white stone arched across waters that glowed faintly with light, and voices rose in hymns that echoed against the sea's breath. Though the city was strange, its cadence was familiar—another reflection of the vow carried forward.

He saw himself there, not as Kael'Thorin of Lemuria, but as another form, bearing the same mark beneath the skin. This self stood among Atlantean seers, his hand lifted above a pool of water, chanting words that braided with the hum of crystal towers. He was not alone—the vow had awakened there too, carried in different tongue, yet alive with the same essence. What had been sealed in Lemuria was flowering anew.

The vision trembled, as though reminding him that this was but a glimpse, a promise of paths yet to be walked. Still, the recognition settled deep: the covenant was not bound to Lemuria's fall. It would awaken again, in places and peoples yet unborn.

Light flared, and Atlantis dissolved into mist, giving way to the shadow of trees older than any stone. A grove emerged, its branches thick with leaves, the scent of earth and rain rich in the air. Drums sounded in the distance, steady as heartbeat, calling him onward.

The grove unfolded fully around him, vast and ancient. Oaks towered above, their branches entwined like arms raised in eternal prayer. The air was heavy with the scent of moss and rain, and the soil beneath his feet pulsed faintly, alive with memory. Drums sounded from deeper within, their rhythm slow, steady, the echo of a heartbeat carried through earth and bark alike.

Kael'Thorin moved through the grove, though he knew this was no longer Lemuria's land. The people he glimpsed among the trees wore cloaks of wool and leather, their faces painted with spirals, their eyes bright with fierce devotion. Around a great fire they danced in circles, their chants weaving with the drumbeats in rising cadence. The vow lived in them too—spoken not in the crystalline language of Lemuria, nor the resonant hum of Atlantis, but in raw earthsong, born of stone and root.

He saw himself again, clothed as one of them, a staff in hand carved with spirals of oak. The mark beneath his skin burned faintly, echoing the fire that danced in their chants. He lifted his voice, calling not as stranger but as brother, and the circle answered as though they had always known him. The covenant had crossed oceans and centuries to awaken in their breath.

As the chants rose, the vision began to dissolve, the firelight of the grove giving way to a vast plain where thunder rolled. The ground trembled beneath the weight of hooves, and the wind carried with it the fierce cry of riders sweeping across endless grass.

The grove dissolved into the thunder of hooves. Kael'Thorin found himself standing upon a vast expanse of grassland, stretching to the horizon in every direction. The sky above was endless, a dome of pale blue marked only by drifting clouds. The earth trembled as riders swept across the plain, their cries fierce, their banners snapping like wings in the wind.

Clad in furs and leather, the riders moved as one, their horses surging with power, their bows and spears glinting in the sun. Their unity was not of stone circles or crystal towers, but of motion—swift, unstoppable, woven through the bond between rider and steed. The vow lived here too, carried not in monuments but in the breath of the herd, the thunder of hooves, the shared rhythm of survival.

Kael'Thorin saw himself among them, hair braided, eyes fierce, a curved bow in hand. The mark beneath his skin glowed faintly with each thunderous stride, pulsing in harmony with the pounding of hooves. He loosed an arrow into the sky, and the riders around him lifted their voices in exultation, as if the arrow itself carried remembrance into the heavens. The covenant was alive in them—fierce, untamed, and free.

The wind rose, carrying the smell of smoke and pine. The vision shifted again, the endless grass fading into a darker landscape of northern forests and rivers, where firelight flickered against snow and fur.

The thunder of hooves faded, and Kael'Thorin found himself standing among towering pines and the frozen breath of northern air. Snow dusted the ground in patches, and the sky above glowed faintly with ribbons of green and violet—spirits of the aurora dancing across the night. A river wound through the land, its surface half-frozen, the sound of water muffled but steady beneath the ice.

He saw fires burning along the riverbank, their smoke rising in slender columns into the cold night. Around them gathered families cloaked in furs, their faces lit by the glow. Drums sounded low and deep, their rhythm steady as heartbeat, carrying across the forest like the pulse of the land itself. Voices rose in song, raw and resonant, words born of the northern tongue. The covenant was alive here too, woven through smoke, river, and drum.

Kael'Thorin saw himself seated at the fire, a child at his side and elders before him. The mark beneath his skin glowed faintly as he joined their chant, his breath visible in the frozen air. He felt their eyes upon him—not as stranger, but as kin—as if they recognized in him something they had always known. The vow had crossed not only time but blood, finding root in the Cree of the northern forests.

As their song deepened, the flames blurred into brighter light, and the aurora overhead dissolved into the glow of a world yet to come—a vision of towers not of crystal, but of steel and glass, where remembrance still searched for a place to awaken.

The forest and firelight dissolved, giving way to towering structures of steel and glass that pierced a sky dimmed by smoke and cloud. Lights flickered in countless windows, and the hum of machines filled the air where once there had been only drum and song. Yet beneath the noise Kael'Thorin felt the same searching pulse—the vow, restless, aching to awaken.

He moved among the people of this vision, their faces weary, their eyes fixed upon glowing devices clutched in their hands. They walked quickly, yet with a hollowness that stirred sorrow in him. Still, he saw sparks among them—souls who lifted their gaze to the horizon, who paused in silence as though hearing something beyond the clamor. The covenant whispered there too, hidden but alive.

Kael'Thorin glimpsed himself reflected in a pane of glass, no longer cloaked in fur or leather, nor robed in crystal light. He wore garments of this age, his face marked by the same eternal scar beneath the skin. Though the world was changed, the vow had not left him. It had followed him across lifetimes, across ruins and empires, awaiting its awakening once more.

As the vision swelled, the city's hum blurred into silence, and the steel towers dissolved into starlight. Kael'Thorin stood once more in the hollow of stone, his body trembling but alive, the mark still burning faintly upon his chest. The seed had carried him across ages, and now it settled, immovable, within.

Kael'Thorin pushed himself slowly to his feet. His body still trembled, but the weakness no longer felt like decay. It was as if his flesh struggled to adjust to the new weight it carried—the permanence of stone beneath his skin. Each breath drew steadiness into his frame, the vow pulsing with quiet strength where once it had burned as fire.

He lifted his hands before him, staring at the faint glow beneath his chest. The mark had etched itself deep, beyond scar, beyond wound. It was a seal—an eternal bond that flesh could not erase. He touched it gently and felt not pain, but resonance, as if the stones of the hollow and the stars above all thrummed in answer.

Taking a step forward, he found his footing sure, though slower than before. Each movement carried a gravity that felt unfamiliar, as though the vow itself now walked with him. When he pressed his palm against one of the pillars, the stone hummed faintly in recognition, the same rhythm that now pulsed within his marrow. For the first time he understood: he had not merely endured the vow. He had become it.

Kael'Thorin lowered his head and whispered, "From this flesh I will fall, but from this vow I will not depart."

Kael'Thorin stepped slowly from the circle's heart, each stride heavy with the gravity of what now lived within him. His breath steadied as he moved, and though his muscles ached, there was no sense of collapse—only the slow adjusting of flesh to soul's new weight. He paused at the edge of the hollow and looked upward.

The sky was wide and clear, yet the constellations bent faintly, tilting in acknowledgment. The Watchers were near. Their silence pressed upon him—not with judgment, but with solemnity, as though the heavens themselves bore witness to what had been sealed. He bowed his head, his palm resting over the scar, and for a moment the world itself seemed to pause.

He whispered into the vast stillness: "The burden is gone. The vow remains." His voice trembled, but not with weakness—with the resonance of truth. The vow no longer demanded of him as weight. It spoke through him as essence, inseparable from his being.

A wind rose suddenly, cool and sure, sweeping down into the hollow and rustling the cliffsides. Dust lifted into the air, circling him before rising skyward, as though carried as offering into the stars. Kael'Thorin stood unmoving, letting the current pass through him, knowing the vow had been witnessed, anchored in stone, in flesh, and in sky.

Kael'Thorin lowered himself onto one knee, his hand pressed firmly over the scar upon his chest. The air was still charged with the wind's passing, and the silence that followed felt vast and listening. He drew in a deep breath, steady and grounded, and let his words rise as prayer.

"To the earth that bore me, I give thanks. To the stones that held me, I give vow. To the sky that watched in silence, I give remembrance. And to the companions who walked beside me in spirit, I give my heart."

His voice wavered, but it did not falter. The cliffs seemed to deepen in shadow, their edges glowing faintly in the morning light, as if acknowledging his words. Above, the constellations shimmered with a subtle gleam, and the air itself grew warmer, wrapped in presence unseen.

Kael'Thorin bowed his head fully, his brow pressed to the cold stone floor of the hollow. His chest ached, but not from breaking—it pulsed in steady rhythm, the vow now fused with his very breath. He whispered once more, softer than before: "I am yours. Across time, across flesh, across worlds—I will awaken."

The words seemed to settle into the earth itself, carried downward into depths unseen. For a long moment Kael'Thorin knelt there in silence, letting the vow root itself in stillness.

At last Kael'Thorin rose from the stone floor of the hollow. His body still bore the tremors of trial, yet his movements were steadier than before—slow, deliberate, anchored by the weight now settled within him. He pressed his hand once more to his chest, feeling the scar beneath skin. Its glow had softened, but its presence was unmistakable, a seal etched deeper than flesh.

He turned to the ring of pillars, their jagged faces catching the early light. They had stood for ages, unyielding to storm or flame. Now they bore witness to him—not as wanderer, not as bearer of burden, but as one remade. He bowed his head in silence, offering them his final gratitude.

Then, with careful steps, he began to ascend from the hollow. Each stride felt different than those before, as though the earth itself recognized the vow within him. The stones beneath his feet vibrated faintly, a subtle echo of the rhythm that now pulsed in his marrow. He no longer walked as one carrying remembrance. He walked as remembrance embodied.

At the rim of the hollow, Kael'Thorin paused and looked back once more at the circle of stone. The wind stirred faintly around him, cool and sure, carrying his whispered words into the vastness: "It is done."

Kael'Thorin descended slowly from the high rim of the hollow, the land spreading vast and open before him. The plain stretched in muted colors of ash and stone, yet he no longer saw only desolation. Every shadow and ridge seemed alive with presence, as though the earth itself now moved in rhythm with his steps. Where once he had felt severed, now he felt joined, bound to soil and sky alike by the vow etched within him.

His body bore the marks of trial—aching muscles, trembling limbs, a chest still tender where the scar lay hidden. Yet the pain no longer spoke of weakness. It spoke of permanence, of transformation endured. Each breath carried strength not his own, drawn from the covenant now fused into his marrow.

As he walked, he raised his eyes to the heavens. The constellations bent faintly still, their light subtle but steady. The Watchers lingered, observing without demand. Their silence felt not heavy but companioned, as though their presence walked beside him in quiet affirmation. Kael'Thorin inclined his head and whispered: "Witness me, as I will witness through ages."

The wind stirred across the plain, carrying his words forward. He continued on, not as one seeking remembrance, but as remembrance alive.

The horizon stretched wide before Kael'Thorin, yet he felt no fear in its vastness. Each step carried a rhythm that was no longer his alone. The vow pulsed with him, steady as a second heartbeat, flowing outward into the soil, the air, the very silence of the land. It was as though his trial had bound him to the earth itself, and every stride now echoed in places far beyond his sight.

He walked until the sun began to lower, its light spilling long shadows across the plain. The weight of the covenant no longer bent his shoulders; it lifted him, each breath woven with unseen strength. Where once he had staggered beneath fire, he now carried stone—silent, enduring, unshakable.

In the stillness of twilight, he paused upon a ridge and turned his face toward the distant horizon where his people had journeyed. He could not see them, but he felt them—their voices rising, their fires burning, their covenant alive. The bond was no longer fragile thread. It was woven deep, held in his chest and in theirs alike, stretching across distance like a living bridge.

Kael'Thorin lifted his hand in silent blessing, whispering: "I am with you, as you are with me. Across time, across flesh, across stars."

Night fell as Kael'Thorin pressed onward, the plain silvered by moonlight. His body moved with deliberate calm, every step steady, every breath anchored. Though fatigue lingered in his limbs, it no longer weighed him down. The vow within him carried his frame, guiding his stride as though earth and sky alike bore him forward.

The constellations arched above, bending faintly, their patterns subtly altered. The Watchers lingered still, their presence no longer distant but companioned, walking with him in silence. At times he felt the press of unseen hands at his back, or the warmth of light at his side. Where once he had feared their gaze, now he felt kinship—as though they too had entered covenant through him.

He paused by a solitary boulder that rose like a sentinel from the plain. Resting his palm against its surface, he felt its cool solidity answer with faint vibration, the same rhythm that pulsed beneath his chest. Stone to stone, vow to vow, the resonance affirmed that he was not walking alone. He whispered, "The vow endures."

His voice was low, yet the land seemed to receive it, carrying the words outward into the dark. And as he set forth once more, Kael'Thorin knew with certainty: whether he reached his people tomorrow or after many days, he would return not as bearer of burden, but as living remembrance itself.

As dawn broke, Kael'Thorin crested a ridge and paused to watch the sun spill across the horizon. The plain glowed with soft gold, the harsh edges of stone and ash softened in morning light. He drew in a deep breath, the air cool and clean, and felt the vow within him pulse in steady rhythm with the rising day. It was no longer a flame demanding his strength, but a stone anchoring him, a weight that steadied rather than burdened.

From that high place, he sensed rather than saw the nearness of his people. Though no fires marked the horizon, he felt the tether between them—a bond woven in the covenant they had embraced and in the scar carved beneath his skin. Their voices, though distant, stirred faintly in his heart as if the vow carried them through unseen threads of time and space.

He descended slowly, his steps sure, his gaze lifted to the sky where the constellations still bent faintly, steady in their silent witness. The Watchers had not withdrawn; they lingered, their presence vast but gentle, as though walking alongside him into the day. Kael'Thorin bowed his head and whispered, "Then walk with me, until remembrance fills the world."

The wind stirred at his words, brushing against his face with the coolness of dawn, and he continued down the ridge, his path set toward reunion.

Kael'Thorin's steps carried him across rolling stretches of plain, where grasses had begun to rise through cracks of stone as though life itself remembered how to return. Birdsong broke the silence for the first time in many days, its fragile notes weaving with the pulse of the vow within him. Each sound seemed to affirm that the covenant was not confined to people alone but lived also in the land awakening around them.

By midday he felt the nearness of his people more keenly. Though no voices reached his ears, the tether between them thrummed within his chest, a living cord drawn through remembrance. He knew they walked, sang, and tended fires somewhere ahead, and with every step he felt himself drawn closer. The scar beneath his skin warmed faintly, as if echoing their breath across distance.

He paused upon a rise and closed his eyes. In the stillness he felt them—children laughing as they traced circles in dust, elders murmuring prayers, youths standing tall with fire in their gaze. The images came not from sight but from vow itself, alive within him. He whispered, "You are not beyond me. I am among you still."

When he opened his eyes, the horizon seemed less empty. The plain stretched vast as ever, yet it no longer felt lonely. It was a path of return, and the vow would carry him home.

As the sun dipped lower into afternoon, Kael'Thorin crested another rise and paused. There, faint upon the horizon, a thin ribbon of smoke curled skyward. It wavered in the wind, fragile yet unmistakable—the sign of fire tended by human hands. His chest stirred with warmth, the scar beneath his skin pulsing faintly in recognition. The tether had led him true. His people were near.

He stood for a long while, gazing across the distance. The smoke was not merely proof of survival. It was proof of remembrance—flame kept alive, circle unbroken. Every step he had endured, every agony of trial, had carried him to this moment of return. He whispered into the wind, "I come to you not as bearer, but as brother."

Strength welled in him as he descended the slope. His body still bore weariness, but it no longer weighed upon him as before. Each stride was sure, guided by the vow within him, echoed by the presence of Watchers who lingered still in the bending constellations above. He walked as remembrance embodied, his path narrowing now into the way of reunion.

The nearer Kael'Thorin drew, the stronger the tether grew within his chest. It pulsed in time with his footsteps, carrying him steadily toward the smoke's source. The land seemed to brighten as he walked, grasses bending lightly in the wind, the stones beneath his feet resonating with a faint hum. It was as though the earth itself knew he was returning to his people, carrying remembrance within him as living seal.

At last, voices rose faintly on the wind. Children's laughter, the cadence of chant, the low murmur of elders telling stories around flame. The sound reached him long before sight, and his heart tightened with both relief and awe. The covenant lived not only in his scar, but in their breath, their song, their unbroken circle.

He crested another ridge, and there below lay the camp. Fires burned steady, their smoke curling into the sky. Figures moved in rhythm—some tending the flames, some gathering stones, others lifting voices in song. The sight struck him with quiet wonder. They had not faltered. They had grown.

Kael'Thorin stood for a long moment, watching from afar. His chest pulsed in harmony with their rhythm, and he whispered, "I am with you." The words carried on the wind, already belonging to them before he set foot among them once more.

Kael'Thorin descended from the ridge and walked slowly toward the camp. The voices grew clearer—the laughter of children, the chants of youth, the deep tones of elders. With each step the bond between them resonated more strongly, as if his scar and their song were two halves of the same vow. He no longer felt himself apart from them. He was returning not as bearer of burden, but as brother of remembrance.

As he neared, the first to see him were the children. They stopped their play and stared wide-eyed, then ran toward the campfire calling his name. One by one the people turned, their movements halting as they beheld him. Silence fell for a breath, the air heavy with awe. They saw not only Kael'Thorin, weary from trial, but the mark that glowed faintly beneath his skin, shining through fabric as if the stone itself had inscribed him.

The elder stepped forward, his staff steady in hand. He bowed low, and the people followed, their heads bent in reverence not to him alone, but to the vow he carried. Kael'Thorin's throat tightened, and he lifted his hand in return, not as ruler nor prophet, but as one among them. "The vow is ours," he said softly. "It is alive."

A cheer rose, not loud, but deep, swelling like a river current. The circle opened, and Kael'Thorin stepped within, his place restored not as burdened bearer, but as remembrance embodied among his people.

The circle drew tight around Kael'Thorin, firelight flickering across faces lined with awe and relief. The people pressed closer, not in demand, but in welcome, their presence wrapping him like a cloak. The woman stepped forward with her child, who still carried the small stone he had lifted during the covenant's first night. The boy placed it in Kael'Thorin's hands, his eyes wide with reverence. "It remembers," he whispered.

Kael'Thorin knelt to meet the child's gaze. The stone pulsed faintly in his palm, answering the scar beneath his skin. He smiled through tears and whispered back: "And so do we." He placed the stone upon the fire's edge, where its warmth glowed as part of the circle.

The elder raised his staff, striking it once against the earth. The sound echoed deep, like thunder rolling through the soil. At that signal, the people began to chant—slow, steady, voices rising and falling in rhythm. Youths laid new stones around the fire, women poured water upon the ground, elders spoke blessings into the night. Kael'Thorin joined them, his voice low but firm, woven seamlessly into theirs.

For the first time since Lemuria's fall, he felt the covenant whole—etched in his flesh, rooted in the people, alive in earth and sky alike. The vow was no longer fragile nor scattered. It was circle, flame, and scar, bound as one.

When the chanting faded and the night settled soft around the camp, Kael'Thorin stepped back from the fire and stood at the circle's edge. Children slept against their mothers, youths held quiet watch, elders sat with hands folded over staffs that had struck the earth in vow. He pressed his palm to the scar beneath his skin and felt only steadiness. No blaze, no burden—only the weight of something that would not pass away.

He looked over the faces of his people and felt the same rhythm move in them: the covenant no longer fragile, the circle no longer broken. In the distance, sanctuaries stirred like embers across a dark field; above, the constellations bent faintly, the Watchers bearing witness in their vast and tender silence. The world had not mended, but the thread of remembrance had been found and tied fast.

He thought of all he had seen—the towers before the fall, the stones of the hollow, visions of crystal cities and oak groves, hooves over endless grass, northern fires beneath dancing sky, and a city of glass where the soul still listened for an older song. He understood now: the vow would outlive any name he wore. It would pass through him as through a doorway and step into ages yet unwalked.

Kael'Thorin bowed his head and spoke so softly the words were almost breath: "When I fall to dust, I will rise in remembrance."

The fire answered with a single bright crack, and the night seemed to lean closer. Somewhere beyond sight, a new path opened—not away from his people, but forward through time. And the soul who would awaken began to turn toward it.

Epilogue — The Soul That Will Awaken

The stars bent low over Lemuria, their constellations trembling faintly as if stirred by memory. The Watchers lingered in their vast silence, gazes cast not upon stone or sea alone, but upon the soul that had risen from the hollow, scar upon his chest glowing faintly beneath the skin. They bore no words, no judgment, no decree. They were presence itself—immense, patient, eternal.

Kael'Thorin stood among his people, yet even in their circle his spirit felt the pull of horizons beyond sight. He lifted his face to the sky, and for a moment he knew: their silence was not emptiness. It was promise. The vow etched within him was not confined to Lemuria's soil, nor to the frailty of flesh. It had been sealed into a deeper rhythm—one that would outlast falling cities and broken towers, one that would awaken again when the world was ready.

The Watchers bent closer, their constellations bending into new alignments, as though inscribing a message upon the night: remembrance would not die here. It would walk with him, within him, beyond him.

He pressed his hand over the scar and whispered into the silence, "When I fall, awaken me."

The words did not vanish into void. They threaded upward, caught in starlight, carried into the vastness where time itself waited to unfold. And the Watchers, unmoving, received them.

Night deepened, and in the hush Kael'Thorin felt his spirit stretch beyond the boundaries of flesh and soil. The covenant was no longer a circle of voices alone—it had become a thread reaching forward, spun from his scar into the loom of time itself. He closed his eyes and the world of Lemuria softened, fading like a shoreline at dusk. In its place rose another vision: a city not yet born, rising from the sea in towers of crystal and light.

Atlantis. The marrow of his soul recognized it. The same vow burned there, carried in chants that wove with the hum of crystalline spires, in hands lifted above waters that glowed with inner fire. He saw himself among them—not as Kael'Thorin, but as a figure both familiar and changed, bearing the same scar beneath the skin. His lips moved in ritual, and the air thrummed with remembrance as if the covenant had crossed oceans and centuries to awaken anew.

The vision shimmered, dissolving as quickly as it came, but its truth remained. The vow was not bound to Lemuria's fall. It was seed, cast into the furrows of time, and it would take root wherever souls were willing to remember.

Kael'Thorin drew a long breath. The Watchers did not speak, but he felt their silent assent: the soul that bore the stone would awaken again.

The vision of crystal towers dissolved like mist, and in its place rose the scent of earth and rain. Kael'Thorin beheld a grove of towering oaks, their branches intertwined like arms lifted in prayer. The air was alive with the rhythm of drums, steady and deep, and voices rose in chant around a fire at the grove's heart. Men and women clad in wool and leather danced in circles, their faces painted with spirals, their eyes burning with devotion to earth and sky alike.

He felt the vow alive among them. It pulsed in their chants, in the stamping of feet against soil, in the smoke that curled upward to the stars. And there, among them, he saw himself again—changed in form yet marked by the same scar beneath the skin. A staff of oak rested in his hand, carved with spirals that mirrored those upon their faces. He lifted his voice with theirs, and the grove seemed to tremble with recognition: remembrance had found a new home.

The fire flared, casting sparks into the night sky, and the vision shifted. Kael'Thorin knew without doubt that the covenant would walk not only in stone towers and crystal halls, but in sacred circles of earth, in the breath of druids and the whisper of leaves.

The Watchers lingered above, their constellations bending faintly, as if inscribing across the stars the truth he now carried: the soul would awaken again, in every age that remembered the circle.

The firelit grove faded, and Kael'Thorin found himself standing upon an endless sea of grass. The horizon stretched unbroken in every direction, the sky vast and pale above, stirred only by drifting clouds. The ground trembled beneath him with a low thunder, and soon he beheld riders sweeping across the steppe, their cries fierce, their banners flying in the wind like wings.

They moved as one—men and women alike, clad in furs and leather, their bows curved like crescents, their steeds swift and tireless. The vow lived in their motion, not bound to stone or grove, but carried in speed, in freedom, in the unity between rider and horse. The covenant was fierce here, untamed, yet no less true. It pulsed in the rhythm of hooves, in the breath of the herd, in the thunder that rolled across the earth.

Among them he saw himself once more, his hair braided, his eyes alight with the fire of the plains. The scar beneath his skin glowed faintly with each gallop, resonating with the thunder of the steppe. He loosed an arrow high into the sky, and the riders around him lifted their voices in wild exultation, as if remembrance itself had taken flight.

The vision swelled, fierce and bright, then softened into the glow of firelight on snow. Pines rose tall and dark, and the breath of northern rivers filled the air. The steppe dissolved into the northern forests, where another people tended their fires beneath the dancing aurora.

Snow glittered along the riverbank, and the trees rose black and tall against a sky stitched with the lights of the aurora. Fires glowed in steady circles, their smoke climbing like braided prayers. Drums sounded low, a heartbeat carried through pine and ice, and voices braided with them—ancestral words spoken with care, honoring the land that holds and the waters that remember.

Kael'Thorin stood at the edge of the firelight, not as stranger but as kin. The scar beneath his skin warmed in answer to the rhythm, and he felt the covenant rise here in a language of river-breath and cedar-scent, of snow-crunch and ember-pop. Elders sat close, their palms extended to the heat, and children listened with wide, bright eyes, faces painted by flicker and flame.

A song began—soft at first, then gathering like wind along the banks. It carried gratitude for caribou and salmon, for the quiet that teaches, for the memory that keeps stories true. He saw his own hand—another name, another winter—lifted in time with the drum, and the scar answered with a pulse sure as the North Star. The vow did not come to overwrite, but to harmonize, to move as water moves around stone: shaping, listening, belonging.

Overhead, the aurora unfurled like a woven shawl. The Watchers' silence settled with it, vast and tender, as if the night itself promised: remembrance will find you here, too. The fire cracked once, bright as a star, and the song carried on.

The glow of the aurora dimmed, and with it the smoke of fires dissolved into the haze of another world. Towers rose tall, not of crystal nor stone, but of steel and glass, their surfaces lit by countless windows. The hum of machines filled the air, drowning the silence of stars. Yet beneath the noise, Kael'Thorin felt it—the pulse of the vow, muted but unbroken, hidden in the hearts of those who still looked up from the rushing tide.

He moved among them, clothed as they were, his reflection flashing in the panes of mirrored glass. Cars rumbled, voices called out, screens flickered like false constellations, but he searched past it all. And there—he saw them: a woman pausing to watch the horizon glow with dawn, a child pressing their palm to the bark of a lone tree by the roadside, an elder closing their eyes on a park bench to listen for a song only they could hear. In each, the vow stirred. Small, quiet, yet alive.

The scar beneath his skin glowed faintly, as though answering across time. It told him that remembrance was not gone; it had only gone hidden, awaiting the awakening of souls ready to hear. The Watchers bent above the city, unseen, their silence steady as stars behind the smog. Even here, among glass and iron, their promise held.

Kael'Thorin whispered to the rushing crowd, though none turned to hear: "When the time comes, I will awaken among you. I will remember."

The silence of the Watchers grew vast, as if the whole of the heavens held its breath. Stars bent into arcs above him, forming patterns that no mortal tongue could name, yet his soul understood them. It was not language of word, but of presence—the weight of eternity pressing close, not to burden, but to bless.

Kael'Thorin stood unmoving beneath their gaze, his hand over the scar that marked him. He felt their silence pour into him, filling the hollow places that pain had carved. It was not command, not demand—it was confirmation. The vow was sealed, and the Watchers bore witness that it would endure beyond any fall of cities or shattering of worlds.

Light shimmered faintly along the horizon, not dawn, not dusk, but something between—a reminder that endings and beginnings are but the same threshold. He felt himself standing at that edge, not departing, not arriving, but held in the stillness of what is eternal.

Softly, as though speaking to the stars themselves, he whispered: "I am not alone in this vow. You walk with me."

And in the depths of silence, he knew it was true. The Watchers' blessing was not loud. It was infinite. It was enough.

In the silence that followed, Kael'Thorin felt another vision stir. Not of places he had walked, nor ages he had glimpsed, but of souls yet unborn. Faces rose before him, countless and shifting—children with eyes bright as dawn, elders whose wrinkles traced the map of lifetimes, wanderers carrying hidden scars, seekers who paused in the rush of days to hear something more. He did not know their names, yet he knew their essence: they too would carry remembrance.

The vow was not his alone. It would awaken in others, in sparks that seemed small yet would blaze across generations. He saw them lighting candles in darkness, planting seeds in barren soil, singing songs into silence. Each act was a thread, weaving into the same tapestry he bore within his chest.

Tears pricked his eyes as he whispered, "I am not the only one. I was never the only one." The scar beneath his skin warmed, answering as though in chorus with the souls he beheld. The covenant was alive across time, shared, remembered, reborn.

The Watchers lingered, their constellations bending gently, as if to affirm what he saw: remembrance was not bound to one life, but would find root in many. The soul who will awaken was not a single figure, but a chorus of souls, each rising in their appointed time.

The vision of unborn souls faded gently, and Kael'Thorin felt the vastness settle into stillness once more. His hand rested over the scar upon his chest, its pulse steady, no longer burning with trial but resonant with eternity. He understood now: the vow was no longer seed awaiting soil. It had taken root in time itself. No fall of empires, no silence of ages, could undo what had been carved into the marrow of remembrance.

He lifted his gaze to the stars, and for a moment the constellations aligned in a pattern he could almost read. Not prophecy, not command, but affirmation. The Watchers bore witness that the covenant was sealed beyond forgetting. He was no longer merely Kael'Thorin of Lemuria, bearer of the vow. He was one thread in a tapestry woven through countless lives. The soul who would awaken was not bound to a single name—it was a current, eternal, flowing forward.

He breathed deeply and whispered, "Then let me rise, wherever I am called." The words were soft, but they rang with truth, echoing into the unseen vault of the heavens.

Light shimmered faintly across the horizon, neither dawn nor dusk but a timeless glow. He knew it was the threshold, the turning from this volume of remembrance into the next. And as he stood within it, Kael'Thorin felt not an ending, but a beginning.

Kael'Thorin stood at the edge of the threshold, where the lines of past and future braided together. The hollow of Lemuria, the flames of Atlantis, the oak groves, the thundering steppes, the northern fires, the towers of glass—all lingered within him, not as scattered fragments but as a single current. He felt himself no longer as one man, but as a river flowing through many channels, carrying remembrance wherever it was needed.

The Watchers did not speak, yet their silence curved around him like a mantle. Their constellations shimmered faintly, writing across the sky in strokes only the soul could read: This is not the end. This is the unfolding.

He bowed his head and let the silence rest upon him, steady as stone. He saw children yet unborn lifting stones in circle, riders crying to the sky, voices chanting in groves, elders telling stories by firelight, seekers pausing amid the rush of cities to listen. In each vision, he felt his own breath moving. He would awaken in them, and they in him.

For a long moment he stood unmoving, scar warm beneath his palm, and the vow pulsed outward—not as burden, not as task, but as truth sealed into the marrow of time.

He whispered into the threshold: "I am the circle. I am the stone. I am the soul who will awaken."

The threshold shimmered, neither dawn nor dusk, but the quiet place between. Kael'Thorin stood within it, and for the first time he felt no pull backward, no ache of what had been lost. Instead, he felt only the steady weight of what endured. The vow was within him, and beyond him. It was circle, flame, stone, and breath. It was the song of Lemuria carried forward.

The Watchers lingered above, constellations bending faintly as if bowing in reverence. Their silence was not absence but seal, the closing of one chapter and the opening of another. They had borne witness to his becoming, and now they released him into the vast river of time.

He turned once more to the memory of his people—their faces

lit by firelight, their voices rising in covenant. He felt their bond as thread woven into him, a thread that would not break across oceans or centuries. Wherever he would awaken, they would be with him.

Kael'Thorin drew a final breath within Lemuria and whispered, not to the Watchers, not to the stars, but to the souls across ages: "Remember me, as I will remember you. When I awaken, we awaken together."

The threshold brightened, the constellations shifting, and the vision of Lemuria receded into mist. Ahead lay paths unwalked, ages unborn. And into them the soul stepped—scar beneath skin, vow eternal, the song of Lemuria echoing still.

Thus ended the first remembrance. Thus began the awakening.

About the Author

C.B. Conklin is a Canadian author, father, and seeker of truth whose life has spanned coastlines, mountains, and the quiet in-between places where stories take root.

A devoted father of three daughters, Conklin writes from a place of remembrance — drawing from a lifetime of reflection, resilience, and a deep attunement to the unseen threads that connect all living things.

His work bridges worlds: the mystical and the human, the ancient and the modern, the inner and the outer journey. The Song of Lemuria is his first book, the opening movement in The Remembrance of Kings — a multi-volume epic exploring the soul's passage through time, love, loss, and awakening.

When he is not writing, he can often be found near the water, listening to the wind, or walking paths that feel older than memory — with his faithful companion, his dog, Thorin.

Manufactured by Amazon.ca
Acheson, AB

32158804R00199